BOOK ONE IN A SERIES

ANIMAL CHARMER

A NOVEL

RAIN NOX

CASTLE BRIDGE MEDIA
DENVER, COLORADO, USA

CASTLE BRIDGE MEDIA
Denver, Colorado

Cover photo by Holly Kuchera/Shutterstock
This photo has been modified.

ANIMAL CHARMER
© 2023 Rain Nox

ISBN: 979-8-9872083-5-9

Chapter 1

LUCY OFTEN GAZED ACROSS THE landscaped garden tucked between the two office buildings, the prime spot near the window a reward for her fourteen years of service at TerraPlaya. Most days she saw the typical back yard birds—cardinals, blue jays, mockingbirds, and doves, and occasionally she saw a rabbit that lived in a burrow beneath the raised deck. Once she even saw a spiny lizard sunning itself on a limestone rock.

But she had never seen a woman argue with a bird.

Until today.

Lucy had been lost in her work when she was startled by a thud on the window next to her cubicle. She swiveled her chair and jumped up to see what had made the sound and spotted a small grey bird lying stunned in the grass.

"Oh no!" Lucy gasped, concerned for the poor creature. She momentarily froze, unsure how to help; she was never one for dealing with emergencies.

Luckily, before she could decide what to do, a woman she had never seen before dashed across the courtyard and knelt down in front of the bird. She was only three feet from Lucy's face, but Lucy knew the woman couldn't see her behind the tinted office window. Even so, Lucy's heart raced as she worried the woman would look up and see her spying.

The woman murmured something unintelligible. Then she sprinted across the courtyard to the parking lot. Lucy looked down at the bird, her face pinched with worry, wondering if she should be doing something. She felt her panic returning as her brain flooded with possibilities. Was the woman coming back? How long should she wait to see? Should Lucy go outside and check if the bird was still alive? Should she take it to a veterinarian? Should she call the building manager?

Lucy breathed a sigh of relief when she saw the woman sprinting back carrying a shoe box. This woman clearly knew how to handle the situation, so Lucy's pulse started to slow, and she watched on with interest as the woman gently scooped up the fallen bird, placed it in the box, and covered it. The woman began walking towards the courtyard exit when a second bird swooped down from a tree and dive bombed her head, causing her to duck down to avoid the attack.

The woman frowned and waved her free hand around emphatically. Lucy thought the woman seemed to be having an argument with the bird. Lucy could see her lips moving but didn't see anyone else that she could be talking to. The woman seemed to pause while listening to a response, then spoke and gestured insistently again.

After what Lucy imagined was a heated discussion, the gray bird flew back up into the tree and the woman exited through the gate with the stunned bird still in the shoebox. Lucy continued to stare out the window, waiting to see if anything else would happen. When nothing did, she turned back to her computer and resumed her work. She tried to concentrate, but the scene nagged at the back of her mind for the rest of the day.

When she left work to head home, Lucy saw the second gray bird as she walked through the courtyard. Thinking of the mysterious woman from earlier, Lucy looked at the bird and whispered, "Hey little bird. I hope your friend is okay."

She immediately felt silly and glanced around to make sure no one heard her. The bird looked at her with a cocked head for a moment and then flew off into a tree. Lucy couldn't stop thinking about the woman and the bird as she drove home, but she knew she was being ridiculous. So what if the woman did talk to birds? That wasn't so unusual. People talk to animals all the time.

4

But as far as Lucy knew, they usually don't talk back.

*   *   *

The next two days flew by as usual. Lucy woke up with the sunrise, was in her cubicle by 7:30 a.m., and immersed herself in mapmaking. Working at an environmental consulting firm sounded pretty glamorous when she mentioned it to other people outside the industry, but in truth, her position was more of an office mouse.

While her coworkers ventured out into nature with their specialized knowledge of salamanders or stream restoration, Lucy stayed in the office making maps. Neat, organized, informative maps that went into technical reports and told the story of the information her colleagues had collected in the field. Not fancy, artistic maps like you would hang on the living room wall, but plain, functional maps that simply served their purpose. It wasn't unpleasant work at all.

Most days passed quickly as she lost herself in choosing the right colors and symbols for her maps, and focusing on every tiny detail of the labels, legend, and north arrow. She was good at her job, and her office mates were smart and generally kind people.

But some days she still looked out into that courtyard garden and wondered how she ended up here at forty years old and if this is all her life would ever be. Some days she longed to be the one doing the field research, traipsing through the forests, collecting samples from streams, or identifying birds with a spotting scope.

On the third day Lucy looked out at the courtyard as she sipped her morning tea and she saw the same woman. This time the woman was entering the courtyard from the parking lot. She stopped near the raised deck and crouched down.

Lucy stood up in her cubicle and strained to see what the woman was doing. Lucy could just barely see rabbit ears poking out from the long grass. Again, the woman seemed to be talking with the animal. Then she stood up, glanced at her watch, and hurried towards the building.

A notification popped up on Lucy's computer, reminding her that she was almost late for a staff meeting. She grabbed her notepad and pen and headed down the hallway to the conference room. She rushed in and took the last available chair just as the department manager, Anuk, was starting the meeting. As she scanned the room, she jumped in her seat a tiny bit when she saw the woman from the courtyard sitting at the conference room table.

"Good morning, everyone! I'd like to first welcome our new employee, Maya Morales, to the team. Maya is our new wildlife biologist. Please everyone take the time to make Maya feel welcome," said Anuk.

A chorus of welcomes and greetings filled the room and Maya tucked her long, wavy dark hair behind her ear as she smiled back at all the new faces.

"Lucy, since you are usually here in the office, I'd like you to be her orientation buddy, helping her with timecards, expense reports, showing her where office supplies are, and answering any questions she might have over the first few weeks."

"Of course, no problem!" Lucy smiled at Maya, who returned the smile readily.

While everyone turned their attention back to Anuk as he covered his agenda, Lucy took the time to study Maya more closely. Maya was wearing a button-down blue plaid flannel shirt with black pants. She wasn't wearing any makeup, and her only adornment was a beaded hemp bracelet tied around her wrist. Even though she looked perfectly professional, Maya maintained a more outdoorsy style compared with Lucy's typical office wear.

As usual, Lucy looked plain, but neat, in crisp gray slacks and a white blouse with a frilly collar, with a long black sweater to keep the office chill at bay. Lucy wasn't overly interested in clothing or fashion. She usually just bought her office attire from the discount rack, selecting pieces that were in her size, in conservative monotone colors that she considered professional. She kept her strawberry blonde hair pulled back into a neat ponytail at the nape of her neck.

"Lucy, can you give us an update on your projects?" asked Anuk, snapping Lucy out of her thoughts and back into the conference room.

"Sure. The maps for the Pine Ridge trail system report will be done today, and I should be getting the data from Elijah for the Blue Bayou watershed study tomorrow so I will start on those maps next."

"Great. Maya, Lucy here is our mapping guru, so you'll work with her for anything you need for your projects, from preparing field maps to exhibits for your final reports. We keep her pretty busy, so make sure to let her know about upcoming projects so she can put them on her schedule."

"Okay, will do," said Maya.

After the meeting, people were filing out of the conference room and Maya held back, waiting for Lucy. "Well, looks like you are the person to know."

Lucy smiled. "I don't know about that, but I'm happy to help—I've worked here a long time and know the system pretty well. Most important thing is timecards. I can help you with that tomorrow since they have to be done by 10 a.m. on Fridays."

"Thanks. Yep—a gal's got to get paid! I also will need to talk with you about my bird survey at Sienna Falls Forest. I'll be going out next week and I need to get some field maps together."

"Sure, I can help with that. I am actually free right now if you want to tell me more about the project."

"That would be great. Let me get my laptop and I'll meet you at your cubicle in five."

"Okay. I'm in that back corner next to the courtyard." Lucy pointed toward her desk.

Maya nodded and headed to her cubicle in the other wing of the office.

Lucy rushed back and opened her filing cabinet drawer to rummage through her tea collection. She scanned the boxes, contemplating which one would be best for meeting a new person. Tea was an important ritual for Lucy. Something about making the tea, holding the warm cup in her hands, and smelling the hot, fragrant liquid was soothing to Lucy. She drank white pear tea in the morning, herbal tea before lunch, orange chocolate green tea in the afternoon, and chamomile in the evening. But different situations called for different teas.

Even though Lucy was, by most standards, a successful professional, and appeared calm and confident on the surface, Lucy was often anxious about both work and social interactions. The tea helped her get through each day without falling prey to her anxieties. She spotted the perfect blend and took off for the break room to prepare it.

When she returned to her cubicle, Maya was waiting with her laptop. "Mmmm—that smells delicious! What kind of tea is that?"

"This is peach cobbler. One of my favorites. I have boxes of it if you ever want to try it." Lucy set her teacup on the coaster she kept on her desk.

"I might take you up on that."

"So, tell me about your project." Lucy sat ready with notepad in hand.

Maya's whole face lit up as she spoke. "Sienna Falls Forest is the perfect habitat for the endangered Silver-winged Warbler. The Southwest Regional Conservation Coalition hired TerraPlaya to do surveys so they can have a baseline for how many birds nest there each spring. Then they can compare the data with future surveys to develop population trends." Maya pressed her hand to her heart. "One of the reasons I decided to take this job was because of more opportunities to do fieldwork like this. If I could see just one Silver-winged Warbler…" She sighed.

Lucy could tell Maya was deeply passionate about this project, and Lucy felt a passing twinge of emptiness because she didn't care deeply about anything in particular. "That sounds like really important work. You're making me jealous that I can't go out and look for birds in the forest."

Maya looked puzzled. "Why can't you?"

"Because I'm forty. It's a little late for me to start stomping through the woods now."

"That's ridiculous! Forty isn't too old to do anything. Really, it's not as fun as it sounds though—mosquitos, muddy boots, heat, humidity. Days where you spend hours looking through binoculars and see absolutely nothing of interest. But still, I wouldn't trade it for anything!"

Maya explained to Lucy how she usually did her survey, what she needed to see on her field maps, and what data she was hoping Lucy could find to load into her GPS unit. Lucy took copious notes and assured Maya that she would have it ready for her by Tuesday afternoon so Maya could head out Wednesday morning.

Maya stood up and stretched her legs. "I'm starving! I'm going to eat my lunch out in that pretty courtyard. Want to join me?"

"Sure." Lucy usually ate her lunch in her cubicle, looking out at the courtyard, people watching and bird watching. But it did sound fun to be the one out there for once, especially since it was a gorgeous spring day. Spring is short in Northbrook, while summer is long and unbearably hot. Every year by early June Lucy lamented how she let spring go by without spending enough time enjoying the pleasant temperature and cool breeze.

Lucy and Maya sat quietly eating their lunch, taking in the peaceful atmosphere of the courtyard, sitting among the spring flowers, and admiring the carefully crafted landscape. The courtyard was a really special feature for a suburban office park. Lucy had watched them create it after they built the adjacent office building.

The courtyard had limestone paths and a raised deck with iron patio furniture nestled beneath two large oak trees. There was even a covered area with picnic benches where they had trained purple wisteria to grow over the top, giving the area a more whimsical, almost wedding-venue like feel.

The whole courtyard was fenced in with wrought iron on the sides between the two buildings, with vines growing up the posts, creating a secret garden only open to those with a keycard.

Lucy looked up from taking a bite of her apple as a fluttering motion caught her eye. A tiger swallowtail butterfly flew from the flower it was feeding on and hovered over the women before landing on Maya's arm. Maya sat perfectly still, admiring the velvety yellow and black wings with powdery iridescent blue near the tail. Lucy looked on with wonder and admiration. Then the butterfly suddenly ascended, flying away from the deck and over the courtyard fence.

"Beautiful!" Lucy exclaimed. "How did you do that?"

"Do what?"

"Get the butterfly to land on you."

Maya smiled. "I didn't do anything, she just thought I was safe to land on, I guess."

"She?"

"Yes, only the female tiger swallowtails have the blue near their tails."

Lucy's face fell. "Oh. I thought maybe she introduced herself to you."

Maya raised an eyebrow at Lucy but didn't respond.

In the silence, Lucy could feel the anxiety starting to wash over her, so she rushed to explain, talking faster and faster until she was practically babbling. "The truth is the other day I saw you talking to a bird, and this morning, a bunny. I wasn't spying on you or anything, but I can see from my cubicle window, and I know it sounds crazy, but I got it into my head that you can talk to animals. Not just talk to them like people talk to their dogs or cats, but like maybe they talk back? I know, I'm weird, just forget I said anything." Lucy stared down at her shoes in embarrassment.

"Lucy, it's okay. You're not weird or crazy. I can talk with animals, at least sort of. Maybe not like you are thinking, but I can communicate with them on a certain level."

Lucy was stunned. Less by what Maya had said, but more that Maya could freely say it without seeming at all concerned that she would be viewed as irrational or crazy, or a liar. Was Maya crazy? She only just met her, so maybe Maya was crazy.

Or maybe she was just slightly delusional in a harmless way. Maybe Maya just spent so much time with animals and out in nature that she started to imagine that she had a special connection. Who doesn't want to be unique, right?

Or maybe it was more like those TV shows with the cat whisperer—a person who spent so much time with cats that he could recognize their patterns of behavior more deeply than the average person, and it came across as animal telepathy.

Maya looked down at her watch. "Shit! I have a meeting in one minute with Anuk to talk about upcoming proposals. I can teach you if you like."

"Teach me...?"

"To talk with animals."

"Uhm..."

"Tomorrow, lunch, right here, same time." Maya grabbed her insulated cooler and sprinted off to the building, leaving Lucy with her mouth hanging open.

Lucy could barely focus on her work for the rest of the day. But since deadlines don't care what new excitement may have come into your life, she slogged through the rest of her assignments and was grateful when five o'clock came and she had time to properly process her conversation with Maya.

*   *   *

After she arrived home, Lucy started preparing dinner, penne pasta with tomatoes. She never liked cooking very much, so she ate mostly simple foods. She considered boiling water the maximum effort she was willing to put in, so she ate mostly salads, cereal, and sandwiches.

While she sliced the tomatoes, she let her mind wander to Maya and lunch tomorrow. The situation was certainly anxiety-provoking. Once she placed the pasta in the boiling water, she took out a notepad and pen and sat down at her kitchen table.

Decades of therapy taught Lucy the best way to manage her anxiety was to weigh her options with objectivity. She started by listing the potential actions she could take. Then she wrote down each of their advantages and disadvantages.

The first option was that she could pretend it never happened, eat lunch somewhere else, and see how Maya reacted. But she still would have to work with Maya and the last thing she needed was awkwardness at her job.

The second option was that she could tell Maya she wasn't interested in her lesson, but then Maya might be offended or think Lucy didn't believe her.

The thing is that Lucy really liked Maya. More importantly, Lucy couldn't help feeling like Maya really could communicate with animals, even if Lucy didn't really believe Maya could teach her to do that too. In the end, Lucy decided the least potentially damaging third option would be to meet Maya for lunch and see what happens.

Lucy circled option three on her notepad and sat back. As usual, once Lucy made a decision, her mind was immediately calmed, although an overall excitement and nervousness about the possibilities remained.

After dinner, Lucy curled up on her purple velvet loveseat and scrolled through streaming options. She most enjoyed black and white movies from the 1940s, starring sophisticated women. Even though Lucy would never conceive of torturing herself with three-inch heels or trouble herself with pantyhose, or even curl her strawberry blonde hair, she still loved and admired the glamour and style of the period.

As she flipped through, an old favorite caught her eye, *Cat People*, starring the mysterious Simone Simon as a newly married woman from Serbia who arrives in New York and is haunted by the legend that her people transform into panthers when aroused with passion. With her chamomile tea in hand, Lucy let herself be lost in the film.

By the end of the movie, Lucy was so drowsy that she could barely keep her eyes open. She managed to crawl into bed and snuggle under her comforter, then drifted into sleep. At 2 a.m. she startled awake, thinking she heard the snarl of a wildcat. *It's just because of the movie sillyhead*, she told herself. Even so, she tossed and turned the rest of the night, dreaming of Maya with a jaguar by her side, its sharp teeth gleaming in the moonlight.

Chapter 2

LUCY WAS GRATEFUL THE NEXT morning that she was so busy with her work that she didn't even have time to fret over her lunch training with Maya. Anuk had given her an urgent request from a client before she had even made her morning tea. Really, the deadline was somewhat unreasonable, but that was consulting. You always just said yes, and somehow made it work. If Anuk didn't say yes to the client, then next time they would hire a different company. And if Lucy didn't say yes to Anuk, then she would be out of a job.

Luckily, years of experience meant she could be highly efficient when needed, knowing exactly what corners she could cut and still produce an acceptable, high-quality product. Lucy sent the final version to Anuk just before lunch.

She glanced out the window and saw Maya already in the courtyard. Lucy gulped. She got her lunch from the refrigerator, even though her stomach was too tight to possibly think of eating, and she headed outside.

"Hi Lucy! How's it going? Looked like you had a busy morning," said Maya from the patio chair under the tree.

"Yeah, last minute requests keep me on my toes." Lucy sat down on the other chair and set her lunch down but didn't make a move to open it. She tried to look relaxed, but her stomach was in knots by now, worrying about what weird things Maya may ask her to do. And if she was about to discover Maya was cuckoo as a cuckoo bird.

She took a deep breath, ready to dive into whatever this was. "Okay, so what's the first step?"

"First you need to tune in to your surroundings. Close your eyes and listen. Notice all the different things you can hear. Listen for sounds close to us and as far away as you can," Maya instructed.

Lucy closed her eyes. She tried to focus her mind on what she could hear—the rustling of leaves in the tree, cars leaving the parking lot, voices as employees entered and exited the office doors around the corner from the courtyard.

As she continued to listen, she started to become more aware, as if her sense of hearing was heightening. She noticed the buzz of a lawn mower in the subdivision behind the office park. Even farther away, a truck horn honking on the highway. Focusing back in closer, she heard Maya unpacking her lunch. A bird chirping nearby. The sound of her own breathing, out and in, out and in.

After a few minutes, Maya spoke gently, "How did that feel Lucy?"

Lucy opened her eyes, feeling like she had been in a trance that was now broken. "Okay, I guess. I'm not sure what was supposed to happen, but I felt like in the beginning I could only hear a few of the more obvious noises, but after a while I started to notice a deeper level of sounds."

"That's great! Perfect really. That is a promising sign." Maya was smiling brightly.

"Does that mean not all people can learn to do this?" Lucy worried. If something took some rare and special talent, then she would not be the person to be successful at it. Lucy knew she was smart and was willing to work for things, but she just never stood out from the crowd.

Maya looked thoughtful for a moment before responding. "I believe all people can learn to have a more sophisticated relationship with animals, but most people don't really pay attention to what is happening around them. They walk around with their earbuds in, swiping their smartphones. They don't make eye contact. They shut out everything. Even people communing in nature are often too busy trying to take the perfect photo to post to really see."

"I know exactly what you're talking about! Even with the 'mindfulness' trend, most people are still living in the future or past, or worrying more about preserving memories, and always on their phones!"

"That's right. And animals live in the moment. Sure, instinct tells them to hoard food for winter or migrate to the south, but for the most part they only live in the here and now. So, if a person can't be in the moment, at least for a short while, then they probably won't be able to talk with an animal. It would be like two trains passing by each other on different tracks."

"That makes sense. Does that mean I should practice being in the moment?" Lucy loved to practice things. She loved anything that had a method where a normal person like her could follow it and have a reasonable chance at success.

That's why Lucy loved school. Each professor provided a specific set of criteria for evaluation and there was a body of knowledge that was expected to be acquired over a certain timeframe. How much time and effort were necessary to achieve the goal was variable, but Lucy thrived on this system and had consistently achieved 4.0s in all her courses.

She didn't really expect talking with animals to have a formal curriculum, but if there was something to practice, Lucy was in.

"Yes, that is a good place to start. You can do the same exercise with each of the senses. Focus on what you can see, what you can smell, what you can feel. Once you can really be aware of what surrounds you, then you will be in the same space and time as our animal friends." Maya took a swig from her aluminum water bottle. "For now, let's start by building a relationship the old-fashioned way—through food!" Maya pulled a bag of nuts from her lunchbox and handed it to Lucy.

Lucy took the bag and thought to herself, "Nuts from one nut to another!" Then chuckled at her own pun, while Maya looked at her quizzically. Lucy tossed some nuts on the patio deck and the two women waited silently for a creature looking for an easy snack. It didn't take long for a squirrel to edge down the tree and keeping a cautious eye on Maya and Lucy, started to eat the nuts.

"Stay still and don't make any sudden movements," warned Maya. The squirrel looked less nervous after a few minutes and started eating the nuts more aggressively, inching closer to the women. Without moving,

Maya instructed, "Now get back to that same place of mindfulness you were before. Once you are there, try to focus your attention on the squirrel without losing that state of mind."

Lucy closed her eyes again and listened for the sounds around her. It didn't take as long this time to notice the different layers of noise. Finally, she focused on the sound of the squirrel eating the nuts, then opened her eyes and carefully examined his little chestnut brown nose, the wavy whiskers, the way he picked up each nut with tiny dexterous claws.

She noticed that his ears were turned towards her and Maya, and he was watching them from the corner of his eye as he munched. She could tell that he was on alert and any sudden movement or sudden noise would spur him to run. Silently, in her mind, Lucy tried to send a feeling of safety to the squirrel, to let him know that she had no intention of harming him. The squirrel suddenly turned to face Lucy; his tiny ears perked up as if surprised.

There's no way the squirrel heard me, right? Lucy thought to herself. Maya hadn't said anything about trying to send the squirrel messages, it just seemed right to Lucy to extend a friendly gesture.

Before she could consider the situation further, the courtyard door swung open, and the squirrel sprung back up the tree. Lucy tried to follow him with her eyes as he climbed. She spotted him on a limb, where he momentarily turned to look at her.

Thanks for the nuts.

Then the squirrel raced back up the tree and was out of view.

Lucy spun around to Maya to see if she had heard the same thing.

"What is it?" asked Maya with concern.

"Nothing," replied Lucy, shaking her head. She probably just imagined it since she was so wrapped up in this silly fantasy. But it seemed like the words appeared in her brain. Not exactly words in English, but the intent of the words. But that was crazy.

Wasn't it?

Maya didn't seem to hear the squirrel, and she was the one who suggested the whole thing. No, Lucy was letting her imagination run wild.

She briefly considered telling Maya what she heard, but it was just too ridiculous to say out loud. She needed to think. "Thanks for bringing the squirrel food, Maya. I have to get back to work now—lots of things to get done before five." Lucy scooped up her uneaten lunch and went back into the building, leaving Maya alone and bewildered.

*   *   *

On Sundays Lucy volunteered at the Northbrook Retirement Home. As a forty-year-old woman with no children, Lucy often thought about what it would be like when she was older and how lonely it would be to have no one to visit her.

She made a point of visiting with seniors at the home who didn't have any family. Her favorite person was Mrs. Kleinbaum. She was 83 years old, sharp as a tack, and uncommonly open-minded. At first, Lucy had visited her as part of the volunteer program, but now Lucy considered her a true friend and often saw her outside of the regular program hours.

Lucy knocked on the door. "Good morning, Mrs. Kleinbaum! It's Lucy."

"Come in!" a voice shouted from inside. Lucy opened the door and was immediately greeted by Mrs. Kleinbaum's cat, Frederica, as she rubbed against Lucy's leg. Lucy reached down to scritch the cat's ears.

"I brought your magazine." Lucy handed it to Mrs. Kleinbaum, who put it on the table.

"Thank you dear. Come in and have a seat." Mrs. Kleinbaum patted a chair. Before Lucy could sit down, Frederica leapt up on the chair and immediately curled up as if she had been there for hours. Lucy and Mrs. Kleinbaum both laughed. It wasn't the first time that Frederica had stolen a seat from an unsuspecting guest.

Lucy shrugged and sat down on the floor next to Frederica and pet her cheeks, which was rewarded with a rumbling purr.

"She likes you, Lucy. Frederica doesn't like everyone, you know."

"I like her too. She's a good kitty. So, how have you been?" asked Lucy.

"Well, things don't change much around here. Mr. Oxert broke his hip, and Mrs. McNally's son bought a new house with a mother-in-law design, and she moved in there. I'm waiting to see who moves into her suite. What's new with you?"

17

"I got a new coworker. Her name is Maya, and she is a little unusual."

"In what way?"

"Well...do you ever talk to Frederica?"

Mrs. Kleinbaum laughed. "All day long! Who else am I going to talk to? Plus, she's a great listener."

"But does she ever talk back?"

"Not so far, but I keep trying. What is this about?"

"It's nothing, really. Maya just has some interesting ideas, that's all." Lucy wasn't ready to confide in anyone about the squirrel, even though Mrs. Kleinbaum was the most non-judgmental, easy to talk to person she knew. "On the other hand, Maya is really passionate about wildlife and preservation. She's a biologist and gets to do all sorts of cool fieldwork."

"She sounds like a neat lady. But do I detect a tiny bit of the green-eyed monster?"

"Busted!" Lucy laughed. "I guess she makes me wish I were doing something different. Maybe I always chose the safe path and not the fulfilling path. But that is just me. The risky path would make me too anxious."

"Hmmm. Well, take it from me, you do not want to look back at your life and regret not having followed your passions, that's for certain. And it's never too late. I started painting after decades of thinking I couldn't. Now my only regret is that I didn't start sooner. Shall we have tea now, dear?"

Lucy nodded, and Mrs. Kleinbaum poured two cups. Lucy sat sipping the tea, the warm cup in her hand, with her arm resting on the chair. Frederica propped her head on Lucy's arm, still purring. It was such a peaceful feeling that Lucy's mind felt at ease for once, listening to the rumbling purr and breathing in the warm steam through her nostrils.

Suddenly Lucy started and sat up straight. "I think Frederica has an ear infection."

"Oh no! My sweet girl. I will take her to the vet as soon as possible."

Lucy was grateful that Mrs. Kleinbaum didn't question how Lucy knew about the ear infection, but then that was Mrs. Kleinbaum's way. She didn't need a lot of explanations for things, she just accepted people for who they were.

Chapter 3

MONDAY CAME TOO FAST, AS always. Sometimes it seemed like the weeks and months blended together, with little to differentiate them. To Lucy, it seemed it was always Monday again. She could barely remember where the weekend went, but it certainly wasn't long enough to replenish her soul. That's how fourteen years had gone by at TerraPlaya.

Lucy was prepared with her tea ready, five minutes early to the Monday morning meeting. Maya came in and sat beside her, and one by one the rest of her colleagues trickled in.

"Good morning, everyone!" Anuk always sounded like he was genuinely excited to start each work week. Lucy used to wonder if he was just putting on a front, but eventually she realized that many people found work fulfilling. Anuk was one of those people. Lucy guessed she wasn't.

"This week is going to be busy. Maya—since Tyler finished the wetland delineation early, he will be your second on the Sienna Falls survey. Lucy—we'll need you to download Tyler's data and start the mapping for the delineation so he can complete the report when he is back in the office."

Lucy stole a glance at Tyler, who seemed to be only half listening while he checked his phone.

She had nothing personally against Tyler. Not really. Well, maybe just a little. It was just that Tyler started out with the same degree as Lucy, and without the specialized biology training that Maya and most of the other staff

19

had. He used to mostly make maps like her, but somehow, he transitioned into doing fieldwork, surveys, and wetland delineations. The company had even paid for his training and certifications.

Maybe Lucy could have done the same, but she never advocated for herself the way that Tyler had. And someone had to stay in the office to make the maps and support the production of the technical reports. Lucy reminded herself that it wasn't Tyler's fault that he was confident and pushy, and Lucy was the opposite. But even though she knew it was unfair, she resented Tyler for it.

As Lucy was leaving the conference room, she caught up with Tyler. "Hey, can I get your GPS?"

He looked up at the ceiling as if looking for the answer, then a lightbulb went on in his mind. "Oh yeah, I think I left it in the car. Can you stop by my cubicle and get it later?"

Even though it seemed like an innocent statement, it made Lucy grind her teeth. Why couldn't Tyler bring the GPS to her cubicle after he went to his car? And why would he leave company property in his car to potentially get stolen?

It wasn't worth it to make a big deal about it. "Yeah, sure," she replied.

Lucy tried to put Tyler out of her mind and instead she focused on the field maps for Maya's visit to Sienna Falls Forest. She downloaded the aerial photography and made base maps that Maya could mark up in the field. She loaded the second office GPS unit with boundaries that would help Maya stay within the survey areas, and with points that represented the locations with suspected quality habitat for the Silver-winged Warbler. She changed the settings on the GPS to match the coordinate system for the Sienna Falls area and made sure the battery was charged.

She showed Maya where the field supplies were kept, including clipboards, waterproof notebooks, binoculars, and cameras. The field preparation kept Lucy busy for most of the day.

After procrastinating as long as she could, Lucy finally went to Tyler's desk a little after four. It was important to her to do a good job on all of her assignments and for that she needed his field data.

Tyler was engrossed in texting on his phone and didn't see her walk up. Lucy cleared her throat. Tyler jumped in his chair and looked up at her. When he saw it was just Lucy he relaxed again and finished typing his text.

Rude, Lucy thought. "Hey—can I get your GPS?" said Lucy casually, careful to keep any irritation out of her voice.

Tyler threw his hand in the air. "Oh yeah. I forgot to get it from the car. I'll be right back." Tyler jetted out of his cubicle and down the hall.

Lucy stood waiting, annoyed at Tyler's forgetfulness. This is why Lucy had lists and sticky notes and electronic reminders. There are a lot of things to keep track of in this job. She looked disdainfully at Tyler's desk. No wonder, she thought as she looked at the piles of papers strewn haphazardly, an old coffee cup tucked in the corner, and not one, but three sweatshirts stuffed beneath the desk.

Tyler returned and handed the GPS to Lucy. "Here you go. Yeah, I think I forgot to change the coordinate system, so you'll have to reproject all the data."

That wasn't a super big deal, but it was unnecessary work for her just because Tyler hadn't bothered to do his job properly. Why someone like him got so many opportunities was beyond her. The best she could tell was that people who were loud and appeared confident were often rewarded, even though Lucy had frequently observed that those people were often the least capable.

Lucy took a deep calming breath in and released it. "Okay, will do," Lucy responded.

"Cool. And also, can you do as much of the editing as possible since I have so much field work this month? After Sienna Falls, I am going with Bethany to take samples at Crystal Beach." Tyler pushed his shaggy hair out of his eyes so he could see his phone and started texting again.

Lucy rolled her eyes, knowing Tyler wouldn't see anyway. Lucy secretly fumed—he gets to go to a forest, then the beach, and in between he just looks at his cell phone? Let it go, she told herself, it only hurts you to fixate on how other people behave.

"I'll see what I can do," Lucy said, then turned on her heels and walked away.

*　　*　　*

After work, Lucy went to her voice lesson. She had always enjoyed singing in school choirs when she was a child, and she thought maybe someday she could join the Northbrook Community Choir. Lucy had always been a very goal-oriented person. She knew that the Northbrook Community Choir held auditions in September, so her goal was to have two songs prepared to try out.

This was her sixth lesson and so far, she loved it. Singing was good for Lucy. Not only did it make her feel good to sing but exposing herself in that way helped to challenge her anxieties. Her teacher Carlos was easy going and supportive, and he celebrated all her little improvements with her.

Lucy was working on the song "So in Love" from the 1940s musical Kiss Me, Kate. The song was challenging, because it required efficient breathing to sing the long musical phrases smoothly, and the harmonies were rich and often unexpected.

"Lucy, I know you haven't been my student for very long, but I wanted to let you know that my studio will be having a recital at the end of August," Carlos said.

"You want me to sing in a recital? I'm not ready!" Lucy immediately felt panicky, her heart rate rising.

"Slow down! First, you don't have to sing, it's optional. I have a few other adult students who will be singing also. It will just be friends and family. I think you will be ready by then, plus it will be great practice for your audition. Just think about it."

"Okay, I will consider it." Lucy started to calm back down. What's the big deal, she thought. The worst thing that could happen is that she sang and was terrible. Or even that her mouth opened, and no sound came out and she stood there like a fool.

She knew the world wouldn't end. And she didn't even have to invite anyone she knew. But on the other hand, it seemed terrifying and just thinking about it felt like she might have a panic attack.

As Lucy grew older, she became more aware of how anxiety controlled her life, preventing her from doing so many things she wanted to do. Once she noticed that, she started consciously making the effort to push against those feelings and go after what she wanted.

Except at TerraPlaya. Things at work were just so balanced and comfortable right now and she couldn't bear to think of upsetting that part of her life.

Lucy decided she was going to practice her song as often as she could and by the end of August, she would be ready for the recital.

*   *   *

Later that evening, Lucy was rewatching the movie version of *Kiss Me, Kate*, starring Kathryn Grayson. The story was based on Shakespeare's *The Taming of the Shrew* and was one of Lucy's favorites. She had even gotten the chance to see it in stereoscopic 3-D a few years back, which was quite a treat.

She was halfway through the film when the phone rang. She didn't recognize the number, so she didn't answer. She hated talking on the phone even with people she liked, so she had no intention of answering to a stranger. They could leave a message if it was important. A minute later her phone buzzed. Lucy pressed play on the message.

"Lucy—this is Maya. Please call me back."

Why would Maya be calling her? Something about the field work? That wasn't until Wednesday so that couldn't be it. Lucy took a deep breath and hit the call button. Maya answered right away.

"Lucy! Thanks for calling me back!"

"No problem. What's up, is everything okay?"

"Tyler sprained his ankle. He won't be able to come with me to Sienna Fall Forest."

Lucy immediately felt guilty for all the bad thoughts she had about Tyler earlier that day. "That's terrible. Poor Tyler. What happened?"

"He was skateboarding and twisted it the wrong way. He has to stay off it for at least three weeks."

"Ugh—that's rough. How can I help?"

"I was wondering if you wanted to come and do the fieldwork with me?"

"Me?"

"Why not? You said you always had wanted to."

"That's true, but I'm not prepared. I don't have the right clothes or supplies. Plus, I don't know anything about birds!"

"That's okay, Tyler didn't either. I am the bird expert—he was going to help take field notes and photos and use the GPS unit."

"I don't think Anuk would like it. I'm not a field person. Plus, I have a lot of mapping work to get through."

"Well Tyler is going to need work to do with his sprained ankle. Can he help with some of that?"

"I guess, yes, he used to do mapping with me before he started going into the field. But still, I'm not sure this is a good idea."

"Why not? Come on Lucy, it will be fun. You have to see how beautiful Sienna Falls Forest is."

Lucy had seen photos of the site and she had to admit it was beautiful. And she really did want to get out from behind the desk for once.

But it was so last minute, and she could feel the anxiety creeping up on her again, filling her brain with a hundred reasons why she couldn't do this. That made Lucy mad. If Tyler could do this, so could she! She was pretty sure she could do it even better than Tyler.

"Okay, I'll do it! But only if Anuk says it is okay."

"Awesome! Leave Anuk to me—I'll talk with him in the morning. This is going to be great!"

The second she hung up the phone, Lucy started to have second thoughts. She paced back and forth across her living room. What if she got poison ivy? What if she couldn't remember how to use the GPS? What if she was just in the way? What if she and Maya had nothing to talk about on the long car ride there?

Calm down, she told herself. All these things can be handled if they happen, and chances are they won't. Let's just leave it up to fate. If Anuk approves it, then she would go. If he doesn't, then she would know it wasn't meant to be.

*   *   *

When Lucy arrived at work the next morning, she went to find Maya, but her cubicle was empty. Lucy went back to her own desk and waited impatiently to find out how the discussion went. Either way it turned out would be fine, but she just wanted to know.

She checked her e-mail and made a list of the tasks she needed to complete today. She had several maps she needed to make, but she knew she wouldn't be able to concentrate, so she went to fix her morning tea. On the way to the breakroom, she passed by Anuk's office and paused when she heard Maya's voice through the closed door.

"I think you are underestimating her," Maya said emphatically.

"Maya, you just started at this company. I am the manager and I make the decisions on how to distribute work to my team. Lucy is of greatest value to us with her mapping skills, and she isn't cut out for field work. That's my final decision."

Lucy rushed down the hall so she wouldn't be caught standing there when the door opened. She escaped outside to the courtyard to get some fresh air. After a few minutes, Maya pushed through the door and walked over to Lucy.

"Hey. I went to your cubicle and saw you out here."

"Yeah, I heard what Anuk said."

"I'm sorry Lucy, I made a case for you, but he didn't feel it was in the best interest of the office. He wants Bethany to go with me instead, but then I have to wait until next week when she is back from vacation. It's so dumb that they put people in such narrow roles here."

"I won't say I'm not disappointed. But thanks for trying, Maya. I really appreciate it."

"You sure you're okay?"

"Absolutely," Lucy lied. "I'd better go do some work. I'll see you later."

"Okay. I'm really sorry Lucy. I'm the one who got your hopes up. I should just mind my own business."

"Really, don't worry about it. It is what it is." Lucy shrugged and went back inside to her desk.

As Lucy was waiting for her mapping software to load, the glass paperweight etched with "10 years" caught her eye. By now she had been at the company for fourteen years.

She thought back to when she received the anniversary gift, thinking *Really? This is what ten years is worth?* Then she had felt bad because they treated her well at the company, she had decent pay, and decent benefits, and it didn't seem right to complain.

But then she imagined being sixty and getting a "30 years" present and it made her sick to her stomach. She wanted more, could be more, could do more. Who was Anuk to limit her potential? Why did Anuk think Tyler could learn new things, but Lucy couldn't?

It wasn't like she was trying to go to space on a rocket, she just was going to help with a field survey for Pete's sake! Lucy took a deep breath, stood up, and marched to Anuk's office.

The office door was open, and Lucy strode in. "We need to talk," Lucy stated matter-of-factly.

"Lucy. Come in, sit down. What can I do for you?"

Lucy remained standing. "I want to know why I can't help with the Sienna Falls field work."

Anuk looked surprised at her directness but responded quickly. "Okay. For starters, you have no field experience, you haven't taken the safety training, you don't have any field gear. You are also our best mapmaker, and we have a lot of maps that need to be produced right now."

Anuk's logic temporarily froze Lucy as her mind struggled to overcome her anxiety and produce a sound response. Then she took a deep breath and spoke calmly but assertively, "Hmm, those are all good reasons. But I really want to do this. Maybe I should have brought it up before, but it bugs me that Tyler gets to do all sorts of different things, but I am always just here in the office making maps. Tyler has the same degree as me—he isn't more qualified."

"I never said he was. I also didn't know this is something you really wanted," Anuk responded.

"Fair enough. Well, now you know. Can't Tyler cover for me on the mapping? He will need office work for at least three weeks."

"That's true, we will have to accommodate his situation. I'm still concerned with your lack of experience and training though."

"I can take the safety training this afternoon. And Maya has tons of experience. We'll be fine!"

"Okay, okay," Anuk relented. "This obviously means a lot to you, and we don't want to lose you, so we'll try this and see how it goes. I'm not saying this can be a permanent change in your responsibilities, but we can talk more about it in the coming months."

"Really?! Thank you so much. I promise it will go smoothly." Lucy practically skipped out of Anuk's office and down the corridor to Maya's desk.

She couldn't believe she had the guts to ask for what she wanted. Much less that it worked out in her favor. This felt like a new beginning for Lucy. She hadn't even known how much it mattered to her before Maya joined the company. It felt like the chance to shake things up a little, get some more adventure into her life. Find out what she is capable of.

Lucy snuck up behind Maya and whispered, "I'm going."

Maya turned around, a big grin on her face. "Anuk agreed? How?"

"I changed his mind!"

"That's awesome! You're going to love it."

"I hope so. If I mess this up, I'll never hear the end of it. I have to take some safety training this afternoon and I will need to buy some field gear."

"No problem—let's go shopping during lunch."

*   *   *

The rest of the day flew by, filled with the trip to buy hiking boots, a good hat, and an insect repellant long sleeved shirt, taking the safety training, printing out the final field maps, and testing the GPS unit in the parking lot.

She even spoke with Tyler on the phone, and he begrudgingly agreed to take over some of her projects while he was resting his ankle. Lucy couldn't believe it had all come together so fast. She couldn't wait for the next day to come.

After cooking a quick dinner of macaroni and cheese, Lucy took the tags off her newly purchased items, packed her overnight bag, and checked and doubled checked her to-do list.

Put more food in bird feeder. Clean dishes. Charge laptop. Check for extra cell phone charger and battery pack. Set alarm for earlier than normal. Set second alarm on phone in case anything went wrong with the first alarm.

She checked the weather and it still looked sunny and mild. By eight she had gone over everything multiple times and knew she was too excited to think about trying to go to sleep early. She turned again to her favorite ritual of tea and an old movie.

In keeping with the theme of her life, she decided to watch *Creature from the Black Lagoon*. One of her favorite monster movies, this one was black and white from 1954 and starred Julie Adams as marine research scientist Kay Lawrence, who travels with her boyfriend to the Amazon to look for an amphibious humanoid creature of legend.

One of Lucy's favorite scenes in any movie ever has Kay swimming in the lagoon, enjoying the respite from the Amazonian heat, while unbeknownst to her, the creature is silently swimming just beneath her in the depths of the water, stalking and admiring her.

Lucy was glad she and Maya were just looking for birds and not sloshing through any wetlands tomorrow. That got her thinking of other things she hadn't considered. Were there bears in these woods? A quick internet search of the county told Lucy there were no bears, which made her feel better, but there were mountain lions, which did not calm her nerves whatsoever.

She read about what to do if you see a mountain lion—make yourself look bigger by holding your jacket above your head. Make a lot of noise. Don't turn your back. Throw rocks or sticks near it.

Lucy started to feel sick to her stomach. Maybe Anuk was right. She didn't have any experience and there were a lot of things that could go wrong. She shook herself.

Get it together Lucy! Do not psych yourself out. This is going to be fine.

Lucy made herself a second cup of chamomile tea and breathed slowly in and out, eventually managing to fall asleep just past midnight.

*   *   *

Lucy woke up with the first alarm clock and hopped right out of bed as always. Morning person was an understatement. She was the most energetic within two hours of waking. Her mind was immediately running on overdrive the second she opened her eyes.

Lucy made some tea, checked her list one more time, and headed to the office to meet Maya in the office parking lot. Maya was already there with her trunk open, and the field gear loaded. Lucy waved hello and threw her overnight bag in the back.

"Are you ready?" Maya asked.

"Absolutely! Let's go!" Lucy climbed in the passenger side with excitement, put her teal insulated water bottle in the cup holder, and buckled herself in.

Maya handed her smartphone to Lucy. "Since I'm driving, you are in charge of two things: directions and music."

Lucy took the phone, already opened to a streaming music service. She didn't know Maya well yet and had a moment of panic. This could be the first thing to go wrong on the trip—that they didn't share any musical tastes in common! "Any requests? Not sure what you like to listen to while driving," Lucy said, trying to avoid being the one to pick the wrong song.

"Nope," said Maya. "You can pick anything from the library saved on there—it's all music I like, and I like lots of different styles, so put on whatever you want."

Lucy smiled at how easy it was to get along with Maya and turned on her favorite road trip music and set the navigator to start the four-hour drive to Sienna Falls Forest.

"Great choice, Lucy!" Maya pulled out of the parking lot, and they were on their way.

Over the next four hours they listened to some great music, and conversation flowed easily. Lucy always thought that nothing was better than a road trip for getting to know someone.

She learned that Maya had two brothers and that she ate dinner with her grandmother every Saturday. She learned that Maya's parents inspired her love of nature. They both worked at a sustainable nature resort that tried to balance tourism, environmental education, and economics while still benefiting the local community.

Lucy was usually awkward talking with people she hasn't known for long, but she felt comfortable with Maya. Before she knew it, they arrived in Sienna Falls Village, just outside of Sienna Falls Forest.

Lucy gaped out the window as they turned into the lodge parking lot.

Maya glanced over at her. "Don't get used to it. We don't usually stay at places like this during our field work. This is the only lodging near the forest, so our travel department negotiated special rates since we are making multiple trips."

"It's not what I was expecting, that's for sure." Since Maya had worked with corporate on the travel arrangements, Lucy had been expecting the typical rural chain hotel. Not anything like Sienna Falls Lodge.

The massive timber frame building was a perfect blend of traditional and modern architecture, mixing wood, glass, and stone features seamlessly. The front steps led to a wide limestone patio with inviting wrought iron benches. Large ceramic planters overflowed with trailing rosemary and yellow lantana.

The women grabbed their luggage and entered through the heavy wooden doors with glass panels into the foyer. Lucy's mouth fell open as she took in the extravagant stone fireplace in the room adjacent to the reception area, imagining how cozy it would be on a winter night. The floors were a dark hardwood, and the front desk was carved with intricate designs and covered with a marble slab. There was a traditional brass bell on the desk, but there was no need to ring it.

Behind the desk was a short woman with a sleek bob of salt and pepper hair. She wore cat-eye glasses with a silver chain adorned with blue glass beads. "Welcome ladies! Is this your first time here at the lodge?" asked the woman.

Lucy nodded and Maya responded, "It is. This place is stunning!"

"Why thank you ma'am. It is, isn't it? My name is Sylvia and if you need anything while you're here just give me a holler, okay? Let's get you checked in."

The women dropped their luggage in their rooms and grabbed a quick lunch at the lodge café. Fortified with a sandwich and calmed with some lavender tea, Lucy was eager to start her very first day of fieldwork.

Chapter 4

"WOW! THIS IS EVEN MORE beautiful than I imagined," Lucy remarked. Sienna Falls Forest was practically bursting with spring. The forest was dense with the twisted trunks and dark green foliage of ashe junipers, and shady limbs of the majestic live oaks. Beneath the forest canopy wildflowers blossomed, the bright red blossoms of the Turk's cap, and the clusters of iridescent-purple fruit of the American beautyberry.

Bald cypress trees lined the crystal-clear Sienna River, their roots reaching like long fingers into the water's edge as the river snaked through the forest. The babbling of the river joined the chorus of birds, croaking frogs, and leaves rustling in the breeze to create a quiet symphony of nature. Lucy breathed in the serenity and peacefulness and felt more relaxed and refreshed than she had in a long time.

Lucy tried not to be too distracted by her surroundings, instead focusing on the GPS unit in front of her. She wanted her first trip to be successful. "The first survey area is up ahead."

"Okay, here are the data sheets. Let's go see what's out there." Maya handed Lucy a clipboard with a pen attached with a string.

A few minutes later Maya stopped in front of a large ashe juniper tree. "You see how the bark is peeling? The Silver-winged Warbler makes its nest out of that bark. That's why this is such good habitat. Okay, I see a nest in that tree. Let me take a look."

Maya brought the binoculars to her eyes and shifted the focus knob. "That one looks empty but go ahead and take a GPS point there and mark on the data sheet that there was an empty nest."

Lucy took the GPS point and filled out the data sheet for that point. Maya walked on, stopping again, and listening, then looking through her binoculars. "There's a nest. Hold on—I can see an adult bird. It's a mockingbird."

Lucy took another GPS point and filled out another data sheet. And another, and another. The women walked in neat transects throughout the survey area, collecting data on any birds or nests they saw. That afternoon they spotted a Red-bellied Woodpecker, a Carolina Wren, a Hermit Thrush, a Ruby-crowned Kinglet, and a few sparrows and cardinals, but no Silver-winged Warblers. Lucy was starting to feel disappointed.

As if mother nature herself was warding off Lucy's despair, the women stumbled upon a White-tailed deer fawn curled up, waiting for its mother to return. It looked adorable with its little white spots and chin resting on its back legs.

The fawn raised its head when it heard the women. Lucy instinctively sent the animal a feeling of safety. At the same time Maya said, "Hey, little guy. We won't hurt you." The fawn lowered its head and drifted back to sleep. The women moved on with their survey, knowing the doe would return soon to find her fawn undisturbed.

Lucy started to think again about Maya's claim to be able to talk with animals. They hadn't had a chance to talk about it since the squirrel incident, but after the event with Mrs. Kleinbaum's cat Frederica, Lucy was starting to accept that not only was it possible to communicate with animals, but that she herself might actually be able to do so. "If you can talk with animals, can't you use that for this survey somehow?" she questioned Maya.

"Hmm. Well, honestly, I never thought about it. The most important thing is to avoid disturbing wildlife as much as possible during the survey, and that might be pretty upsetting if a human started talking to them. I usually only talk with pets or urban wildlife that are around humans on a regular basis, like in my yard or at the office park. But also, we need to be able to document our findings in a scientific way and it would be hard to explain if I was like 'hey—how many eggs you got in there, lady?'"

Lucy laughed. "Good point! But it still seems like it should come in handy."

"Maybe you're right." Maya scrunched up her forehead in consideration. "I bet we could use it to find the birds without even trying to talk to them, and that would help. Let me think on that."

"Cool. We could try it tomorrow."

"Definitely. We should start to head back to the lodge before it gets dark."

*   *   *

Having completed her very first day in the field without any mishaps, Lucy felt more accomplished than she had in ages. They had walked about six miles through the forest that afternoon after a four-hour drive.

She crawled into bed and turned on the television in her hotel room. After flipping through all the channels twice, she finally settled on an old rerun of Bewitched. As she watched, she thought the show was a good reminder of how careful she needed to be with this whole talking-to-animals situation. Maya might be not care what people think of her, but Lucy spent a considerable amount of energy trying to hide her anxiety and didn't need anything else to make her feel different from other people.

Today felt good, though. She had done something really different from her normal routine and it went fine. She got along with Maya well on the car ride and she didn't get poison ivy, at least that she knew of yet. She didn't get eaten by a mountain lion, she had no problems with the GPS, and they didn't get lost. Just a normal day of field work. No big deal.

Lucy wrote in her notebook a reminder to herself the next time she was worried about a laundry list of potential bad things that could happen, at least this time, nothing did.

Lucy was exhausted and her shoulders ached from carrying the GPS and backpack of supplies. Even so, she was looking forward to getting back to the forest tomorrow. She soon fell asleep with the television on.

That night she dreamt that she woke up in a field of wildflowers. The sun was shining, and meadowlarks were fluttering by. Every little breeze made the grasses sway back and forth with color, and she could feel the energy of the bees buzzing among the flowers, and the birds hunting for insects. She could hear the sing-song bird calls of dawn and smell the fresh morning dew and she knew she was part of it, that she belonged.

*   *   *

At 6 a.m. there was a knock on the door. Lucy opened it. "Good morning!" she said cheerfully.

Maya looked surprised. "Looks like you are all ready to go! I thought you might be tired after your first field outing."

"I've never slept better, and I can't wait to get back out there." Lucy slung the backpack over her shoulder.

"I feel the same way. But first, I wanted to talk with you about what you said yesterday."

"You thought of a way we could talk with the birds without disturbing them?"

"Sort of. I was thinking more of using it to locate them."

"Let's experiment and see what happens," Lucy agreed.

The women ate quickly at the lodge's breakfast buffet and headed out towards the second survey site. It was a two-mile hike to the next location. Lucy again marveled at how beautiful Sienna Falls Forest was. Since it was just after dawn, the forest had a different feel, like a pot of water just beginning to simmer.

The early birds started to sing as the nocturnal critters tucked into their holes for a nap. As they walked near the Sienna River Lucy spotted tiny fish in the water. Around the bend in the river the women startled a snowy egret, who took flight from the log that was sticking out from the shoreline.

"As we walk, I want you to start tuning into the different bird calls you are hearing. It's much easier to identify birds by their call than by trying to find them in the binoculars," Maya instructed.

"Okay. I don't know that many bird calls though, mostly just the ones that come to my feeder in the backyard."

"That's fine, I just want you to start noticing and differentiating among them."

As they walked on Lucy did start to notice more sounds. She heard cooing that she knew was probably a dove of some kind, she heard chirping sounds that seemed to her like a warning—'humans in the forest, humans in the forest!'

She heard whistles, clicking, and chattering, and short and long songs that repeated, perhaps a handsome fellow trying to attract a mate. Once the women heard the shriek of a hawk flying somewhere nearby, but they couldn't see it through the tree canopy.

Lucy was still navigating the GPS and announced to Maya that they were reaching the second survey site. Lucy got out the clipboard and data sheets and waited for Maya to proceed.

"Let's try something, Lucy. Let's close our eyes and listen to the birds in this area. Then tell me what you hear."

"Okay." Lucy took a minute to get back to the mindfulness state that Maya had taught her. It was easier to attain the more often she attempted it. First, she smelled the cedar-like scent of the ashe juniper, and felt the bark of the nearby tree, then she closed her eyes and focused on sounds. Before long she knew her sense of hearing was heightened, and she started to notice many more aural details than she had before.

On the surface there was the gurgle of the river where it was running over rocks, and the rustle of the leaves in the wind, and a few loud birds, like the cheep of a cardinal that she recognized from her yard feeder, but beneath that there were other sounds. There was a cricket chirping, a mosquito buzzing too close to her ear, and trees making slight creaking sounds when the wind gusted.

She focused in now on only bird sounds, and she heard one that sounded like a slow trill behind her, and another that was four parts—long, short, short, short to their right. Further in the distance she heard one that was a downward slurring sound. She opened her eyes.

"What did you hear?" asked Maya. Lucy explained to her as best she could without the proper terminology that she assumed experienced birders probably had.

"Whoa—that's amazing for a beginner. I think you might have a knack for this. Let's track these down and see if we can ID them." They started with the cheep, which Lucy had correctly identified as a cardinal, to her delight. The slow trill Maya thought was a sparrow, but she couldn't get a good enough look to identify the species.

The long, short, short, short Maya was particularly interested in since many warblers have similar calls. After what seemed to Lucy like forever of Maya looking through the binoculars from different angles, she announced that it was a Golden-winged Warbler. But Maya said that was still a good sign because that meant it was the right habitat.

They continued working their way through the second survey area, with Lucy documenting all the nests and sightings, but still no sign of the elusive Silver-winged Warbler. As they worked their way to the third survey area, Lucy wondered again if they were using their special skills to their advantage as much as they could.

"I don't know much about birding, but doesn't everyone listen for birds to identify them? Isn't there more you could do with your specialized abilities?" asked Lucy.

Maya nodded. "Yes, of course all birders listen for birds—that's part of how I said that anyone could learn to communicate with animals if they could be in the moment. Most birders build that skill as they stay quiet listening for hours on end. The rest get bored and find a different hobby. Think of this as the most basic level of animal communication—just listening and awareness."

Lucy bit her bottom lip. She knew she was already way past basic level on this but still didn't want to tell Maya about the squirrel's voice in her mind, or about what happened with Frederica the cat. "You said talking with them would be too disruptive, and that makes sense. But could we somehow let them know we are not here to harm them?"

"Hmm, I could probably communicate that we come in peace without directly talking to individual birds. Maybe then they would be more visible and easier to identify. Silver-winged Warblers are known for being shy and elusive."

"Exactly. Let them know they don't need to hide from us."

When they arrived at the third survey area, Maya put down her backpack and sat down on the forest floor. She closed her eyes and Lucy could tell she was slipping into a state of mindfulness as her face relaxed and a serene look washed over her.

Lucy felt the slightest change in energy of the forest, so minor it would have been undetectable had Lucy not already been well in tune with her surroundings. Without thinking, Lucy also sent out waves of calm to the forest floor. Maya opened her eyes immediately.

"Did you do that?" Maya asked, her eyes wide.

"What? I just let the forest know we were not here to hurt it." Lucy felt unsure of herself. Did she do something wrong? She didn't want to disturb the birds or mess up the survey.

"I know—I could feel it. It was powerful!"

"Really? I didn't even mean to do it, it just seemed right."

"It was perfect. Let's try it together and maybe it will be even more effective and extend even further."

Lucy sat down in front of Maya on the ground. Maya clasped her hands. Both women closed their eyes and once again sent out currents of peaceful energy as far as they could imagine. As they did, they heard subtle shifts in the sounds of the forest. The birds changed from the alarm calls warning of predators to the tuneful songs of mating. They opened their eyes in wonder.

Without speaking, the women stood up. Maya nodded to the right and Lucy grabbed her backpack and started walking in that direction. Maya lifted her binoculars and held her gaze for what seemed like an eternity to Lucy. Finally, she lowered them, a wide grin on her face.

"We found one. That is a Silver-winged Warbler nest!!!" Maya whispered with excitement. "Here, take a look." She handed the binoculars to Lucy and showed her which tree to look in.

"I see it! She's beautiful!" Lucy's heart filled with joy. She couldn't believe they had actually found the rare bird, that she was lucky enough to be here in this moment to share it, instead of sitting in her cubicle staring out the window.

Lucy took the GPS point and filled out the data sheet, and Maya took a lot of extra notes about the area where they found the Silver-winged Warbler. She took out her camera stand and zoom lens and took photos of the nest, the tree, and the area. The smile never left her face the whole time. Even though she hadn't known Maya for long, Lucy sensed that this was a special moment in Maya's career, and maybe even her life.

That afternoon they found two other Silver-winged Warbler nests in the third survey area. As the sun started to set, both women felt elated. The walk back to the lodge felt effortless because they were practically floating on air. They spoke very little, both happily savoring their time spent in Sienna Falls Forest.

*   *   *

Back at the lodge the front desk clerk greeted them. "Welcome back. You ladies look like you had a good hike! Are you enjoying your vacation?" Sylvia asked.

"It's beautiful here. But we're actually here for work," Maya replied. Maya explained about the survey as the clerk listened with interest.

Lucy stopped listening as she noticed out of the corner of her eye two men on the other side of the lobby looking their way. Both were wearing blue jeans with flannel shirts and baseball caps.

"That sounds pretty exciting! I didn't even know there were endangered birds in our forest," the clerk was saying as Lucy tuned back into the conversation.

As the women started back towards their rooms, Lucy leaned over to Maya and whispered, "Did you see those two men in the lobby?"

"Hmm—maybe—not sure, why?"

Lucy worried about sounding paranoid, but she trusted her intuition, and she trusted Maya. "I swear they were listening to our conversation."

"Huh. That's weird. Who do you think they were?"

"I have no idea."

Maya looked thoughtful. "Let's ask Sylvia tomorrow morning if she knows. But for now, let's have dinner and get some sleep."

After dinner Lucy was far from tired. She was still high from their amazing day, but also troubled by the men in the lobby. Maybe she was just feeling overwhelmed by all the unexpected changes in the past week, and this was just her anxiety manifesting itself.

Lucy busied herself with downloading the GPS data from the receiver and entering the datasheets into her laptop, then uploaded the files to the TerraPlaya server. By the time she was finished it was midnight and she was finally exhausted enough to sleep.

*   *   *

After breakfast the next morning, the women stopped by the front desk.

"Good morning, ladies," said Sylvia.

"Good morning!" replied the women.

"We had a question. Yesterday there were two men here in the lobby in flannel shirts and blue baseball caps. Do you know who they were?" Maya asked.

Sylvia shook her head. "Sorry, but I can't give any information about other guests."

Lucy started to apologize and walk away but Maya pulled her back.

"Oh, we totally understand, it's just Lucy here thought one of them was really cute and they shared a moment, and we were hoping to find out where they work," Maya lied.

Sylvia's eyes lit up. "You got me—I am a sucker for romance! They have been here before, so they probably are on a corporate account. Let me check. It couldn't hurt anyone just to give you the name of the company." Sylvia checked her computer and then nodded. "Looks like they are from Sepharine Holdings Inc."

"Thank you so much, Sylvia!" said Maya.

"Of course! Don't forget to invite me to the wedding," Sylvia laughed.

The women smiled back and walked quickly towards their rooms.

"I can't believe you did that, Maya!!!" Lucy scolded along the way.

"What? You wanted to know and now we do."

Lucy snorted in disbelief at Maya's gumption. But she was also glad her new colleague pushed a little past her comfort zone.

Lucy opened the door to her room and gasped. "What the hell?" Her face paled in shock as she took in the scene. Someone had been in her room.

39

Her neatly stacked datasheets gone. Her laptop was gone. The GPS unit was gone. Lucy's hands started shaking and she felt like she might pass out. She ran down the hall.

"Maya!" she shouted outside her door.

Maya swung the door open "You too? I can't believe this!" Her room was also in disarray.

"Did they get your laptop?" Lucy asked.

"Yes, and they took the camera too." Maya was shaking her head in disbelief.

"We were only gone for a few minutes for breakfast. How could this happen?"

"Someone must have been watching us to time it so well. Let's go tell the front desk so we can file a police report. We shouldn't touch anything."

Lucy was grateful for Maya's composure. Lucy felt like she was going to throw up her breakfast and her hands were still shaking. Maya seemed more angry than anything else.

The police came and the women filed a report. Sylvia was apologetic and assured them that this had never happened before. Maya got Lucy some tea to help calm her down and told her on the bright side at least the women had their purses with their wallets and car keys at breakfast, so they didn't have to change all their credit cards or anything like that.

Lucy sat with her hands clutching the tea and she had a sudden look of dread on her face. "Anuk! He is never going to let me go out again when he hears about this."

"This isn't your fault—hotel rooms get broken into—that could happen to anyone. It has nothing to do with you," Maya reasoned. "Plus, the actual field work went fine. Although I guess we lost the data." Maya's face fell.

"No—I uploaded all the GPS data and entered the data sheets before I went to bed. It's all on the server."

"You did? You are awesome, Lucy!" Maya beamed at her. "I also uploaded all the photos to the server. So, we didn't lose any of the data. They aren't going to be happy about the laptops, camera, and GPS, but I'm sure they have insurance for those things. The important thing is we have the survey data. Nothing can change that we found Silver-winged Warblers."

Chapter 5

"HI MRS. KLEINBAUM!" LUCY SAID as the door opened.

"Lucy dear, come in." Mrs. Kleinbaum closed the door and motioned for Lucy to have a seat. As if on cue, Frederica jumped on the chair again and both women laughed.

"Hi sweet girl! How are you feeling?" Lucy asked the cat. Frederica purred and rubbed her head on Lucy's hand.

"We owe you a thanks, Lucy, she did have an ear infection. My little Frederica isn't too happy about me putting drops in her ear, but I can tell she feels much better now."

"I'm so glad!" Lucy pet the cat's chin as she flopped on her side like a furry rug. She noticed that once again, Mrs. Kleinbaum refrained from asking Lucy how she knew about the ear infection. Lucy desperately wanted to tell someone everything that has been going on, but she was worried she would sound crazy.

"Is there something on your mind?" Mrs. Kleinbaum looked at Lucy with earnest concern.

"That is putting it mildly. A lot has been going on lately."

"I'm happy to listen if you want to tell me about it. I've seen a lot in my life and nothing you say will surprise me."

Lucy knew that Mrs. Kleinbaum would probably accept her story without judgment. She did really want to say it all out loud to hear how it sounded outside of her head.

Before she knew it, she was telling Mrs. Kleinbaum about Maya, and the squirrel, and Frederica, and the birds in the forest. Mrs. Kleinbaum listened intently until Lucy was completely empty of words.

"That's exciting! First of all, I'm so proud of you for standing up for yourself and getting this wonderful opportunity. Sienna Falls Forest sounds magical."

"So, you don't think I'm nuts?" asked Lucy.

Mrs. Kleinbaum shook her head. "Of course not! At my age you realize as long as you've lived there is still so much more to know and each one of us just scratches the surface. And I could always tell from watching you and Frederica that you have an affinity for animals. Hey! Can you tell me what Frederica is thinking now?"

"It doesn't exactly work like that, but I can try to ask her and see what happens." Lucy closed her eyes and focused on Frederica's soft rumble purr, quickly falling into that special state of mindfulness that was getting easier to find each time. Then she opened her mind to Frederica.

Treats!

Lucy threw back her head and started laughing uncontrollably.

"What is it? What did she say?" Mrs. Kleinbaum demanded.

"She wants treats!" Lucy croaked out between laughs.

"Ha! You don't need special powers to know that." Mrs. Kleinbaum joined in the laughter and the two of them roared while Frederica, looking quite insulted, jumped down from the chair and stormed off with her tail held high in the air.

"Aww—come back, Frederica my dear." Mrs. Kleinbaum went to the cabinet, took out two treats and gave them to the indignant cat.

*   *   *

Lucy was relieved that Maya had been right. Anuk was not happy about the loss of equipment and the delay in the project schedule, but he was more concerned that the women were safe than anything else. And he agreed that the same thing could have happened if Tyler had gone instead, so it had little to do with Lucy.

However, the remainder of the Sienna Fall Forest survey was postponed until they received the new laptops, camera, and GPS, which was disappointing for Lucy. She started on the mapping based on the data they had collected, while Maya set up the report and data tables. Since both Lucy and Tyler were doing mapping for a few weeks, the upside was that her workload was light, and she had time to focus on other things.

She tried to find out more about Sepharine Holdings Inc. All she found on the internet was a generic looking property investment company. Nothing that would provide any clues as to why they would be interested in Lucy and Maya's conversation with Sylvia.

On a whim, Lucy searched through the archives of the local town paper, the Sienna Falls Herald. She wasn't sure what she was looking for, but she figured she'd know it when she saw it. Most of the articles were about typical small-town happenings, like the antique car show, or the spring dance, or features on the homecoming queen or a pumpkin that looked like FDR. But then she found a headline that caught her eye. It was an obituary from three years ago.

Grady McWalter III, largest landowner and descendant of the founding family of Sienna Falls dies at 87.

Grady McWalter III was a rancher, a philanthropist, and an upstanding member of the Sienna Falls community. He sat for twenty-two years on the town council. In 1978 he donated 1,900 acres of his family's land to the town to be forever preserved as Sienna Falls Forest.

The article went on to talk about his many charitable ventures, but what Lucy was interested in was what happened to his remaining land when he died. The article said his wife and only son had tragically been killed in a car accident years ago. She was guessing that if he owned the land that Sienna Falls Forest was on that he probably had owned the adjacent land as well.

Since Lucy worked with land parcel data for her job all the time, she knew to look at the county appraisal district website. Before long she was viewing a web mapper of land in Sienna Falls Village. First, she clicked on the actual forest, and sure enough the county records showed the transfer from Grady McWalter III to the town in 1978. Then she clicked on the large parcel to the west. The owner was listed as Boxultor Properties, Inc. It appeared that the land had transferred from the McWalter Family Trust to Boxultor five years ago and the land had already been plotted for a subdivision.

Lucy recalled from the drive to Sienna Falls that some of the land was already being cleared and she remembered billboards advertising the future subdivision.

Lucy clicked on the parcel east of the forest. It still showed as being owned by the McWalter Family Trust, with no transfers in recent years. She wondered who was managing the land and what would happen to it in the future. She made a mental note to investigate further, but right now she had a team meeting to attend. She grabbed her pen and notepad and made her way to the conference room.

Lucy noticed immediately that Anuk didn't seem like his normal positive cheerleader self today. When he started the meeting, she knew that she was right.

Anuk stood at the head of the conference room. "Everyone, I have some news." The room immediately stirred with the buzz of nervous employees fearing the worst. Anuk continued, "I don't want to alarm anyone. No one is losing their job right now. But corporate is not as happy as they could be with the performance of our region, and they will be sending a representative to spend some time here in our office next week. It is important that we put our best foot forward and show them that we have what it takes to perform at a higher level in the next quarter."

Bethany spoke up first, pointedly asking, "Like, what does that mean? Is this, like, some kind of Office Space situation?"

"I don't think so," Anuk replied, "but this is the first time since I've been here that this has happened so I can't honestly say for sure. I don't think anyone who has been busy and delivers quality products to our clients needs to worry. And as far as I'm concerned that is every person in this office."

Lucy glanced at Maya, and Maya gave her a worried look back. In the fourteen years that Lucy had worked for TerraPlaya, corporate had generally left her office alone. But when the company was acquired by an even larger firm, she started to see some changes. They expected much higher profits and much lower overhead and were less willing to invest in their employees.

She felt bad for Maya, who had only been at the company for a few weeks and was probably wondering what she had gotten herself into. She also felt bad for Anuk, because although he seemed to be taking it in stride, she knew that corporate held him partially responsible for the disappointing office profit since he was the department manager.

After the meeting, Lucy tried to reassure Maya that there was nothing to worry about and that Maya's skillset was critical to the success of the office. Maya seemed to feel a little bit better, but understandably left for the evening still looking unsure.

*   *   *

After the troubling news at work, Lucy arrived home glad to have other things to focus on besides her job. Most evenings Lucy practiced her voice lessons, still determined to sing in the student recital. Today Lucy felt more than ever the pleasant distraction of losing herself in the music. She also noticed that the feeling she had when she was lost in her singing was quite like the feeling she had when she worked on communicating with animals.

To sing, Lucy had to be in touch with her breathing, with her body, careful not to hold any unnecessary tension. At the same time, she had to focus on the words, and the music, and her technique, as well as the feeling she was trying to project to her imagined audience.

Lucy also practiced a technique her voice teacher taught her about preparing for a performance. She was supposed to visualize getting up in front of the audience, confident and tall, then imagine singing through her song with emotion and intensity, all the way to the end.

Carlos had said that the more detail she could imagine in the performance, the stronger the benefit would be. She tried to focus on the timbre she wanted her voice to have, the inflection of each word and phrase, and the connection with the audience.

She didn't know if this practice would help her in the recital, but she did notice that the more that she practiced it, the less intimidated she felt about singing in front of an audience. Perhaps because in her visualization, the audience was engaged and appreciative of her performance, and gave her some heartfelt warm applause when she finished singing.

Practicing her voice lessons and her animal communication felt like cross training to Lucy, as each one seemed to benefit from the other. Lucy was finding these days that she could slip into the mindfulness state needed to communicate with creatures in seconds rather than minutes, and she could stay focused more easily and for longer periods of time.

This evening Lucy was microwaving popcorn to snack on while she watched a movie when she saw something move on the floor out of the corner of her eye. "Eeeek!" Lucy shrieked as she jumped back. A brown scorpion was crawling near her kitchen door, apparently having slipped under the door sill.

It was about three inches long, and when it saw her, it raised its tail showing her its stinger. Its front pincers reminded her of a tiny lobster.

Lucy had seen her fair share of scorpions, but that lifted stinger, ready to strike, never failed to instantly raise her pulse and make her skin tingle all over. She knew that although scorpion stings in Northbrook would hurt like hell, none of them were particularly dangerous. Still, she did not want it in her house. Nor did she want to harm it.

Quickly shifting states while still keeping an eye on the tiny beast, Lucy sent it a message in her head, and since she was alone, out loud, "I'm sorry but I'm going to have to ask you to leave. I do not want to hurt you, but as long as you are here in my house, I will be afraid of being stung. Please go back the way you came."

Lucy waited to see what would happen. She hadn't ever asked an animal to do anything, but she reasoned that just because you can talk to something that doesn't mean it will necessarily obey, just like with people.

The scorpion moved its pincers and for a moment Lucy thought it was going to run towards her. But then the scorpion turned around and started moving towards the kitchen door.

Fair enough. It is in my nature to sting, after all.

And the scorpion slipped back under the door sill to the back yard.

Lucy vowed to get a better seal for under her door. Then it dawned

46

on her how incredible what had just happened really was. She had not only communicated with an animal, but she had an actual conversation that resulted in a positive outcome. She was starting to realize that there was limitless potential for how this skill could be used.

She longed to talk more with Maya about this, but she had a gut feeling that she had already surpassed Maya's skillset. Her intuition said she should explore this avenue deeper on her own and see how far she could take it, and then she would probably have a thing or two she could teach Maya.

Lucy retrieved her popcorn from the microwave and in keeping with her ongoing theme, she decided to watch *Them!*, one of the first of the Atomic Age monster movies, this one about gigantic, irradiated ants in the New Mexico desert.

Lucy knew it would probably give her nightmares, especially after seeing a scorpion in her house, but she also felt comforted by watching black and white movies and imagining how much scarier they probably were to viewers at the time.

Chapter 6

IT WAS LUCY'S GREATEST HOPE that they would get the new GPS unit in time to go back to Sienna Falls Forest and conveniently miss the visit from corporate. But although they had their new laptops up and running, the GPS delivery was delayed, and Bethany was using the other one for a different project that week. When corporate came, both Lucy and Maya were stuck in the office.

Mitchell Price was the chief operating officer of the corporation that had bought TerraPlaya. He was accompanied by a consultant specializing in corporate efficiency.

Lucy would have laughed because it seemed Bethany was right on point with her Office Space comment. But given that they actually did schedule one on one meetings with each employee, it didn't seem funny at all.

On one hand, Lucy wasn't too worried because she was always highly utilized, but on the other hand she was very anxious because justifying herself to a stranger was her worst nightmare.

The day began with a meet and greeted in the conference room. Mitchell introduced himself and explained that they were just there to help us all fulfill our potential. He thanked everyone for their hard work and expressed that he believed that this office was capable of great things. Lucy had to stop from gagging on the corporate mumbo jumbo this guy was spouting.

Then he introduced the consultant, Hyun Shim. She had a bright smile and gave a warm greeting, but Lucy could tell this woman was smart and tough and probably ruthless, which is what her job required. Lucy respected that, and as long as she was also reasonable, they would get along fine.

First Hyun sent out an employee survey that everyone would need to fill out before their individual appointments. Lucy knew she would need to be careful completing it because the consultant was looking for certain traits that would indicate problem employees.

Once corporate decides to use metrics they tend not to listen as much to supervisors, even though they were the ones to see employees in action. Even her fourteen years of good reviews from Anuk may mean nothing to the parent corporation. TerraPlaya was just one of several smaller firms they had acquired, and she was just one of thousands of employees.

After the meeting Lucy made some more tea and settled down to complete the survey. Sure enough it had a lot of statements that you could agree or disagree with on a scale of one to five. Things like 'I want to give more than 100 percent to my company.'

"Really?!?" Lucy mumbled under her breath. "First of all, it's not even possible to have more than 100 percent of something. Second of all, why do corporations feel the need to suck all the life blood out of a person? Why isn't it enough that I do consistently high-quality work for forty hours a week? Why do they also need me to act like this job is the highest purpose a person can have?"

That was part of what she always appreciated about TerraPlaya—they valued that she did her job efficiently and with care, but they didn't push her to become a manager or work sixty hours a week. That was before the company was acquired, though. Now Lucy really started to worry about her interview with Hyun.

As her anxiety started to build, she took out her notepad and started to brainstorm ways she could get out of the meeting. One option was that she could say she was sick and go home but that might draw unwanted attention. Another option was that she could ask for the appointment to be moved because she had a big deadline. But that might make her look like she couldn't manage her schedule.

In the end, Lucy decided that third and best option was that she would go to the evaluation. In this case, making the decision didn't calm her nerves at all.

Her meeting with Hyun was after lunch so she had several hours to become even more anxious than she already was.

As if reading her mind, Maya stopped by her cubicle. "Want to eat in the courtyard? I could use a break."

"Yes!" agreed Lucy immediately, desperate for any distraction. Sitting outside in the peaceful garden was exactly what she needed.

The women got their lunches from the kitchen and made their way outside, welcoming another beautiful Northbrook late spring day. It was almost summer, and soon it would be too hot to eat outside.

Neither woman seemed talkative since they were both preoccupied with Hyun Shim. Lucy ate half of her sandwich before her anxious stomach complained.

She closed her eyes and felt the warm breeze wash over her. It was hot enough that the birds were quiet by noon. She opened her eyes again and saw a little green anole on the tree watching her drink out of her water bottle.

She took the lid from her Tupperware and poured some water in it. "Would you like some water?" she asked the anole out loud, setting down the lid at the base of the tree. "We won't bother you. We'll sit right here and wait for you to get a drink." Lucy sat back down and waited.

Maya looked on as the anole scampered down the tree, drank out of the Tupperware, and scampered back up. "How did you know he was thirsty?" she asked.

Lucy smiled. "I saw the way he was eyeing my water bottle. Poor little guy. They really should have put a water feature back here. Maybe we could put a little bird bath and fill it up every day."

"That's a great idea," Maya replied. "You've become much more attuned to animals in a such a short time. It's really impressive!"

Lucy felt kind of bad that she hadn't told Maya everything yet, but she really wanted to keep it to herself for now. Still, it felt great that Maya was complimentary of her progress. "Thanks! I have been practicing."

This was true, especially since the scorpion incident, Lucy practiced animal communication regularly, just like she practiced her voice lessons.

She practiced going into the state of mindfulness whenever she had a free moment. She tried talking with her backyard birds at the feeder.

And of course, she had become fast friends with Frederica, Mrs. Kleinbaum's cat. As much as one can be friends with a cat, anyway. Nothing as successful as her interaction with the scorpion had occurred, but she was starting to intuitively understand animals, even when she wasn't communicating with them directly.

*   *   *

At first the questions that Hyun asked Lucy seemed innocent and impersonal, like did Lucy have all the software and hardware she needed to do her job. Then she moved to questions about her supervisor Anuk, and if he provided the support she needed to do her job.

Lucy tried to answer carefully to protect Anuk, since he was a kind person, and had always been a great mentor to her, not to mention letting her have this recent opportunity to go to Sienna Falls.

Lucy started to open up a little, but in her mind, she knew that is what Hyun wanted, to start with the softball questions first and build trust between them.

And then it came.

"Where do you see yourself in five years?" asked Hyun.

Lucy could feel her anxiety escalating as she knew there was a "right" answer to the question, and her honest answer would not be well received. The fact was she wanted to continue making maps, and if Sienna Falls worked out, occasionally assist with the field work.

That's it.

She didn't have any serious ambition to move up the corporate ladder, or to make work a bigger part of her life. Anuk never pushed her because he valued the work that she did and the expertise that she brought to the team.

Lucy decided to go with that angle, because if she outright lied, she would start sweating as her anxiety went through the roof and she would look even worse to Hyun.

Lucy was aware that too much time had passed when she finally answered, "I hope to continue to build my technical skills as the mapping technology improves, and help the company stay on the forefront of the mapping industry."

She felt gross as she said the words, but it wasn't untrue. She really did intend to keep up with the latest tech and even improve processes as she had in the past.

Hyun was typing notes in her laptop as Lucy responded. She looked at Lucy as if she could see right through her. "You see your role as a technical expert?"

"Yes," Lucy replied plainly, trying to keep her rising emotions out of her voice.

"Do you do programming or customization of the mapping software?" Hyun questioned.

"No, my job doesn't require that, but I do frequently create models that automate processes within the program to make things we do often more efficient," Lucy responded.

Hyun kept typing. "Did you know your company has a corporate level team that does advanced customization of mapping software?"

"Yes, I have worked with them on occasion."

"But you haven't tried to develop any new markets for the types of work your company is capable of doing relating to map products?"

Lucy was starting to sweat through her blouse and her hands were starting to tremble as she felt like she was being attacked. But she tried to keep a level head. "I focus on producing quality deliverable for our clients so we can have repeat business, and that in turn helps us get more work from those clients," Lucy answered with satisfaction.

Hyun didn't seem happy with Lucy's answer. "You consider yourself a technical expert, but you don't have any advanced technical skills?"

Lucy's mouth was parched so she paused to get some water. While she was tilting her head up to drink, she saw a huge cockroach crawling along the ceiling. She was not a big fan, but they were unavoidable in Northbrook, so she wasn't squeamish about them either.

Lucy started to form an idea in her head. She was starting to panic and needed to get out of this interview as soon as possible before she said something she would regret.

Without waiting for Lucy's answer, Hyun fired another question at her. "You've worked here fourteen years and you have never made any move into management or other leadership positions. Why is that?"

Lucy felt like her brain was going to explode with anxiety and she might throw up her half sandwich. She reached out desperately with her mind, hoping that her plan would work.

Hyun screamed as the giant cockroach "fell" off the ceiling onto her lap. She leapt out of her chair, still shrieking, brushing the creature to the floor.

Hyun's eyes followed the cockroach as it ran back up the wall, then she grabbed her laptop and darted for the door. "We will finish this conversation later, Lucy. I can't work in these conditions!"

Lucy waited as long as she could for Hyun to be far enough away before she started laughing. It felt great to release all that tension that had been building, and she unclenched her hands that she hadn't even realized were all balled up into fists in her lap.

She could finally breathe again. "Thanks, I owe you one," Lucy told the cockroach, shaking her head because that was not something she had ever imagined saying in her lifetime.

When she arrived back at her cubicle, she grinned. On her desk was the GPS unit that had just been delivered. She and Maya could finally return to Sienna Falls.

*   *   *

"Ladies! I'm surprised to see you. Welcome back," Sylvia said when she saw Lucy and Maya.

"Hi Sylvia!" Lucy and Maya responded. Lucy continued, "We are here to finish the survey now that we replaced our equipment."

Sylvia sighed with remorse over the recent theft. "Thanks for giving us another chance. We have new security cameras, and we hired an additional security officer since you were last here, so please don't worry about a thing. That was not a normal event for our little town," Sylvia assured them.

"That's great to hear," Maya replied.

Lucy had a sudden thought. "Hey Sylvia, how long have you lived in Sienna Falls?"

Sylvia smiled. "All my life, I'm lucky to say! Why do you ask?"

"Did you know Grady McWalter III?"

"Sure. Everyone in town knew Grady. His family pretty much founded the town, and if it weren't for him there wouldn't even be a Sienna Falls Forest."

"Because he donated the land, right?" prompted Lucy. Maya looked curiously at Lucy, wondering what she was getting at.

"That's right," said Sylvia. "You've been learning your Sienna Falls history. Not just that though, without Grady, this whole area would probably be one big logging operation."

Maya gasped at the thought of Sienna Falls Forest cut down. "That would be a real shame. Thank goodness for Grady or we would never have seen a Silver-winged Warbler."

"Indeed," Sylvia continued. "There was a time when the other town council members almost agreed to sell part of the town, but Grady convinced them not to. It's already sad enough that part of his land is now being developed for subdivisions. But people have to live somewhere I guess, and who can blame them for wanting to live somewhere so beautiful?"

Lucy nodded in agreement "True enough. That's a nice way to think about it. So, what happened to the rest of his land? To the east of Sienna Falls Forest—did it go to his heirs?"

Sylvia shook her head. "It's quite tragic really. Grady's wife and son died in a car accident, and he lived alone for the rest of his years, mourning, becoming more and more of a hermit as he got older. Last I heard that land was tied up in court, with siblings and their children trying to lay claim to it since Grady never updated his will."

"The land is just sitting empty right now?" asked Lucy.

"Yep, and I bet it stays that way for years while the lawyers make all the money."

"Thanks Sylvia. We'd better get set up to do our survey now."

"Have a great day, ladies." Sylvia waved as Lucy and Maya headed to put their things in their rooms.

Lucy wondered how many more Silver-winged Warblers they would see today. She couldn't wait to find out.

Chapter 7

AS LUCY AND MAYA STARTED the trek to the fourth survey area, they felt the tranquility of the forest and the babbling of the river soothe their city stresses. Even carrying the equipment and hiking for miles seemed relaxing to them compared with working in a cubicle all day.

The worries about Hyun the efficiency expert faded from Lucy's mind as she started to focus on the sounds of the birds chattering and the trees rustling.

Again, the two women walked mostly in silence, with Lucy leading the way with the GPS unit. They recognized some of the forest features, like the big bend in the river, and the grassy area where they had seen the spotted fawn. They heard a variety of the more common birds and saw a few nests along the way.

Once they heard a splash near the river and they walked over to see a moss covered Red-eared Slider paddling away from them. Lucy had always been fond of turtles. In Northbrook there were often dozens of turtles sunning themselves on rocks in the park pond near her house and she loved to admire them.

As they hiked on, the forest started to slowly change. After a minute, Lucy turned to Maya, who shook her head.

"Something's not right," Maya said.

"It's too quiet," replied Lucy, as she realized she could no longer hear the chirping or songs of any birds.

As hard as she strained to hear something alive, she could only hear the river continuing its ceaseless flow, but not so much as a single sound of a bird calling. The forest seemed unnaturally still.

"Where are we compared to the third survey area?" asked Maya.

Lucy looked down at the GPS then widened her eyes as she whispered, "We're in it now."

"But there's nothing here!" Maya looked through her binoculars with distress, hoping to find some remnant of the vibrant forest they had seen just a short time ago. "You have the GPS points from the previous survey on there, right? Where was one of the Silver-winged Warbler nests?"

Lucy nodded and pointed to the left, leading Maya's gaze towards a large tree. Maya looked through her binoculars. "I see the nest. It's empty," she said as the blood drained from her face.

Lucy frowned. "Are you sure? Maybe the mother is out getting food?"

"No. The nest is destroyed," Maya said with quiet rage.

"How long do they stay in the nests, could the babies have fledged?" Lucy asked in desperation, not wanting to believe the birds they had been so thrilled to witness could have met a tragic end.

Maya shook her head. "The eggs incubate for twelve days or so, and then the young leave about nine to twelve days after hatching." She squeezed her eyes shut, trying to make sense of it. "They should still be here. But even if my count is off, this nest was destroyed. That is not what a natural decay looks like."

Lucy started to feel sick to her stomach. "Are you saying they were purposely destroyed?"

"I don't know what to think, but this is not normal." Maya was struggling to keep her composure with anger, panic, and sorrow welling up inside of her. "Where are the other two nests?"

Lucy directed her to the other two points. Maya looked at the trees through her binoculars, shook her head and crumpled to the ground. "They're all gone. Destroyed."

In the brief time Lucy had known her, she had never seen Maya look so lost.

A tear started streaming down Maya's cheek as she lamented, "I can't believe we lost them. We had found hope, Lucy. Hope for a beautiful bird that had done nothing wrong but make their homes in forests that humans want to cut down. And we found them. And now they're gone." Maya put her head in her hands and wept.

Lucy put her arm around Maya and consoled her. Even though Lucy didn't have a lifetime of experience looking for endangered birds like Maya did, she still had been deeply moved when they had found the Silver-winged Warbler nests.

It hurt her deeply that they were gone. But there was nothing she could say to make it better, so she simply let Maya cry on her shoulder and release her pain.

When Maya's weeping subsided, Lucy handed her some water and some trail mix from the backpack. "Eat. You need energy for the hike back."

Maya forced a half-smile in thanks and reluctantly ate a small handful. She chewed thoughtfully and Lucy could practically see the gears turning in Maya's mind.

"But we aren't hiking back yet," said Maya. "First, we need to take some photos of the destroyed nests. Then we need to push on to survey area four. I need to know if there is anything out there. What if this is an anomaly? I can't give up hope that there are more Silver-winged Warblers in this forest." Maya stood up with determination.

Lucy was speechless with admiration for her new friend. If Maya wasn't giving up, neither would she. Lucy gathered up the gear, turned on the GPS and brought up the data for the next survey area, while Maya suppressed her feelings enough to take the photos to document the damaged nests. When Maya was done, Lucy pointed the way.

They pushed on to survey area four and walked the transects as they had done for the first three survey areas, but they found nothing. No inhabited nests of any kind, not even the common birds that had been plentiful before.

It was like something had washed through the area, removing everything in its path. Since Lucy had become so attuned to her senses, the emptiness and silence of the forest was deeply unsettling. It was horror-movie creepy.

Their hearts were heavy with sadness as they were forced to accept that there were no birds in this part of the forest, and they had no hope of seeing any more Silver-winged Warblers. They completed the survey of area four with nothing to show for it.

"Did you hear that?" Maya asked.

"Yeah—it sounded like a truck somewhere over there," Lucy said, pointing to the east.

"You have the forest boundary on the GPS, right? How close are we to the edge?"

Lucy looked at the GPS unit and zoomed out to see the eastern boundary. "Maybe like a quarter of a mile to Grady McWalter's property."

"Let's go check it out."

"Is that a good idea? We should really get back. It's a long way."

"Just to the fence line. It won't take long. I have a gut feeling about this. Trust me, Lucy."

Lucy sighed. "I do. Let's go."

Lucy led the way with her GPS unit and after a while they could see the fence line posted with signs that said, "Private Property, No Trespassing." They had walked along the fence for ten minutes when Maya stopped short.

"Get down!" Maya pulled Lucy lower to duck behind a bush. From their hiding place the women watched as a navy-blue pickup truck drove down the ranch road on the other side of the fence.

Lucy gasped. "Did you see that guy?"

"Yep. That's one of the men who was in the lobby listening to our conversation before our stuff got stolen. What are they doing here? I thought no one was supposed to be on that land?"

"There could be a legitimate reason—taking care of the property or lawyer stuff. I don't know." Lucy was thinking out loud, not wanting to jump to conclusions.

Maya looked at her incredulously. "You don't really believe that do you?"

Lucy shook her head. "Nope. Something bad is going on here, and it definitely has something to do with them. But I'm not sure we should get involved in this."

Maya snorted. "We already are, Lucy! Do you still think it was a random coincidence that our laptops and GPS unit were stolen? When no one else's rooms were broken into? And now the birds that we had surveyed are mysteriously gone?"

"Of course not! I just don't know what we can do about it, that's all." Lucy was battling feelings of helplessness and anxiety, complicated even more because she didn't want to let Maya down.

Maya took a deep breath in and let it back out. Then she spoke with the calm resolution that Lucy had observed many times during their short friendship, "I don't either, but I'm going to figure it out. Are you in?"

In seconds, Lucy's anxieties flashed through her mind—they could get in serious trouble, or even get hurt. But when she replayed watching Maya see the Silver-winged Warbler nest for the first time, she knew there was no going back to who she was before. No sitting in the office and watching the world go by. She had to help her friend and help the birds.

"I'm in," Lucy replied.

Chapter 8

"HAPPY BIRTHDAY MRS. KLEINBAUM!" LUCY sang when the door opened. She handed Mrs. Kleinbaum a small clear vase full of sunflowers.

"Thank you, Lucy! These will really brighten up the room." Mrs. Kleinbaum said as she admired the bouquet.

Frederica the cat sauntered in and looked at the flowers with interest. "Now Frederica, you stay away from these flowers, alright?" Lucy warned.

Frederica started washing her paw and pretended she didn't hear Lucy. Lucy and Mrs. Kleinbaum laughed at Frederica's typical behavior.

"Sunflowers aren't toxic to cats, but she could still get an upset stomach if she eats them," Lucy explained to Mrs. Kleinbaum.

"I'll make sure she can't get them. Would you like some tea, dear?" asked Mrs. Kleinbaum.

"Yes, please. I brought a mini angel food cake topped with strawberries and whipped cream."

"You spoil me, Lucy! While the water is heating up why don't you tell me what has been going on with you."

Lucy filled Mrs. Kleinbaum in on what had happened at Sienna Falls Forest while they ate cake and drank tea.

"I'm worried you are getting into a dangerous situation," Mrs. Kleinbaum said, her brows furrowed.

Lucy nodded, "I don't disagree with you, but we can't let this go—we need to figure out what happened." Lucy spoke with a resolve that Mrs. Kleinbaum hadn't seen before.

"I can see that. You've changed a lot over the past few months. You seem to have found a sense of purpose."

Lucy considered this for a moment. "I guess I have. I hadn't really noticed until now. I thank Maya for that," Lucy replied.

Mrs. Kleinbaum had a faraway look in her eyes. "You bring back memories of me and my best friend when I was younger. Before I was married, Trish and I both taught high school. I taught English and she taught Social Studies. Since we had summers off, we used to travel across the country. We went to the Grand Canyon, Mount Rushmore, Carlsbad Caverns, we saw shows on Broadway in New York City, went to the top of the Space Needle in Seattle, and ate beignets at Café Du Monde in New Orleans."

"Gosh—that sounds amazing," Lucy replied.

"It was. Although I had a wonderful marriage until Andrew passed away, I will always cherish those summers with Trish. Nothing is more valuable than a true friend."

Lucy nodded in agreement. Her life was certainly richer since Maya had started working at TerraPlaya. Not only because of the fun they had together, but because Maya introduced her to the world of animal communication, and that changed everything for her.

Maya had pushed her outside of her comfort zone and as a result she got to experience the beauty of Sienna Falls Forest. And now, even though they faced the unknown, Lucy felt right knowing they would take the challenge on together and somehow, they would prevail.

"You know what, Mrs. Kleinbaum? I'm thankful that you and I are friends. It's always nice to come here and visit."

Mrs. Kleinbaum nodded in agreement. "I am too, Lucy. You always keep me entertained with your stories."

"And I didn't forget you either, Frederica, my cat friend. I brought you a little present too! It's a toy turtle stuffed with catnip." Lucy took it out of her purse, opened the package, and put it on the floor in front of Frederica.

The cat looked aloof for a few seconds, walked past it as if she were going to reject the gift, and then slyly attacked the turtle from the side.

Thank you, Lucy.

*   *   *

Lucy had already had her mid-morning tea and was working on some maps when Maya appeared next to her cubicle.

Maya told Lucy that she had called her friend Brandon at the state wildlife department to see if they could investigate. But without any evidence that someone was purposely trying to harm an endangered species there wasn't anything to be done. The agency was severely short staffed so they would need some real proof that something was amiss to even open an investigation.

Brandon called the ranger who covered the region that included Sienna Falls Forest to let him know to be on the lookout for anything unusual, but that is all he could do for now.

Lucy was disappointed, but at least Maya had tried. They were still voicing their frustrations when Lucy's desk phone rang.

Lucy picked up the phone. "Lucy—get Maya and get in here now!" Anuk ordered.

Lucy's stomach immediately tied in a knot. She looked at Maya, who shrugged her shoulders, and they headed to Anuk's office.

Before the women had even finished entering the room, Anuk barked at them, "What happened out at Sienna Falls Forest???"

Maya answered first, "What do you mean? The birds were gone and—"

"And they just fired us," Anuk snapped.

"What?!" exclaimed Lucy and Maya.

Anuk was shaking his head. "They terminated our contract. We are to turn over any data you collected immediately, and you won't be completing this survey or any of the surveys we hoped to do next season."

"But I don't understand," Lucy said in bewilderment. "We haven't even submitted the report yet, so they don't know what we found."

Maya turned to Anuk with disbelief. "We actually found Silver-winged Warblers. It's what they were hoping for! This doesn't make any sense."

"Sense or not, this project is over," Anuk shook his head even harder as if it would somehow change the situation. "This is the last thing we needed with corporate breathing down my neck, and the efficiency expert evaluating our office. I should have trusted my gut—it was a mistake to send you out, Lucy."

"That's unfair! I didn't do anything wrong!" Even though she knew she was right, Lucy couldn't help feeling like a total failure. First, they lost the company laptops, camera, and GPS, and now they lost the contract.

She couldn't exactly blame Anuk for trying to place the blame on her. She could feel tears welling up in her eyes but tried to hold them back. She didn't want Anuk to see her cry.

Maya's face was starting to turn red with anger. "Look, I don't know what happened, but Lucy certainly didn't do anything wrong out there. We did our job. We found three nests of an endangered bird. They should be happy. I'm not going to stand here and get reprimanded for...I don't even know what!"

Lucy considered that Anuk rarely got upset or yelled so she knew he must be really feeling the pressure from corporate to lash out them like this.

She choked back her tears and said as calmly and professionally as she could force, "Maya's right. You should be on our side. Let's find out why they really cancelled the contract. Maybe we can fix it. And if we can't, at least we'll know why."

Anuk slumped back in his chair and sighed. His voice changed from angry to defeated. "It still doesn't change the fact that we lost a big contract at an unbelievably bad time. This doesn't look good. For any of us."

Maya still looked angry but even she softened. "We'll figure this out. This is my career and my life, researching endangered birds, and this means everything to me. We will fix this."

"Okay, but you are not to return to Sienna Falls Forest until we work this out, agreed?" Anuk warned.

"Absolutely," said Maya, while Lucy nodded. But Lucy could see Maya had her fingers crossed behind her back and that made her smile inwardly. They weren't going to let this go without a fight.

*   *   *

Lucy wiped the dust off the entertainment center. She didn't have company at her little house very often, so she usually only had her own standards of cleanliness to meet, and they were fairly low. As long as nothing was unhygienic, and things were not too messy or cluttered, it was fine. She wasn't a person who mopped the kitchen floor once a week or washed the windows every month.

She did like things organized. Things were less stressful if she knew where everything was. If she cut herself, she knew exactly where the antibiotic ointment was, and if she was on her way out the door and found it chillier than expected, she could just grab her favorite sweater off the hook at the end of the hall.

Since she rarely had guests over, her anxieties were flying a mile a minute. About the house being clean enough. About being a good host. About offering the right food and drink. About picking the right movie. What if her guest got bored? Or overstayed her welcome? Lucy knew she was being ridiculous, because her new friend was one of the easiest-going people she had ever known.

She was setting out some snacks on the coffee table when the doorbell rang.

"Come on in, Maya!" Lucy said as she answered the door.

"Hi Lucy! Should I take off my shoes?"

"Only if you want to. I'm an avid sock wearer so I'm never barefoot in the house anyway." Lucy ushered Maya into the living room. "Would you like something to drink?" she asked.

"Is that root beer?" Maya said eyeing the six pack on the table.

"Yep, my favorite brand. And I have frosty mugs."

"Nice! I'll have one of those please."

Lucy smiled. She was already relaxing, remembering how easy it is to hang out with Maya. She went to the freezer to get the mug as Maya followed. "I have a few movie choices for you. You said you haven't seen that many black and white movies, right?" asked Lucy.

"That's right. I never watched many movies growing up since I spent so much time outdoors at the ecolodges where my parents worked. I am still getting caught up on everything I missed. I'm open to anything,"

Maya replied.

"Have you seen *The Picture of Dorian Gray?*"

"No, I don't think so."

"It's a 1945 horror drama—pretty creepy," Lucy warned.

"Sounds perfect."

"Great! Do you want popcorn? I have a special recipe—I top it with melted ghee and parmesan."

"Delicious! Yes, please," Maya replied enthusiastically.

Lucy made the popcorn and the women sat down to watch the movie. Maya was engrossed as the main character descends into debauchery, causing his portrait to become more twisted and disfigured until it is a horrific painting of pure demonic evil. When the movie was over, Lucy turned on the lights.

"What did you think?" Lucy asked.

"I loved it! I didn't know they made movies like that in the forties."

"Absolutely! Some of my favorites are on the darker side. We can watch the 1935 *Mad Love* next time."

"Cool."

Lucy sat lost in thought for a minute. Then she popped out of her seat. "That movie gave me an idea. Hold on—I'll be right back." Lucy left the room and returned with her laptop.

"What's up?" asked Maya.

"I was just thinking that it would be worth comparing old aerials of Grady McWalter's property to the east of Sienna Fall Forest with recent aerials." Lucy logged into her computer and navigated to an imagery program. In just a few minutes she had pulled up an aerial view of the property from six months ago.

"Look! This building here is pretty new. You can see how the vegetation is cleared and hasn't grown back yet. Let me pull up an aerial from two years ago." Lucy waited as the image loaded, while Maya looked on in anticipation. "It wasn't there!"

Maya gasped. "Why would someone have built on the property after Grady died while the will is still being contested?"

"I don't know. And it doesn't look like a house or a barn or something that would support ranching either," Lucy said.

"Where did we see the guys from Sepharine Holdings in the truck?"

Lucy pointed inside Sienna Falls Forest just west of a dirt road that led to the new building. "We were here. The men from Sepharine must have been going to that building."

Maya nodded. "We need to find out what's in there."

"How are we going to do that?" asked Lucy, fearing the answer she knew Maya would give.

"We need to go back to Sienna Falls Forest."

"But we promised Anuk we wouldn't," Lucy argued halfheartedly.

"It's a public park—we would be going as private citizens just taking a hike in a forest. We'll just look around a little more. Now that we know where the building is we can hike right up to the property line across from the new building," Maya insisted.

Lucy grimaced. "I don't know…"

"Come on, you said you were in—just a little hike on public property can't get us in any trouble," Maya implored.

Lucy sighed, knowing she might regret this but that she would give in eventually. "Okay, fine. This weekend then."

"This weekend," Maya agreed.

Chapter 9

"YOU'RE BACK AGAIN, LADIES! SO nice to see you," said Sylvia with a smile.

"Hi again, Sylvia!" said Lucy.

"Hey—did you ever connect with that handsome guy?" Sylvia asked.

Lucy's cheeks immediately started turning red as she remembered the lie that Maya had told. She felt bad lying to Sylvia because she had been so kind to them.

Maya quickly chimed in. "Nope. Lucy lost her nerve. She's a bit shy."

Lucy was thankful for the quick thinking on Maya's part since her anxious brain still hadn't thought of a proper response.

Sylvia chuckled. "Ah well, you might have another chance because they checked in again last night." Sylvia winked as she handed the ladies their room keys.

Lucy and Maya exchanged quick glances.

Lucy paled. "Um, they-they-they did?" Her pulse shot up and she started to feel woozy.

Maya cut in. "Thanks for letting us know. We better be on our way." Maya pulled Lucy down the hall.

Once they were a safe distance from the front desk Lucy exhaled. "Why are they back? What are they doing here?" Lucy asked, starting to panic.

Maya unlocked her room and ushered Lucy in. "I don't know. That's what we are here to find out," Maya replied.

Lucy nodded. "But are we safe here?"

Maya looked serious. "I'm not going to tell you there is no risk. If they broke in and stole our equipment because we were doing the bird surveys, then they certainly aren't the good guys. But that doesn't mean we are in physical danger. We'll be as careful as we can be."

That didn't do much to calm Lucy's nerves. But she had agreed to come, and she wasn't going to back out now. Lucy stood up to put her suitcase in her room. "Meet in the lobby in ten?" she said faking a casual confidence she did not feel, even though she knew Maya would see through it.

"See you in ten," Maya confirmed.

*　　*　　*

Returning to Sienna Falls Forest didn't feel the same to Lucy after experiencing the loss of the Silver-winged Warblers. Gone was the feeling of peace, replaced instead with apprehension about what they might encounter this time.

Instead of feeling in tune with the forest, Lucy was searching for every sign of life, dreading that they may again find the deeper forest still and abandoned.

Fortunately, as Lucy and Maya hiked towards the other side of the forest, they did hear birds singing and bees buzzing. Squirrels hunted for acorns, and ants marched along the leaf litter. Lucy started to relax again as the gurgling of the Sienna River once again calmed her nerves.

Both women were cautiously hopeful as it seemed the forest was already partially recovered since their last visit. It wasn't anywhere near as vibrant as it had been on their first visit, but at least it wasn't deadly silent.

It was a long way to the other side of the forest, where they suspected Sepharine Holdings Inc. was up to no good, doing who knows what in the new building on Grady's land. Lucy knew they would be passing through the survey area where they had been over the moon after spotting the Silver-winged Warblers. As they approached, Maya drooped.

"You okay, Maya?" asked Lucy, even though she knew well enough that she was not.

"I just can't imagine why anyone would want to hurt an innocent bird," Maya replied.

"I know. It's hard to reconcile how terrible some people can be. But then I meet someone like you, and I am reminded that there are still plenty of good people in this world—I just haven't met them yet."

"Aww, thanks, Lucy! I know in my mind that you are right—a few bad apples make it seem like the entire world has gone to hell. But most people are probably good. Or neutral at least!"

"I like that—neutral people!" Lucy laughed.

The women walked on with a lighter spirit after the exchange, encouraged by the energy of the forest that was still going strong as they approached the halfway mark to the other side.

Maya stopped now and then to look at birds through her binoculars, not trying to hide from Lucy that she was still ever hopeful that they would find more Silver-winged Warblers. Lucy was also secretly hopeful every time Maya spotted something, but she never asked, since it would be obvious if Maya found one.

Several miles into their journey the sky began to darken as clouds formed overhead. Maya looked up and shook her head. "It wasn't supposed to rain."

"Ha! That's typical weather here, right? Hopefully, it will blow over soon," Lucy suggested hopefully. But raindrops started forming and it seemed the temperature dropped ten degrees in minutes.

Maya frowned but marched on resolutely, "We're about three quarters of the way there, so let's push on."

Lucy nodded in agreement. The women continued towards the McWalter ranch, their heads lowered to keep the drizzle out of their eyes. Suddenly they heard a noise in front of them. Both women looked up and saw a large buck running towards them with fear in his eyes. Lucy and Maya jumped out of the way as it ran on.

"What was that about?" Lucy puzzled.

"I don't know, I guess something spooked it," said Maya.

It was then that Lucy and Maya both noticed a growing rumble moving towards them, combined with the shrieking soundscape of agitated birds all around them. Maya whispered, "I think whatever happened before is happening again."

"I think you're right," responded Lucy as her eyes widened. Coming towards them was a wall of forest wildlife. Deer, squirrels, birds, insects, all fleeing something unseen, speeding towards the women.

"Lucy. Run!" Maya grabbed Lucy's hand and pulled her back the way they had come. The women ran as fast as they could over the wet forest floor, struggling to see under the dim and cloudy skies.

They tripped on branches and rocks, scraping their arms and legs as they scrambled through the brush, afraid to look back.

Lucy knew they weren't running from the animals. They were running from whatever it was that made the forest react like this. After seeing how the Silver-winged Warblers nests were destroyed, Lucy knew they didn't want to meet who or whatever was responsible for the wreckage.

Still, their immediate danger was getting trampled by the fleeing forest animals who could run much faster than the women. They had to find another way. Lucy reached out her mind to the forest. She grabbed Maya and pushed her to the right, "This way!" Maya followed Lucy down a slope and into a cave.

Breathing heavily, the women listened from inside the cave as the animals continued to rush past them. They were safe for now, at least from the forest animals.

Maya looked curiously at Lucy. "How did you know this was here?"

"The forest animals told me," Lucy replied.

"Whoa. You were able to communicate with them telepathically, not to mention in the middle of a crisis?"

Lucy nodded. Since they were stuck inside the cave for a while, she thought it was time to confide in Maya about how far she had taken her animal communication skills. She told Maya everything and even though they were in a cave in the middle of the forest, hiding from an unknown threat, Lucy felt like a weight was lifted from her.

Maya didn't judge Lucy for not sharing this sooner. Instead, she whistled through her teeth. "That is a rare level of skill. I heard my great-grandmother was like that too. It's time for you to meet my lita. No one knows more about this subject than she does. Come to dinner next Saturday. You will have the best food you've ever tasted, and we can talk to her about all of this."

Lucy nodded. A faint noise made Lucy turn the flashlight on her phone and pointed it up to reveal several tiny bats hanging from the cave ceiling.

"Oh! Tricolored bats. Turn off the light," exclaimed Maya. Lucy quickly turned off her phone. "These must be roosting females. I haven't seen this species very often."

Lucy wasn't sure about being in a cave with bats, but she knew if Maya wasn't worried, then Lucy was safe with her biologist friend.

Maya tugged on Lucy's arm, "Do you think you could ask the animals what is happening out there?"

"Maybe. Let me try." Lucy reached her mind out to one of the bats. Nothing happened and Lucy was afraid she might be disturbing their sleep. But then she heard their response in her mind.

Wolves. Ravens.

"They said wolves and ravens swept through, terrorizing the forest animals."

"That's impossible," countered Maya, "there aren't wolves or ravens in this area!"

Lucy shrugged. "That may be so, but that's what they said."

"No, I believe you, it just doesn't make any sense."

The women sat in silence, taking in the new information, when they both realized the forest was quiet once again. "Can you ask if it safe to leave?" asked Maya.

Lucy paused, her mind reaching out again, then drooped. "I can't. There's no one outside the cave to ask."

Maya's face fell as she realized the force that killed her beloved birds had struck again. The women cautiously exited the cave, scanning the forest for signs of life, or even worse, wolves, but they saw nothing.

"Let's hightail it back to the lodge," Maya suggested.

"Agreed. I've had enough for today."

*   *   *

After a sleepless night for both women, Lucy haunted by dreams of running through the forest, they agreed to head back home to do more research and formulate a plan. As Maya turned down the road that led out of Sienna Falls to the highway, Lucy spoke out, "Stop the car!"

Maya jerked the car over to the side of the road. "What is it?"

"Look at that building." Lucy pointed to a small office that looked like a converted house. The sign read "The Southwest Regional Conservation Coalition."

Maya's face lit up with recognition. "That's the group that was funding our survey!"

"I know. And they are the ones that canceled it. Maybe we can find out why," Lucy suggested.

Maya parked the car and the women walked to the door.

"What are we going to say?" asked Lucy. Even though it was her idea, as soon as she said it, she immediately felt anxious about confronting the people who fired them.

"I don't know—we'll have to play it by ear," Maya said. Lucy sighed since she knew Maya could live like that and not crumble with fear. But that's why Lucy was glad to know her.

The office was small and filled with boxes of files, folding chairs, large metal filing cabinets, a few tables, and clipboards. The walls were covered with posters of wildlife and local maps. There was only one person there, a woman who looked like she was in her mid-thirties, holding a tall stack of papers.

"Good morning! Are you here for some information about volunteering?" asked the woman, placing the stack down on a desk and turning to give the women her attention.

"Not exactly," replied Maya.

"Okay, my name is Skye. What can I do for you today?" She pushed her reading glasses on top of her auburn mop of hair and looked at them with interest.

"I'm Maya, and this is Lucy. We actually work for TerraPlaya."

Skye's glance fell to the floor. She clearly recognized the name and knew why the women were there. "It's not our fault—we had no choice,"

Skye said, her voice filled with regret.

"What do you mean?" Maya prompted.

"We're just a small non-profit. We rely heavily on donations to fund all of our projects and outreach, not just at Sienna Falls Forest, but all over the region."

"What does that have to do with the bird survey?" Lucy questioned.

Skye sighed deeply. "The McWalters were a major source of funding for our group. Grady McWalter was an amazing conservationist and a generous person. You might not know that he passed away a few years ago. For a while we thought his heirs would continue their sponsorship for years to come. But then suddenly after you started the survey, we got a call from the McWalter Foundation saying that we should focus our efforts outside of Sienna Falls Forest if we wanted their continued support."

"So that's why you fired us? Did you know we found three Silver-winged Warbler nests during our first survey?" Maya demanded.

Skye gasped. She looked on the verge of tears. "I didn't know—that is incredible! I have never even seen one before. That's exactly the kind of data we need to make good conservation decisions." She pulled her gray and black striped sweater tighter around her and crossed her arms. "I'm so sorry, but there isn't anything I can do. We have to think of the big picture. Without the McWalter donations we wouldn't be able to fund the surveys anyway."

Maya nodded. "I understand the situation now. I don't blame you, but we also are in trouble at work because of this."

"Again, I'm so sorry. If I can do anything to make it up to you, please let me know," Skye said sincerely.

Maya handed Skye her business card. "Thanks. If you hear anything else about Sienna Falls Forest or the McWalters, please call me."

Chapter 10

MONDAY AGAIN, AS ALWAYS. AT least it felt that way to Lucy. But she had to admit her weekends were more exciting since she met Maya, even if it wasn't always in a good way.

Back at work things seemed slow and tedious compared with all the excitement of Sienna Falls.

Lucy was making maps again. Maya was reassigned to another project and would be doing field work with Bethany later in the week.

Lucy felt restless. This is the risk of taking a chance, she thought to herself, now she knew what she was missing. Although the truth was, she had felt unfulfilled before, she just wasn't able to admit it until Maya showed her another option.

Lucy had to remind herself once again that she was incredibly lucky to work at TerraPlaya and she still enjoyed making maps and working with spatial data. She decided to focus on her tasks and, at least for now, try not to think about field work and Sienna Falls.

Another Monday, another Monday morning staff meeting. Anuk was extra cheery and positive sounding, but Lucy could sense it was a little forced today.

"Good morning team! I hope everyone had a great weekend. This morning I want to kick off a new initiative. As part of the corporate growth directive each office must work on a growth strategy plan. Some of you have helped with these before, but for some of you this may be totally new. We need to look at what our strengths are, who our existing clients are and what additional services we could provide those clients. We also need to identify potential new clients we could market in the future, and how we can position ourselves to serve them."

Lucy yawned without meaning to and Maya kicked her under the table.

It's not that Lucy didn't understand that she worked for a corporation, and getting new business was how she continued to get a nice paycheck every week. It's just that this was her absolute least favorite part of the job and she always dreaded being assigned to attend networking events or board meetings. More like 'bored' meetings, Lucy thought.

In the past, Lucy had gone to great lengths to avoid cold calling potential clients. She had become a great internet sleuth, somehow managing to find e-mail addresses even when they were purposely not listed on potential client websites. Then Lucy would e-mail her questions, or requests for meetings. It had always worked out so far, but she always worried she would be found out.

She thought back to what Hyun Shim had asked her in her interview. Maybe Lucy did need to better understand what the overall company's mapping customization capabilities were so she could market them, even if they weren't all skills she had herself.

Sometimes Lucy started feeling motivated to focus more on her career and try to contribute more to business development, but then she remembered her anxiety and shrank back into just trying to be a good part of the production team. She made a mental note to discuss this with Maya when she had time.

Anuk continued, "It's up to each and every one of us to make this office successful. No one is too junior or too senior to help with business development. Even the most inexperienced intern can make meaningful connections with other interns at our client's businesses. And guess what—someday those interns will be the ones selecting firms to work with, and they will know our former interns who have since become project managers!"

"It's totally true!" exclaimed Bethany, her eyes bright. "One of my classmates from college is now the Assistant Director of Planning for Northbrook!"

"Thanks Bethany—that's a perfect example. That is exactly what I am talking about. I want you each to take some time over the next week to fill out this spreadsheet. Think about the relationships you have at places that could use our services, even if it is someone you haven't spoken to recently. Think about what our clients need and how we could expand our services to fill those needs. Do we need to hire someone with an additional skillset? There are no wrong answers here, I just ask that you try."

Lucy left the meeting feeling a little down. She felt guilty that she didn't care as much as she was supposed to about work, even though she really liked Anuk and her entire team.

She was never really sure if other people were like her—maybe they were just pretending to be enthusiastic about work. Or maybe they were genuinely invested in the success of the corporation. Bethany always seemed super excited about everything, and that made Lucy feel like an Eeyore.

Lucy cared about her projects and strove to produce high quality deliverables, but it was harder to care about meeting some seemingly random corporate metric that no one asked her about.

Since the meeting was so demotivating, Lucy decided to take a minute to see what she could find out about Grady McWalter's heirs. She knew from the newspaper article and from Sylvia at the lodge that Grady's wife and son had died tragically, so she guessed that the relatives fighting for ownership were probably siblings or their children. She went back to the Sienna Falls Herald to find Grady's obituary.

At the end of the article, she learned that Grady's only brother Errol had also passed away, but that Grady was survived by his sister Ellie and her son Jacob and daughter Missy, and his deceased brother's sons Bart and Peter.

She added that information to the notes she had started taking about the Sienna Falls mystery so she could look up those names when she had more time. For now, she needed to get back to her maps.

The rest of the day rushed by her, followed by her voice lesson that evening. Four more days went by the same, full of mapmaking and meetings. As nervous as she was, Lucy couldn't wait for Saturday. She needed help making sense of her new skills and how they fit into her life. She just hoped Maya's grandmother would have some answers.

*   *   *

The door opened and a short older women immediately hugged Maya. "Hi lita! How are you doing?" Maya hugged her grandmother back.

"Wonderful now that you are here, cariño." She gestured towards Lucy, "And this must the woman I've heard so much about."

"I'm so pleased to meet you, Mrs. Morales," Lucy said politely.

"Please—call me Carmela. No need to be so formal—any friend of Maya's is a friend of mine." She gave Lucy a big hug. "Come in, come in. The food is almost ready."

Lucy followed Maya and Carmela into the house. Unlike Lucy's place, which had been painted in a plain beige throughout, this house felt alive with color, the small living room walls a bright blue, leading to a kitchen in an earthy gold color that seemed to bring a bright sunny day right into the room.

"It smells amazing in here!" Lucy exclaimed as they walked towards the kitchen, where the spicy, rich aroma of simmering meat and roasting tomatillos wafted into her nose.

"I hope you are hungry, because lita will expect you to eat until you are stuffed like a turkey," Maya joked.

Carmela poked Maya. "Hush now Maya, that isn't true. Guests can eat what they like, it's just my granddaughter I worry about. I don't know what you eat the rest of the week. Probably something from a can!"

Maya laughed and started to set the table. Lucy came over and together they put out the plates, silverware, and napkins. Usually, Lucy was anxious about being at a new person's house for the first time, but she was so comfortable with Maya by now, and Carmela was so warm and inviting, that she soon forgot to be nervous.

The women ate enchiladas verdes with rice and black beans. It was one of the best meals Lucy had ever tasted, and she kept eating until she felt like the button might pop off her pants. The three women talked and laughed, and Carmela told some embarrassing stories about things that Maya did when she was little.

Eventually they were all full, and Maya and Lucy started to help clean up the meal. Once the kitchen was spotless again, and the leftovers wrapped up for Lucy and Maya to take home at Carmela's insistence, the older woman beckoned for the younger two to sit on the couch.

Carmela sat back in a big green armchair and the mood turned serious as she spoke to Lucy. "It seems we have some things to discuss. Maya tells me you are gifted in animal magic."

Lucy's eye widened. "Magic? No, nothing like that. I seem to be able to communicate with animals but it's not like I am a witch or anything like that."

Carmela pursed her lips. "You young people are so worried about words. What is magic but something that people can't explain? It may seem normal to you, but if others knew what you could do, surely they would call it so."

Lucy considered this and slowly nodded. "I guess that is true."

"Tell me about your magic then," Carmela instructed.

Lucy told her about her first lesson with Maya and how shocked she was that the squirrel thanked her. She told her about Mrs. Kleinbaum's cat Frederica, the incident with the scorpion, and shamefully confessed about Hyun Shim and the cockroach. Finally, she told her about what had happened in Sienna Falls Forest and how she knew to find the cave that she and Maya had hidden inside.

She explained that she had practiced falling into a state of mindfulness regularly, and that since her first lesson she had frequently worked on honing her skills. Lucy admitted that she didn't really know what to do with this power or how to build on it further.

Carmela listened intently and when Lucy was finished, she said, "Child, you have a unique affinity for this. My mother, Maya's great-grandmother, was gifted like you and she could do these things and much more. You have just scratched the surface."

Maya chimed in, "What about you, lita? Doesn't this run in our family?"

Carmela shook her head "No, it's not something you can inherit. You have these skills because your great-grandmother developed them and taught me it was possible. Then you grew up knowing it was a language to be learned just like English or Spanish. To be honest, I was too busy working and raising a family to focus on animal magic, so I never learned to do what my mother could do. But I can tell you some incredible stories and perhaps once you know what is possible you can figure it out for yourselves."

"Please, we would love to hear about your mother," encouraged Lucy, while Maya nodded in agreement.

"My mother could talk with animals, like you can, and also ask them to do things, like you did with the scorpion and cockroach. She could sense when they were near and also sense their moods and their needs. She often was able to help injured animals because of those skills. But in addition to those things that you have already learned, my mother could also see through their eyes."

Lucy and Maya gasped with amazement. "You mean she could get into their minds and see what they were seeing?" asked Maya.

"That's right. She always asked for permission first, but she said there was nothing in the world like seeing the earth from the viewpoint of a hawk in flight, soaring above the ground, or as humbling as watching the world tower over you as an ant in the tall grass."

"That's incredible!" said Lucy.

"Amazing!" exclaimed Maya. She thought for a moment and said, "I'm not sure that is something I could even imagine doing. What about you, Lucy? Could you?"

Lucy blushed. She was uncomfortable thinking she might have skills that surpassed Maya's and Carmela's, but as soon as she heard it was possible, she knew in her heart that she would be able to figure out how, even if it took a lot of trial and error.

"I think I could," she admitted. "I don't know how exactly, but intuitively I just know I could."

Carmela smiled. "I have no doubt that you can. Maya, why don't you take her to see Cousin Jeremy. He might be able to help."

Maya nodded. "That's a great idea. I will set that up."

Lucy saw a flash of a frown cross Maya's face, even though she tried to hide it quickly. "What's wrong?"

Maya looked sheepish. "I have to say I'm a bit jealous," she confessed. "I've spent my entire life working with animals and you come along out of nowhere and are already way more advanced than me at communicating with them."

"Aww. I'm sorry, Maya! I understand, really," Lucy replied. "But it's like you said before—your job is to understand them in their natural state so you can protect them. You can't do that if you interfere with them. Your skills are nuanced to help you in that mission, and nothing could be more valuable."

Carmela nodded in agreement. "Cariño, your magic is your own, and part of your magic is doing your research to help the threatened creatures without voices. It is a beautiful treasure that you found your calling."

Maya's frown relaxed. "When you put it that way, I know you're right. But I'm still going to be envious!"

Lucy laughed. She never imagined someone like Maya would be jealous of her. Then her face grew serious as a thought occurred to her, and her smile vanished. "Do you think it is possible to make animals do things against their will?" she asked.

Carmela's face tightened. "That's very dark magic, Lucy. If my mother ever did that, she didn't tell me, but if I had to guess, then probably yes, it is possible to control animals against their will."

Lucy looked at Maya and could tell they were thinking the same thing. Dark animal magic was afoot in Sienna Falls Forest.

Chapter 11

LUCY WAS FILLED WITH NERVOUS excitement as they pulled up to the entrance at Red Bluff Ranch. Maya got out and swung open the metal gate, drove her car through, and shut the gate tight behind them.

They drove along the dirt road. On the right Lucy noticed the ranch was greener where a stream snaked through the property. The trees were taller, and the understory was lusher.

On the left side of the road the grasses swayed in the wind in shades of browns, reds, and yellows, mixed with a few bright spots of bluebonnets and verbena wildflowers.

As they turned a corner Lucy saw a clearing where a man stood waiting for them. Maya parked the car and the women exited.

"Jeremy!" Maya greeted her cousin warmly from just outside the car but did not approach him as he pointed upward at the small falcon circling overhead.

Lucy held her breath as she watched the bird swoop down and perch gracefully on his outstretched arm, protected by a thick leather glove. "Whoa—that was awesome!" said Lucy in hushed voice.

"This here is Silver. She's a merlin falcon." Jeremy beckoned the women closer. "Approach slowly and stop when I tell you."

Lucy was transfixed as she admired the merlin. The regal bird had silver-grey feathers on her back and her belly was streaked with reddish-brown. Her sharp beak was gray with yellow at the base, and her dark eyes ringed with yellow spoke to Lucy of a profound intelligence not to be underestimated. Lucy felt a deep sense of honor as she neared the bird.

"Silver, it is a pleasure to meet you," Lucy said aloud for Jeremy and Maya, but also directed the words telepathically towards the falcon. Silver nodded her head ever so slightly towards Lucy.

"Thanks so much for having us out, Jeremy. It's been a while since I've seen you," Maya said.

"Anything for you, cousin. And I wanted to meet the talented Lucy. Only you would find someone with animal magic at a new job," he responded.

Lucy blushed, "Actually, I didn't even know about animal magic before Maya came to work with me."

Jeremy nodded in understanding, "Must have been fate, then. Like finds like."

"I suppose it was. So, you must practice animal magic too then?" asked Lucy.

"It's different for me. Like Maya, I grew up knowing about animal magic from an early age. But it wasn't until I was eight years old, and I saw a falconer at a wildlife expo that I knew what I was meant to do. When I saw the special bond the woman there had with her hawk my heart skipped. After that I read everything I could about falconry. Then when I was old enough, I started studying for the exam, and eventually found a falconer to do my apprenticeship with."

Maya beamed proudly. "Jeremy is one of the few master falconers in this region."

"That's quite an accomplishment. Falconry sounds fascinating but also like a serious undertaking," Lucy mused.

Jeremy nodded. "The relationship between falconer and falcon is like no other. A falconer could train with a bird for years but at any time the bird could leave and never come back. There is a lot of potential for sorrow and heartbreak, but also for excitement and joy. And there is never a day off. There are no hawk-sitters. You have to care for your bird 365 days a year."

"I never thought of that! How long have you known Silver?" asked Lucy.

Jeremy looked at Silver with admiration. "Eight years. I've had her since she was a fledgling."

"That's a long time. You must know her really well. Do you talk to her?" Lucy asked.

"Not like you and Maya would. With Silver we don't need to talk in words, I know how she is feeling and what she needs from me. And she knows what I expect of her and that I will always protect her and take care of her."

Lucy nodded. By now she understood that using words was only one of many ways to communicate with animals, and often not the best one since using words is making the animals adapt to human ways, instead of the other way around. "Did Maya tell you why I am here?"

"Yes. She told me what lita suggested. I've already passed the idea by Silver, and she wasn't opposed to it. But you will have to get her permission first."

Lucy wasn't sure exactly what she was asking since she had never done this before. She lowered her head, then briefly caught Silver's gaze before lowered her eyes again. Lucy quickly went to her space of mindfulness and sent Silver feelings of respect. She then asked, not in words as she knew from Jeremy was not something Silver was accustomed to, but instead simply asked for permission. At first, she wasn't sure if Silver responded in the affirmative, but then she felt her answer.

Jeremy spoke softly, "I can tell that she has agreed, and her behavior tells me that she is still calm and not disturbed by the request. You may proceed when you are ready."

Lucy looked at Maya with uncertainty. Maya smiled and nodded, encouraging Lucy that she could do this. Lucy closed her eyes. She once again centered into mindfulness and reached out to Silver. She felt Silver's mind. At first it was like pushing up against a heavy door, but then she felt Silver unlock and Lucy cautiously stepped in.

It was dark and Lucy was trembling in fear. She held her arms out, flailing to find her way. Then she smiled to herself. Just open your eyes, Lucy. And she did. But they weren't her eyes. Instead, she saw the brown leather glove beneath her and looked out into Jeremy's deep brown eyes next to her. She was seeing through Silver's eyes!

Lucy's fear melted into unbridled excitement. She couldn't believe this was happening. Jeremy looked at Silver and seemed to know that Lucy was successful. Jeremy asked Silver telepathically if she was ready, and since Lucy was in her mind, she heard it too. Then Jeremy pushed his arm upward and Silver took off in flight, taking Lucy with her.

Lucy's stomach dropped as Silver soared upwards. She was flying! Before long she could see the tops of the trees and Jeremy and Maya were just small figures on the ground. The wind whipped around her, and the chill of the air sharpened her mind. She could see the tiniest details miles away.

It was unlike anything she had ever experienced. She was both calm and tense at the same time. It was a freedom she had never felt before. She wasn't in control, but just along for the ride. She relaxed into it and felt one with Silver as she circled over the field.

Silver spotted a group of sparrows a few hundred feet away near a clump of trees. Before Lucy realized what was happening, Silver dove down towards one of the small birds with a singular focus and hunger. Lucy felt herself falling at an unimaginable speed, hurtling towards the ground.

As Silver approached the sparrow, Lucy understood what was about to happen. She knew she could jump out of Silver's mind at the last minute. But that felt disrespectful, as if judging the falcon for being a predator refined over millions of years of evolution.

Lucy watched on steadfastly as Silver dove at the sparrow, her talons stretched out. Lucy winced as the talons pierced the bird, stunning it. Lucy felt Silver's pride in a successful hunt and tried to keep her emotions in check as Silver soared gracefully back to Jeremy with her prey.

When Silver arrived back at the clearing, Lucy gave her a respectful thank you and jumped back out of her mind. Lucy fell backwards, landing on the grass. Maya rushed over to her, "Are you okay?"

She nodded, still overwhelmed by the experience. "Yes, I'm okay," Lucy replied with a shakiness in her voice.

Silver ate her prize with relish. Jeremy looked at Lucy empathetically, "I should have warned you, Lucy. I'm sure it wasn't easy to see that up close. It can be quite gruesome if you aren't used to it."

Lucy looked up from the grass and shook her head, "No, that's okay. Silver is an incredible hunter. It was unsettling to see, but I'm also grateful that I could share that experience. For someone who buys her chicken in a package at a grocery store, I don't usually see the circle of life up close like that."

Jeremy chuckled. "That's one way to look at it!"

Maya laughed with them. She sat down next to Lucy. "You realize you did it on the first try? That is a serious achievement."

Lucy was still processing what she just experienced. It was fulfilling in a strange way that she had never felt before. And she also couldn't wait to try it again. Once more, her friendship with Maya was going to change her life in ways she had never even imagined.

*   *   *

Mrs. Kleinbaum shook her head in disbelief as Lucy filled her in on her visit with Jeremy and flying through the air through Silver's eyes. "Well, isn't that something? Just when I think I've heard the strangest thing, you come back and tell me something even more fascinating!"

Lucy nodded knowingly. "When I woke up this morning I wondered if it was a dream. But it's all real!"

"I always believe you, Lucy, but this I would love to see for myself. Do you think you could do it with Frederica?"

Lucy looked at the fluffy white cat. "Maybe—I'd have to ask her if it was okay first."

Mrs. Kleinbaum reached her hand out beckoning Frederica, who wandered over and sniffed her hand, hoping there would be treats involved. "Frederica my dear, would you let Lucy show me her new special skill?"

Lucy reached out to Frederica with her mind and asked her for permission to see through her eyes. Frederica's response felt closest to a teenager shrugging and saying "whatever." Lucy laughed. "She said yes, more or less."

Mrs. Kleinbaum led Frederica into the bedroom room where Lucy couldn't see her. "Tell me what you see out loud."

Lucy slipped into mindfulness and again found a door outside Frederica's mind. This one felt different than Silver's, warmer perhaps because they already knew each other, but it unlocked and let Lucy in the same way.

"I see a toy under the bed. She is picking it up in her mouth. Wait—now she's jumping up on the bed and dropped the toy on your pillow. She's looking at you now—you are holding up three fingers."

Lucy heard Mrs. Kleinbaum applaud in appreciation for her new trick. Then she felt Frederica start to get indignant and impatient and knew she wouldn't allow her to stay long inside her mind. Cats are known for their independence, so it wasn't too surprising.

"Oh, she's jumping off the bed now and walking towards the bathroom. Wait, oh Frederica!" Lucy quickly pulled back from Frederica's view as the cat stepped into the litterbox.

"Frederica, you are such a brat sometimes!" Mrs. Kleinbaum admonished. "Sorry Lucy, you probably didn't need to see that…"

"I should have known better," said Lucy, "and I'm learning that I'm not always going to like what I see."

Mrs. Kleinbaum sat down in the chair next to Lucy, looking impressed. "I'm so glad you are sharing your adventures with me. This is an amazing journey you are on!" An idea lit up her face. "Can you tell the animal where to go so you can see what you want to see?"

"I haven't tried that yet, but I think Maya's great-grandmother could do that. That would require an extra level of permission though. I don't think Frederica would agree to that."

"Probably not. Doesn't sound like a cat thing to do." Frederica came back out to the living room and Mrs. Kleinbaum gave her some treats for letting Lucy experiment on her. "But if you could do that, you might be able to solve a mystery for me."

Lucy was intrigued. "What's the mystery?"

"A few weeks ago, I got a new neighbor, Mrs. Perez. She told me that she keeps hearing weird noises in her bedroom at night. She told the staff in the main office, and they checked out her apartment, but they didn't see or hear anything out of the ordinary. She isn't sure if she is imagining things and it's upsetting her. She's a lovely lady and I don't want her to move away. Maybe you could investigate?"

Lucy was doubtful. She only just started experimenting with this skill and she didn't know how it all worked yet or how reliable it would be. "Hmmm, that sounds complicated. I think it would be a bit much to tell her about my animal magic since I don't even know her. And I can't very well spy in her apartment while she is home sleeping."

"That's true. I don't want to invade her privacy." Mrs. Kleinbaum's eyebrows furrowed as she tried to think of a solution.

"And what animal would I use to see in her apartment and how would I get it in there?"

"These are all good questions and I'm afraid I don't know the answers. It's probably a silly idea anyway."

Lucy hated to see Mrs. Kleinbaum look so disappointed. She loved that Mrs. Kleinbaum's first thought after witnessing her new skill was how she might be able to help a new friend, and that made Lucy want to help too. "Let me think about it. Maybe I can come up with something."

Mrs. Kleinbaum brightened with hope. "Thanks Lucy. You're a kind soul."

Chapter 12

EVER SINCE HER FIRST FLIGHT with Silver the merlin at Red Bluff Ranch, Lucy longed to soar in the clouds once more. She also missed the ocean since she used to spend her summers by the sea when she was a child. Now that she lived in landlocked Northbrook it was a minimum four-hour drive to the water, not counting Northbrook Lake, which was beautiful in its own right.

Lucy decided to stay in Brighton Bay this weekend and spend some time exploring the beach and practicing her animal magic.

As she drove around the final bend of the main road and the long bridge to Brighton Island appeared, Lucy immediately felt calm wash over her like the waves. It was similar to how she felt at Sienna Falls Forest, but she felt even more connected to the ocean than she did to the forest.

She drove to the management office to pick up the keys to a tiny bungalow she rented for the weekend. The little yellow house rested on stilts to protect it from the summer hurricanes and there was a wraparound deck with a perfect view of the ocean.

After Lucy unpacked, she walked down to the beach, the warm sand between her toes, and the sun shining down like a blanket. Lucy put out a large beach towel near the water's edge.

She looked out over the ocean and saw a laughing gull circling near the shore. Lucy couldn't wait to try out her new skill. She gently reached out to the bird. Lucy wasn't sure how it would work on an animal she didn't know, who was also a bit far away from her.

The bird seemed confused at first, unsure where the request was coming from, but Lucy sent feelings of calm and reassurance to the gull and after a moment it acquiesced. Again, Lucy felt the door in the bird's mind, but this time she practically fell through it. Then she could see the ground falling away as the bird rose higher above the ocean.

Lucy took in the view as the bird soared. The ocean beneath her, whitecaps crashing, the water stretched out to the horizon. She felt her stomach lurch as the gull caught a thermal and the current of air pushed her upward. She glided on the thermal until it disappeared and then caught another and another.

She imagined she was hang gliding, forgetting that the gull was the experienced flier, and Lucy only along for the ride. Lucy felt the bird angle to turn and then she flew along the beach as the gull searched for a snack.

As they circled, Lucy saw a brown pelican perched on the fishing pier at the house next door. *Could she switch from one animal to another*, she wondered?

This time she approached the door of the pelican's mind at the same time as she asked for entry, and she was shocked to find that she abruptly left the gull and was now with the pelican. It felt like hopping from stone to stone crossing a stream.

Her entry seemed to compel the pelican to take flight from its post. The pelican's movement felt different as Lucy glided close to the water's surface along the crests of ocean waves. Lucy had never surfed before, but she imagined this is how it would feel to rest on the water, feeling the spray in her face and breathing in the salty ocean air.

When Lucy was flying it was like nothing else in her life existed—no work, no Sienna Falls mystery, no voice lessons to practice, no bills to pay, no anxieties at all to weigh her down.

The pelican started to climb higher and began to circle, its keen eyes scanning for fish. Lucy knew from her experience with Silver what was going to happen next, but this time she was prepared to be a part of nature instead of observing it on a wildlife television documentary.

Through the sharper pelican eyes Lucy could see a school of fish swimming in the water beneath them. She knew the pelican saw it too. Suddenly Lucy was diving steeply towards the water's surface.

From forty feet high the water was like a concrete wall she was about to hit with great force. She braced herself for impact. The bird plunged into the water.

Lucy was surprised that it didn't feel as solid as she had imagined it would be and for a moment, she could only see a darkness of gray and bubbles. Then Lucy saw the sky again as the pelican surfaced, expelled the water, and swallowed the fish it had scooped up in its bill. Lucy breathed in a sigh of relief.

Lucy thanked the pelican and returned to her towel on the beach. She understood now how Maya could make a lifelong study of birds. Each species was unique and had its own way of flying, feeding, and communicating.

Lucy was glad that the pelican's feeding was less gruesome than the merlin, but she was still in awe of the incredible adaptations that each bird developed.

Using her animal magic in this way was exhausting. She wasn't sure why, since on the surface it seemed like she was just sitting still while the bird was the one that did all the work. Somehow it did use a lot of Lucy's energy to connect with animals, and to stay in the state that allowed her to see through their eyes. She suspected that the animals may be siphoning off some energy from her as part of the arrangement, but she couldn't be sure.

After spending time with both the gull and pelican Lucy felt completely drained. It was already late in the afternoon, so she went into the little yellow house to have a snack and relax.

Lucy ate some pretzels and watched the ocean from the wrap around deck. She let her mind wander and reflect on everything that had happened lately. What did it all mean? Maya's grandmother had said she had magic and Lucy felt uncomfortable with that word. Even though she had always read fantasy novels with witches, wizards, and magicians, that was just fiction. It wasn't something she believed existed in real life.

And yet, here she was, developing abilities that defied the typical human experience. *Magic*, she thought. *Magic. Magic. Magic.* As she repeated the word it became less heavy, less weighted with meaning. She had magic like some people have a knack for math or have a flair for theatre. Lucy was still the same Lucy, just with a little magic added.

This weekend was devoted to experimenting with her animal magic. Lucy had decided to stay off her phone as much as possible and didn't even bring her computer. She brought a book from the library to entertain herself when she needed a break from training. But even at the peaceful beach she couldn't keep her mind from wandering to the Sienna Falls mystery.

She still needed to do research on Grady McWalter's relatives. And she knew at some point Maya was going to want to try and visit the strange building they had seen on the aerial on the edge of the McWalter property. Lucy knew she would be scared after the last experience at Sienna Falls Forest, but she also knew that she would say yes when Maya asked her to go.

Her mind also drifted back to the troubles at work. With her unfinished interview with Hyun Shim, getting fired from the Silver-winged Warbler survey contract, and obligation to contribute to the strategic office growth plan, there was a lot to be anxious about.

It bugged Lucy that even on a weekend retreat she couldn't stop her mind from obsessing over things she couldn't do anything about right then. But she knew from experience it was best to let her mind think things through and then just try to let them go, rather than trying to avoid thinking about specific things altogether.

She also thought about Mrs. Kleinbaum's friend and if there was some way she could help her. That got her thinking about what other ways she might be able to help people or animals with her new skill. The possibilities were endless, but she needed to take one step at a time. First, she needed to master her abilities, then she could put them to good use.

With the sound of the ocean waves outside her door, Lucy fell asleep early while reading her book. In her dreams she flew, as she would often do from now on.

*　　*　　*

Lucy was in her cubicle making maps. She huffed as an error message popped up on her screen. Lucy stood up and spoke over the cubicle wall, "Bethany—did you just lose your connection to the server?"

"Yep, I totally did. I'll write IT and see what's up."

"Thanks—let me know."

TerraPlaya didn't have an onsite IT specialist because their office was so small, but usually it wasn't an issue. IT could reset their servers remotely when needed, and most problems could be resolved through the electronic ticketing system.

While she waited, Lucy went to make herself some tea. She shouldn't have been surprised that staff were already congregating in the kitchen since they couldn't do their work without access to the server.

Bethany walked past the break room and headed down the hall. A minute later she returned to the kitchen. "Danny said we need to look in the server room, but it's, like, locked or something. Does anyone know where the key is?"

"Anuk keeps it in his desk," said Tyler.

Bethany headed towards Anuk's office but again returned a minute later. "Anuk's not here and his office is locked too."

Tyler was standing in front of the open refrigerator gazing like a teenager trying to will a tasty snack into existence. Without turning his head, he said, "Yeah, I think he had a client meeting this afternoon and was heading home after."

"Well, that's not, like, super helpful." Bethany threw her hands up in the air.

The staff mulled around trying to decide what to do. Bethany e-mailed Anuk, knowing he would check his work e-mail after his meeting. Lucy finished steeping her tea and headed back to her cubicle with plans to sip it while looking out into the courtyard.

Just a few sips in, her phone chimed that she had a new text message. It was Maya.

Can you C in the server room?

IDK—it's sealed tight.

Lucy focused and went into her state of mindfulness. She reached out within the office for any critters that might be able to help. She shuddered as she sensed cockroaches, flies, millipedes, and silverfish. As she focused close to the server room she suddenly felt tingly all over. She could sense hundreds of minds in there.

Lucy took a deep breath and jumped into one of the creatures. Ugh! She squirmed as she saw what the problem was. There were ants everywhere, crawling from the electrical outlet into the server components.

Lucy jumped back. She had seen enough. No wonder the server wasn't working—it was under attack.

Lucy texted Maya. *Ants.*

Ugh!

Lucy knew that this problem needed to be addressed as soon as possible, before the colony got any bigger. Any downtime when the staff can't bill to clients would negatively impact the office, and her team couldn't afford any more setbacks. They needed the server fixed.

She searched the internet and discovered ants in electronics was a common problem. She was also surprised to discover that if the infestation was new, it was possible that removing the ants could allow the server to reboot without major repairs.

Lucy walked back to the break room. Bethany was sitting at the table drinking coffee and scrolling on her phone. "Did Anuk respond yet?"

Bethany looked up. "Not yet. It's after lunch anyways. We should just, like, call it a day and he can open it in the morning."

Lucy wasn't sure how much worse the problem could get overnight, but her instinct said time was of the essence. "I saw some ants near the server room door."

Bethany furrowed her brows in disgust. "Really? Ewww!"

"You're a biologist—don't you see much worse in the field—snakes and spiders and scorpions?" Lucy asked.

Bethany rolled her eyes. "Yeah, but they're, like, *outside.* Anyways, I didn't notice any."

Lucy imagined kicking Bethany in the shin but refrained from doing so. Instead, she patiently said, "Would the building management have a key?"

Bethany's face lit up, but then fell. Lucy thought she was probably hoping for an excuse to go home early. Lucy couldn't blame her for that. But it was only one-thirty…

"Fine. I'll go see if anyone is in the building management office." Bethany skipped off down the hallway.

Twenty minutes later, Bethany returned with the building manager. The woman had a bundle of keys carefully labeled by office suite. Lucy was relieved when she unlocked the server room door.

The woman whistled through her teeth. "That's not good."

Bethany pushed past her to get a look. "Aaagh! That's a lot of ants. Super gross."

The building manager pulled out her cell phone. "I need an exterminator to Suite 3c server room asap."

There wasn't anything more for Lucy to do—it was up to the professionals now. She returned to her cubicle and looked out the window.

Maya peeked around the corner. "No point in sitting in here doing nothing. Want to sit in the courtyard while we wait?"

"Sure." Lucy followed her outside.

"Sounds like you were getting annoyed with Bethany in there," said Maya.

Lucy chuckled. "Bethany just needs some direction. I like her, but she just has a different style, that's all. Still, I don't envy you having to do field work with her."

Maya smiled. "It's not so bad. Bethany knows her wildlife, it just isn't as easy to see because she's a woo hoo girl."

Lucy lifted her brow. "What's a woo hoo girl?"

"Picture sorority girls drinking in a bar having fun and they put their arms up in the air and yell 'Woo hoo!'"

"Aaah—yes, I know what you mean." Lucy knew exactly what Maya was talking about. When she was a teenager, she was jealous of the woo hoo girls and wished she could be like them. Eventually she accepted she never would be, and that was okay. But it was a good reminder not to assume Bethany wasn't smart and capable just because she spoke differently than Lucy.

Maya suggested that they practice bird identification skills while they waited. Lucy listened to the bird sounds in the courtyard. She knew for certain the cheep of the cardinal. She also saw a mockingbird at the very top of a tree singing its varied tunes. Maya pointed to several birds far away on the telephone pole wire.

"Grackles?" Lucy guessed.

"That's right. Nice!"

Lucy was starting to understand why birding was such a popular hobby. It challenged your mind, gave you a reason to be outside, and it was rewarding when you saw a rare species. She had just started but she was already getting better at identification.

When they had exhausted the birds in the courtyard and the parking lot, Maya challenged Lucy on insects.

"No fair! I haven't studied insects at all."

Maya laughed. She showed Lucy some small craters in the soil under a tree.

"Do you know what these are?"

Lucy shook her head.

"Ant lion pits. The ant lion digs a crater and then waits at the bottom for an unsuspecting ant to fall in and then chomp!"

"Brutal! I have seen these holes before, but I had no idea what they were. Learn something new every day."

Bethany opened the side door of the building "Server's back up." Lucy thought she could detect disappointment in Bethany's voice.

Maya sighed and turned to Lucy. "Back to work."

Lucy moved towards the entrance. "Guess so."

"Good job solving the server mystery. Maybe this is your new calling—solving animal-related mysteries."

Lucy laughed. "Maybe so."

Chapter 13

LUCY TREASURED HER TIME ALONE, and rarely felt lonely. As Lucy's animal magic deepened, she was never truly alone because she always felt the animals near to her, the owl in the tree outside her bedroom window, and the frogs in her garden.

At first it bordered on creepy because she knew every spider or earwig that was in her house, but it was comforting once she got used to it. Even with her ever growing bond with the natural world, it was also really nice to have a friend like Maya.

As much as Lucy had enjoyed her solitary weekend at Brighton Island, she was excited to share it with Maya this time. Lucy rented the same little yellow house on the beach. This time Maya was going to help Lucy with her animal magic, but they were also going to have some fun at the beach.

Lucy hadn't tried her animal magic on anything that lived in the water. That moment when the pelican dove to catch the fish made her pretty anxious and she hadn't wanted to try any sea creatures that weekend. But with Maya there she was emboldened. The women went to the edge of the pier and looked into the water.

"There's a fish, Lucy! I think it's a speckled trout."

"Geez—you know both birds and fish?" Lucy shook her head in amazement. Sometimes she wished she had a really deep knowledge on one subject, the way that Maya had with wildlife.

"I'm not as good with fish, but I used to go fishing in the summer with my grandfather when I was young. The speckled trout is common here. See how it has black dots along its back and fins? That's why it's called speckled. It's hard to tell here, but it also has a sort of purple-ish sheen to it."

"It's kind of pretty!" Lucy shook out her arms and legs as if she was about to run a marathon. "Okay, I'm going to see if I can swim with a speckled trout. Do you still see it?"

Maya pointed in the water and Lucy spied the fish again. Before it could swim out of sight, she quickly knocked on the door of its mind. She started to panic as she was instantly underwater, gasping for air and feeling like she couldn't breathe. She almost jumped out of the fish, but then she recognized that the big blurry shadow on the pier was Maya leaning over the edge, and Lucy wasn't alone.

She took a deep breath and remembered that she was still in her own body, she was just borrowing the fish. Then she relaxed into it as she had flying with the birds, but this time she was moving through the murky bay water.

She saw oysters on the bottom of the bay, and she struggled to make out very far ahead as the fish took her into some reeds near the shore. She saw some other tiny fish swimming away from her and wondered if she was about to experience yet another feast. But the fish changed course and swam back the other direction.

Lucy was starting to feel comfortable swimming with the fish, and she was also feeling ambitious about progressing her animal magic with Maya there to support her. She decided it was time to try seeing if she could control an animal.

Without too much consideration, Lucy willed the fish to head back to the shore. Suddenly the fish leapt out of the water as if it had been spooked. Lucy felt herself forcibly kicked back to the other side of the door and was back in her own mind again.

She was so startled that she started to fall backwards towards the edge of the pier. Maya reflexively reached out and grabbed Lucy's arm before she tumbled into the bay.

"Whoa!" Maya exclaimed as she helped Lucy sit down on the wooden slats. "Are you alright?"

Lucy looked embarrassed. "I'm fine. I think I just tried to control the fish without its permission, and it did not appreciate it. I knew intellectually that I should ask first, but in the excitement of the moment I forgot and just told it what to do."

Maya was incredulous. "Wow! It booted you right out?"

Lucy nodded. "Rightly so. I feel bad now—I hope I didn't traumatize that poor fish."

Maya consoled her. "I'm sure it will be fine. And you'll remember next time to make sure it is okay first."

"Definitely. I feel better now but could use some food and a break. Do you want to get some lunch?"

"Sounds good," Maya replied.

The women walked into town from the little yellow house. Seafood was the regional specialty here on the coast, but Lucy wasn't sure she could eat a fish just after swimming with one. They settled on a place that had both seafood for Maya and hamburgers for Lucy. Lucy made a mental note to never do animal magic on a cow or a chicken or she'd probably have to become a vegetarian.

The patio at the restaurant was almost empty since the lunch rush had already passed, so the women were free to talk about the topic of the day.

Maya looked out at the ocean view as she sipped her iced tea. "I wonder, even if you got permission, if you did something the animal didn't like, could it kick you out at any time?"

Lucy swallowed a bite of her burger and looked up. "That feels right—I can't imagine making an animal doing something that might be against its own self-interest."

"But remember how Iita said that would be dark magic? Controlling an animal against its will? Do you think she was right, and it is possible?"

Lucy was haunted by their last experience at Sienna Falls Forest, and what the bats had told her. *Wolves. Ravens.* If that was true, and as Maya said, there were no wolves or ravens naturally occurring there, then someone brought them there on purpose. And that someone probably wasn't just releasing them and letting them do whatever they wanted.

The question is did these dark magicians control them against their will, or were the animals willing participants? Lucy reasoned that the same way humans are good, bad, and everything in between, that some animals could also be evil. Or was it like Jeremy and Silver the merlin? Did they have a symbiotic relationship of some kind where the animals were getting something in return for doing the dark magicians' bidding?

"I absolutely think it's possible and it is terrifying. And I wonder if some animals might be prone to working with people who practice dark magic."

"Oh—I could see that. Like how some dogs have a better temperament to be guard dogs than pets."

"Maybe so. And those dogs are trained to be extra mean to protect their property, but they still obey their owners."

The women finished their lunch in silence, both pondering the depth of possibilities of dark animal magic. As they stood up to leave Maya remarked, "I think the best thing we can do is train you in controlling animals the right way and understand as much as we can about how it works. Then we can try and find out more about what is happening at Sienna Falls Forest."

After lunch Lucy was reenergized and even more determined to progress on her animal magic. She decided she would try again controlling an animal, but she would go back to birds since she had already had successful interactions with several bird species. They walked back to the little house on the beach and sat on deck chairs on the wraparound porch.

This time Lucy saw a little blue heron in the reeds by the pier, and she cautiously approached it with her mind. She wanted to take her time and build up trust with the bird. She sent out a feeling of calm and good will towards the bird, assuring it that she meant no harm. Then she asked for permission to enter the bird's mind. The heron seemed agreeable, and Lucy was once again on the shore in the reeds, looking out through the bird's eyes.

For a few minutes Lucy just stayed with the bird, who was stealthily stalking along the beach looking for some fish to eat. Then Lucy shyly asked if the bird wouldn't mind turning and walking in the other direction. She didn't ask in words, but in an impression that the bird would understand. She felt a momentary flash of confusion, and Lucy quickly sent out more feelings of reassurance. Then she felt the bird relax again and turn around, still stalking, but in the other direction. Lucy was excited—she did it!

But then she wondered if she really did anything, or if the bird had decided to move of its own accord. She needed more proof. She decided to push farther and asked the bird if it wouldn't mind taking flight. This time she swore she could feel the bird consider her request and then consent.

As the bird took off Lucy could hardly believe it. She was soaring again over the waves. As they flew, she started feeling more comfortable sending directions to the bird as the heron didn't seem to mind. She circled to the right and then flew along the coast, then swooped lower and went right over Maya's head on the porch.

Maya stood up and waved with delight, sure that Lucy had been successful in controlling the heron. She sat back down and watched as Lucy and the heron turned back to the coast.

Lucy didn't want to overstay her welcome or stress the little blue heron, so she thanked it profusely for cooperating, bid the bird farewell and left it to return to fishing. When she opened her eyes, she was looking at Maya, who was wearing a huge smile and clapped her hands together. "You did it, didn't you?" Maya asked.

"I did!" Lucy exclaimed.

*   *   *

This time Lucy had brought her laptop to the beach house. She figured since they had decided to play detective that they may as well spend part of the weekend researching Grady McWalter's surviving relatives. She decided to start with Grady's deceased brother's sons Bart and Peter. Unfortunately, there were quite a few Peter McWalters when she did a quick internet search. She would have to find a way to narrow it down.

She added Sienna Falls to the search even though she suspected that none of the heirs lived there any longer. As luck would have it, she was wrong. It looked like Peter was a history teacher at Sienna Falls High School. She found his profile on the school webpage, and the school social media. He had a wife and children and was the assistant baseball coach at the school.

Lucy showed Maya what she had found, and Maya agreed that Peter didn't seem like the type who would be responsible for the dark magic at Sienna Falls Forest.

Next, she looked up Peter's other brother Bart, which was easier since Peter and Bart were connected on social media. Bart had moved away from Sienna Falls. He was now living in Phoenix and worked as a nurse practitioner at a city hospital.

Even though Lucy knew you can't really tell what a person is like from their online presence, she didn't feel like Bart was a good suspect either. But Maya agreed that they couldn't rule out either Bart or Peter at this point.

That left Grady McWalter's sister Ellie and her son Jacob and daughter Missy. Lucy figured that Ellie was probably in her eighties by now, and although she could potentially be the behind-the-scenes mastermind, it was more likely that she was enjoying retirement rather than destroying a forest.

Lucy searched for Jacob McWalter instead. She found several social media pages but none of the photos looked like they would be the right age. She looked at job networking sites but came up empty there as well.

Lucy was getting frustrated with the search, so she switched to Missy. Again, she came up empty. Maya suggested that Missy may have changed her last name if she married.

Lucy searched the state marriage records, first assuming that Missy may have stayed in state. She did find some Melissa McWalter marriage entries in the right timeframe. So now she needed to look for Melissa Brellham, Melissa Lee, Melissa Rodriguez, Melissa Trawley, Melissa Zimmer.

After over an hour of dead ends, she found the page of a Melissa "Missy" Zimmer, CEO of ZRC Laboratories on a professional networking site. Lucy searched for ZRC Laboratories and found their website. Lucy practically jumped out of her chair.

"Maya—come here and look at this!"

Maya rushed over. Lucy pointed at the screen. "Melissa 'Missy' Zimmer, CEO of get this—a company that does animal testing for cosmetics!"

Maya's eyes widened. "We could be on to something here! Let's see what we can find out about Missy Zimmer and ZRC Laboratories."

"I'm on it." Lucy started typing, encouraged to finally have a lead. But the website for ZRC laboratories didn't provide much additional insight. It had generic info about being a leader in the industry, but it struck Lucy that it didn't seem to be marketing their services.

The page didn't list any cosmetic companies as example clients. The page didn't offer an obvious way to contact the company, which seemed suspicious. She couldn't even figure out where the company was supposed to be located since there was no address or phone number. Lucy threw her hands up in the air.

"This is another dead end. I don't know how we can find the company or be certain it is the Missy we are looking for," Lucy said with resignation.

"It's okay Lucy—we have a lead and that is more than we had before. I may know someone who can help us. My college friend Jason is a corporate lawyer. He probably knows how to find business records. I can call him next week. Let's get some rest so we can work more on your magic tomorrow."

Lucy nodded. She realized how tired she was after a long day of animal magic. Despite the potential dead end, overall, it was a pretty great day. She had swum with a fish, controlled a bird in flight, and had a nice lunch with her friend. Tomorrow she would work even harder to further her magic so they could get to the bottom of the Sienna Falls mystery.

Chapter 14

LUCY AND MAYA BOARDED THE ferry from Brighton Island. It was a free, twenty-minute commuter ferry that took them across the bay to Merrick Peninsula. On the weekend it was mostly tourists looking to do some sport fishing or birdwatching.

But Lucy was there for a different reason. Brighton Bay was home to bottlenose dolphins and now that she had had gotten over her fear of animal magic in the water by swimming with the speckled trout, she couldn't imagine anything more amazing than swimming with a dolphin.

The women looked out over the railing as the ferry left the port. Pelicans lined the poles on the ferry piers and gulls circled, hoping tourists would feed them to get a perfect photo. As the ship moved away from the shore, they both scanned the water for any sign of a dolphin.

The ferry ride was short, so they knew it was a longshot that they'd see any, but Lucy was still bitterly disappointed when they arrived at the opposite shore without any sightings.

Since they were also there to have a fun weekend, Lucy took Maya to her favorite miniature golf course. Located up on a hill, the course had a magnificent view of the ocean. They walked through the giant pirate ship, under the castle door with cannons that the balls shot through, around the giant spider, and admired the ten-foot-tall bright red windmill with moving blades.

Lucy laughed as Maya hit her ball so hard that it flew off the side of the course and landed in the wooded area and she had to go back to the front desk to get a new ball. Maya didn't even care that Lucy beat her by twenty points, especially since neither of them got even close to par. It was fun, and just what they needed.

Next door to the mini-golf course was an old-fashioned ice cream shop with a red and white awning, and black and white checkered floors. Lucy's mouth watered as she eyed the menu with egg creams, shakes, phosphates, and root beer floats. Maya ordered a banana split with three flavors of ice cream, and Lucy ordered a malted milkshake.

They walked around Merrick for a while, their bellies uncomfortably full of dessert, then headed back towards the ferry landing for the return trip.

Again, they leaned on the railing scanning for dolphins, and still nothing. Lucy was starting to get discouraged when she saw three dolphins leap out of the water about twenty feet from the ship. Maya spotted them also.

"Hurry Lucy—now is your chance!" urged Maya.

Lucy nodded and immediately reached out to one of the dolphins. The first dolphin didn't seem too receptive to her, so she tried the second dolphin. This one opened the door promptly and Lucy was in.

Unlike with the speckled trout, who moved from side to side, this time Lucy was in the ocean, moving up and down through the waves, in and out of the water. She was moving fast as the dolphin accompanied the ferry. Then the dolphin dove down under the water, still swimming swiftly.

Rays of sunlight penetrating the ocean's surface made it look like an underwater paradise to Lucy. She was filled with joy as she kept stride next to two other bottlenose dolphins. It was incredible to see the dolphins up close. Their curved mouths made it look like they were smiling at her. One was light gray and had a scar on its side. The other was almost black on top with an off-white belly.

Lucy was surprised when the dolphin she was swimming with reached out to her. So far, it had never happened to Lucy that an animal tried to communicate with her other than answering questions that Lucy had initiated. Lucy responded affirmatively to the dolphin, and the next thing she knew the dolphin used its flippers like wings as it started to slowly roll.

Lucy laughed with delight as the dolphin spun, then broke back up through the surface where she could see Brighton Island ahead of her. She knew the dolphin was playing just for her, a gift from a new creature friend. She also knew the ferry ride was almost over, so she let the dolphin know that was one of the best experiences of her life and thanked it and wished it well.

"Is she okay?" Lucy heard a man asking as she returned to her own sight.

"Yes, yes, she's fine, just got a little seasick, that's all," Maya assured the man who was still looking at Lucy with concern.

Lucy gave a weak smile. "Thank you, I'm okay—we're almost back anyway." Lucy had never considered what she might look like to other people while she was doing her animal magic. Now she realized at best she probably looked like she was taking a nap, and at worst she might look like she was nuts.

As they moved away from the man and got ready to disembark from the ship, she whispered to Maya, "Do I make crazy faces when I'm under? Do I make noises?"

Maya averted her eyes. "Ummm…"

"Why didn't you tell me?" demanded Lucy.

"This is the first time we weren't alone. I didn't think about it. Mostly your eyes are closed, but your face makes expressions like you are dreaming, and sometimes you make little sounds, like an ooh or aah or a shriek," Maya explained.

Lucy started to turn bright red. "Oh my gosh—that's so embarrassing!"

"Maybe you can learn to control that too—we'll work on it. But you swam with a freaking dolphin! How amazing was that?"

Lucy shone. "Indescribable."

"I'm so jealous," Maya confessed.

"I know. Thank you for helping me with all of this, anyway."

"Of course, that's what friends are for," Maya said firmly.

*   *   *

Back at home on Sunday night, Lucy jumped as she always did when her phone rang, which wasn't very often. It was Mrs. Kleinbaum, so she answered immediately. "Hi, Mrs. Kleinbaum. Is everything okay?"

"Yes, I'm fine. I'm calling about Mrs. Perez. I don't want to push you or anything, but she is going to visit her daughter all next week, so her apartment will be empty. That would solve the first issue of privacy," Mrs. Kleinbaum explained.

"This is good timing actually. This weekend I tested out directing animals where to go and I can do it! Not perfectly, and not *all* animals, but it works in theory."

"I knew you could do it, Lucy—you never cease to amaze me with your discoveries! So that just leaves your question of what animal could you use?"

"I'm thinking something small that could get in the walls?"

"Like a mouse?" asked Mrs. Kleinbaum.

"Maybe. But I'd need to find a mouse and it's unlikely there would be one there when I need it. I could buy a mouse, but I don't really want a pet mouse. I will think of something, though. Let's plan to meet at your apartment on Tuesday evening."

"That would be wonderful! Thank you for trying to help. Even if it doesn't work, I am grateful."

"Anytime, Mrs. Kleinbaum! I'll see you then."

Chapter 15

MONDAY, MONDAY, MONDAY. AFTER SUCH a lovely weekend at Brighton Island, it was even harder for Lucy to go back to work this week. But that's what adults do, Lucy thought to herself. So responsible with her 401k that she started in her early twenties.

Maybe it was because she never had children, but she still felt like she was playing grown up. When she put on her office clothes it felt like a costume. When she made her appointments for dental cleanings every year and paid her bills each month it all felt surreal, like she was just going through the motions of what it means to be an adult.

But Lucy loved living in her little house that would be paid off in ten years and she wouldn't change that for anything. And she loved having enough expendable income to go on weekend trips and take voice lessons. So back to work for Lucy. As long as she chose to be there, she would do her best. Today that meant working on the strategic plan.

Anuk had scheduled a brainstorming session bright and early. So far, they determined that Bethany would go with Anuk to visit the Northbrook Assistant Director of Planning since Bethany knew her from college. Lucy hadn't volunteered to go anywhere or meet anyone because the idea terrified her, but she knew she needed to step up and be part of the team if she wanted to continue working there.

Anuk announced, "The state Department of Environmental Resources is having their annual conference in two weeks. TerraPlaya has reserved a booth in the exhibitor's lounge. It's a great way to get our name out there. I need a few people to volunteer to staff the booth."

Maya glanced at Lucy and raised an eyebrow. Lucy considered that staffing a booth could be a safe way to fulfill her obligations, and if Maya was there, it wouldn't be too bad. She covertly nodded just enough so Maya could see.

"Lucy and I can staff it," Maya said.

"Great, thank you," Anuk responded.

The meeting continued with what Lucy found to be somewhat tedious discussions about potential clients and marketing strategies. She couldn't wait to get back to her desk and make maps. That was something she knew she was good at and made her feel like she was contributing to her team's success.

The brainstorming session lasted until lunchtime, when Lucy was relieved to sit in the courtyard and relax for a bit. It was getting quite hot out, but there was some shade, and a nice breeze and cold drink made it tolerable. Maya joined her after a few minutes. Lucy filled her in on Mrs. Kleinbaum and her neighbor.

Maya listened to the story and furrowed her brows in thought. "A mouse isn't a bad idea—the noise definitely could be something in the walls that was quiet when the building management inspected it."

"That's true. But where am I going to get a mouse? Should I buy one? Then what do I do with it after?" Lucy asked.

"I can help you there. I have a friend who runs a pet store. I'm sure I can borrow a mouse for you."

Lucy shook her head in disbelief. "Why does it seem like you have a friend for anything we ever need?"

Maya shrugged. "I have a lot of family and all their friends are my friends."

"Now I'm jealous," Lucy admitted.

"Don't be—my friends will soon be your friends! Jeremy thought you were really cool, and my grandmother loved you."

Lucy felt warm and grateful, and a tad embarrassed. "Aww, that's really nice. I like them a lot too!"

"Let's go by the pet store after work and we'll get you set up for tomorrow."

*   *   *

Armed with a small mouse that Lucy had already confirmed would allow her entry into its mind and let her navigate, she arrived at Mrs. Kleinbaum's door.

"Come in Lucy! Oh my—is that a mouse? I'd better put Frederica in the bedroom, so she doesn't get any ideas." Mrs. Kleinbaum lured the fluffy white cat to the back with some treats.

"Yes. Oddly enough, I borrowed this mouse."

"How unusual, but convenient," responded Mrs. Kleinbaum, chuckling at the absurdity.

"Which apartment belongs to Mrs. Perez? Is it near here?" Lucy asked.

"It is three doors down that way. There is a welcome mat with a flower on it." Mrs. Kleinbaum pointed down the sidewalk to the right. "But how is the mouse going to get in?"

Lucy grimaced and said, "I hate to tell you this, but a mouse can squeeze under a door gap of one quarter inch, and they can fit through a hole the size of a dime. Maya told me today mice have flexible skeletons."

Now Mrs. Kleinbaum made a disgusted face too. "Oh my, I'm not sure I wanted to know that! But I'm grateful to this little one for helping us out today."

Lucy nodded in agreement and looked at the little mouse in the cage. "It's showtime, my friend."

"Good luck Lucy!" Mrs. Kleinbaum said as Lucy scanned the area to make sure no one was around, then opened the cage and put the mouse on the sidewalk.

Lucy stepped back into Mrs. Kleinbaum's apartment and jumped in the mouse's mind. She moved the mouse down one apartment, two apartments, then arrived at the third door with the flowered mat. She asked the mouse if it could squeeze under the door and the next thing she knew she felt like she was being squished. It was momentarily dark, then quickly lighter again as she entered the apartment.

She felt strange trespassing in Mrs. Perez's home, but it was for her own good, so she pressed on. She felt the mouse give a slight pull to the kitchen where there was a pantry full of food that the mouse could smell from here, but Lucy nudged it back to the bedroom where Mrs. Perez had heard the noises.

There, behind the wall.

Lucy realized that she could also hear what the mouse was hearing. As the mouse moved closer to the wall behind the bed she heard it too, a slight buzzing and intermittent tapping noises. Definitely didn't sound like nothing, Lucy thought.

Lucy scanned inside the room from the mouse's viewpoint and spied a vent.

Can you get in there? Lucy asked.

The mouse moved towards the vent and just barely squeezed through the slats.

The vent connected to ductwork so there was not a clear view of the inside of the wall, but as the mouse scurried up the duct, the sound got louder. Lucy knew what it was instinctively. Bees. Buzzing and tapping against the wall. She directed the mouse to leave immediately as she didn't want it to get hurt.

Once the mouse was safely out of the apartment and back in the cage, Lucy walked around the apartment building and inspected the outside of Mrs. Perez's unit. Shining her flashlight, she saw an opening in the bricks that seemed just right for bees, and what looked like a sticky goo that could be honey.

"I'm pretty sure it's bees," Lucy reported to Mrs. Kleinbaum.

"Oh dear! That doesn't sound good. I'll figure out some excuse for noticing them and report it to the management."

"Let me call Maya right now. Knowing her, she has a beekeeper friend. If you tell the management, they will probably just hire someone to exterminate them." Lucy knew that if it really was bees, they could be relocated and help replenish some of the dwindling colonies that help keep the ecosystem balanced and pollinate crops.

Lucy dialed Maya, who picked up right away, knowing Lucy rarely made calls if it wasn't urgent. "What's up Lucy? Did you find something at Mrs. Perez's apartment?" Maya asked immediately.

"I think it's bees. I didn't see them, but I think it is a colony behind a brick wall. Do you happen to know a beekeeper among your long list of friends?"

Maya chuckled. "Oh geez. Okay. Yes, of course I know a beekeeper! Let me call him and see when he can get out there. If he can determine it is bees, he may work out an agreement to remove them for a small amount if he can relocate the hives."

"Thanks Maya—you're the best!" Lucy ended the call and turned back to Mrs. Kleinbaum. "Maya knows someone—I'll update you tomorrow after he takes a look. Hopefully, this will be all wrapped up before Mrs. Perez gets back."

Mrs. Kleinbaum was deeply appreciative. "That's wonderful. She will be so pleased to know she wasn't hearing things. Next time you visit I'll introduce you to her."

"That would be great. And I'm happy to help," replied Lucy. And she really was. This was the first time she had used her animal magic to do something positive and it felt amazing. She couldn't wait to find more ways to help people. But first she had to reward this mouse for a job well done.

Lucy asked her tiny companion, *do mice really like cheese?*

I love cheese!

Lucy giggled. *All right then, let's get you some cheese.* She headed out the door.

"Goodnight, Mrs. Kleinbaum."

"Goodnight, Lucy. And please tell your mouse friend I said thank you!"

Chapter 16

LUCY WAS DRINKING HER MORNING tea when Maya appeared in her cubicle. "I talked with my lawyer friend last night. Jason gave me some good leads on researching corporations. I looked up Missy Zimmer and ZRC Laboratories on the SEC database. I found the business address listed in the initial filings. Here it is." Maya handed Lucy a slip of paper.

Lucy scanned the paper and looked up. "Winkler? That's just thirty minutes away, right outside the city. I guess not surprising Missy didn't move too far away from Sienna Falls."

"True. Winkler is a small university town. And I happen to know that they have an animal science research program there."

"That's too much of a coincidence."

"Agreed. Are you up for a little extended lunch adventure?"

Lucy tensed. She wasn't mentally prepared to do any sleuthing. "Today?"

"Yes, no time like the present," Maya replied. "I thought we could visit the school and at least drive by the business address. I looked at the street view online and it looked like an old office building, nothing interesting."

Lucy considered this. It didn't seem like Maya had anything dangerous in mind, and she was anxious to find out what ZRC Laboratories was all about. "Okay, I guess I can—I don't have any meetings or big deadlines today."

A few hours later they were on the Winkler Tech campus. Maya parked the car and the women looked at the campus directory sign. "There." Maya pointed to the Animal Sciences building on the map. They started walking in that direction and came upon a large brick building with stone lions on either side of the front steps at the main entrance.

Lucy felt uncomfortable. It had been well over a decade since she had been in a college building. All the students seemed so young, their whole lives still ahead of them. Their young, fresh faces, full of hope for their future made Lucy feel old and obsolete. What was she even doing there? "Are we allowed to be here?" she asked.

Maya shrugged. "If the door doesn't require a key card, we are going in. If anyone asks, we are prospective students looking for a career change." Maya pushed open the heavy wooden doors and they walked into a small foyer with hallways leading to the left and right and straight ahead. Signs indicated that the labs were to the left, so Maya led them that way.

As they walked slowly down the hallway, they saw classrooms with lab desks, microscopes, scales, cages, cleaning supplies, biohazard containment, and lots of other equipment whose purposes Lucy could only guess. There were rooms with empty cages and some with cages that held mice, all secured with keycard access at the entrances. Some of the rooms had students hard at work on their experiments and assignments, but the women didn't pause to look too hard in order to remain inconspicuous.

"What are we looking for?" asked Lucy.

"I have no idea. We're just looking right now."

The hallway dead ended into a large, secured laboratory. The women had no choice but to retrace their path and return to the main foyer. This time they took the hallway to the right, but only found typical college classrooms with desks and chairs, electronic blackboards, and podiums. They again returned to the foyer and this time took the main hallway.

"In here!" Maya suddenly pulled Lucy into the open door of an office. The sign read "Career Services."

There was a small waiting room with couches and a table, and a front desk with a chair that currently sat empty. There was a large binder on the counter with a cover that read "Internship Listings" and a note that said students were free to flip through the book, but it was also posted online and gave the website. The room also had a large bulletin board with job listings and career fair postings. Maya started flipping through the binder.

Lucy picked up a pamphlet titled *Career Opportunities for Animal Science Majors*. "Huh. Meat scientist, conservation officer, animal trainer for movies! Real wide spectrum for what you can do in this field."

"Is dark magician who destroys forests in there?" quipped Maya.

Lucy feigned scanning the text as she flipped the pamphlet over and back again. "Let's see. Nope, not listed as a career choice. Are you finding anything in there?"

"Not yet."

Lucy turned her attention to the bulletin board. And then she saw it.

Lab assistant wanted. Must have special affinity for working with live animals. Screening tests required. Apply online.

"Maya—check this out." Lucy pointed to the ad.

"Special affinity? Like being able to talk with animals? Or control them?"

"That's what I'm thinking. And what about the screening test? This is definitely worth looking into."

The sound of dishes being deposited in a sink and a refrigerator opening and closing came from the door behind the front desk.

Maya grabbed the ad off the bulletin board. "Looks like lunchtime is over. Let's get out of here."

The women sprinted out just as the door behind the front desk opened.

Lucy checked the time on her phone. They had already been gone for an hour and twenty minutes and it was still a thirty-minute ride back to the office. In truth, she was tired, and she wasn't sure she wanted much more adventure today. They had found a new lead to explore and she felt good about that. "What do you say we do a quick drive by of the business address and then head back. We can come back another day to scope it out some more?"

"I'm good with that." Maya put the ZRC Laboratories address in her phone and started driving in that direction. "Let's think about what to do with this ad. Do you know anything about catfishing?"

Lucy snorted. "Um—what do you think? Don't you have a friend for that?"

"Ha ha. Let me think." Maya scrunched up her face in thought, then her eyes lit up. "Maybe I do—I think the husband of one of my cousins is in cybersecurity. I bet he could give us some advice."

"I'm sure we could look it up on the internet. I'm guessing we should set up a fake e-mail account and maybe a fake social media account or two. Of a college student in animal sciences. We could also set up a fake phone number that only goes to voicemail."

"You're scaring me how this is coming so easily to you! Getting quite crafty," Maya joked.

"Only since I met you…"

The navigation voice on Maya's phone chimed in, "You have reached your destination."

Maya slowed the car down and pulled to the curb. The women stared at a large, razed lot lined with construction fencing. A small billboard said it was going to be the site of a new city hospital.

Lucy's face fell. "Another dead end."

"At least we have the ad. Catfishing it is." Maya turned the car around and they headed back to Northbrook.

*   *   *

The exhibitor tables lined the hallways outside the Department of Environmental Resources conference session rooms. Each company had a nice crisp white tablecloth, a backdrop with their company name and eye-catching graphics, marketing pamphlets, and most importantly, swag.

The quality of the swag varied, from the standard mugs, pens, and tote bags with the company logo, to phone chargers, waterproof notebooks, reusable metal straws, wildflower seed packets, and insulated travel mugs. Many booths had big bowls of candy or bags of chips. Most of the staff at each booth wore some variation of a polo shirt in company colors, adorned with the company logo.

TerraPlaya was no different, so Lucy and Maya stood behind their booth of pamphlets and swag in their dark green matching polo shirts. Lucy was nervous since talking with strangers was definitely not her forte, but since she had attended plenty of conferences, she knew most attendees already knew all the players in their industry and were just there to be seen.

Maya had assured Lucy that all she had to do was be pleasant and answer any questions, and most people would just bashfully take the swag and move on to the next table. Still, Lucy's palms started to sweat every time that Maya left her alone at the table to take a break. She worried that as soon as Maya left some difficult person would approach her or ask her questions about the company that she should know the answer to but didn't.

Several people came to talk with Maya, unsurprisingly. Some of them were former colleagues or clients from Maya's previous company and some were members of the local environmental professionals group. Lucy smiled and shook a lot of hands as Maya introduced her to person after person.

Lucy was handling it all well, but that level of social engagement was exhausting to her. She couldn't wait for the day to end, but also felt good about fulfilling her marketing duties to help her team.

Most of their swag was gone by 2 p.m. and fewer people were stopping by the booth as most had made their way around multiple times by the afternoon session. An older gentleman with a button-down khaki shirt paused in front of the TerraPlaya booth. He read Maya's conference badge. "Hey, you're friends with Brandon Copperton, right?"

Maya nodded. "That's right, I'm Maya, and this is Lucy, nice to meet you." Maya extended her hand.

"Buck Henshaw. Nice to meet you too. I used to work with Brandon at headquarters in the wildlife department, but now I'm the ranger for the southwest region."

Maya's face lit up with recognition. "You cover the Sienna Falls Forest area!"

"Yes ma'am. Brandon had asked me to keep an eye out for anything strange out there, but the truth is I cover so many properties that I don't make it to each one as often as I'd like. And even then, Sienna Falls is pretty large to cover on foot."

"Sure, that makes sense. Have you been there lately?" Maya asked carefully.

"I patrolled the western portion a week ago and didn't see anything amiss. Have you had any more troubles?"

Lucy and Maya both knew that if he hadn't gone far enough east towards the McWalter property, he probably wouldn't have seen anything other than a slightly quieter forest than usual. "Our assignment ended, so we haven't done any more surveys there," answered Maya, still being truthful but not volunteering any unnecessary information.

"Is that right? That's a shame. It's a real pretty place. My paw knew Grady McWalter III. He was a great man. Real generous. Did you know he donated the land for Sienna Falls Forest?"

Lucy and Maya nodded. Maya added, "Yes, the lady at the lodge told us. She said that the city almost sold part of Sienna Falls to a logging corporation, but he stopped them, and then donated the forest."

"That's right. And he set up a conservation easement for his ranch too. Couldn't bear the idea that the young folk would sell it for subdivisions."

Maya looked shocked. "He did? Are you sure? We heard he didn't leave an updated will and his lands were tied up in the courts."

"Hmm. Well, I could be mistaken, but I'm fairly sure he at least started the process a good ten years ago. Maybe he never finished it. I'll ask some folks back at headquarters if they know. A lot them are old timers who've worked there for decades, and they'd remember."

Maya handed him her business card. "If you find out anything more, can you let me know?"

"Will do. Nice to meet you ladies."

After Buck was out of earshot, Lucy whispered, "Is it possible Grady completed a conservation easement without anyone knowing about it? Doesn't it require a bunch of lawyers?"

"Definitely on the lawyers. If it was finished, then the easement should have become part of the property deed. It must not have been because I'm sure that would have been publicized after his death. It would mean that such a huge part of the Sienna Falls Village would be protected from development, which would have made some people happy, and others super pissed. That would have been big news."

"Still, it's something we should look into. We can find out which land trust non-profits existed ten years ago and talk with them."

"Great idea."

Lucy finished out the conference day without any social faux pas, and she left with a recycled material tote bag full of swag herself. A hot pink stress ball, a pocket-sized bottle of sunscreen, a travel mug, and an assortment of miniature candy bars. It wasn't the worst day, but she was ready to go home, watch an old movie, and not talk to anyone for the rest of the evening.

*　　*　　*

Lucy was sleeping peacefully when ringing startled her awake. She glanced at the clock. Who was calling her at 8 a.m. on a Sunday morning? She reached for her phone.

"Maya—what's wrong?"

"It's Silver. Something upset her on her morning hunt. Jeremy was wondering if you could go out to Red Bluff Ranch this morning and talk with her."

"Oh no! Poor Silver. Of course I'll help if I can."

"Thanks Lucy—you're the best. I can swing by at nine and pick you up if that's okay."

"Sure. See you then."

Lucy wondered what could be the matter with the majestic merlin. She had such fond feelings for Silver since her first experience seeing through a creature's viewpoint was through the falcon's eyes. She had flown for the first time with Silver, and she would never forget it. If there was anything she could do for Silver and Jeremy, Lucy would be happy to help. She rushed to get a quick breakfast and be ready to head out when Maya arrived.

Lucy got in the car, threw her bag in the back, and put on her seatbelt. "Is Silver okay?"

Maya pulled the car out of Lucy's driveway and headed towards the ranch. "Yes, she seems to be, but Jeremy said she is trying to tell him something and he can't figure out what."

Lucy nodded. "I'm glad he called. Let's get to the bottom of this."

The women drove in uncharacteristic silence as they both privately worried about Silver and Jeremy. When they arrived at Red Bluff Ranch Lucy hopped out to open the gate and close it behind the car after Maya drove through. Jeremy was waiting in the long driveway.

"Thanks for coming, Lucy. Silver won't calm down since her hunting flight this morning."

Lucy looked at the regal merlin. Even someone less attuned to animals could tell that the bird was upset. Her feathers were slightly puffy, and she kept moving her head in an agitated manner.

"Hi Silver, it's me, Lucy. Do you remember me?" Lucy asked out loud and in her mind. Silver affirmed that she knew Lucy. "I'm here to help. Can you tell me what happened?"

Lucy turned to Jeremy and Maya. "She wants to show me something. I will let you know what I am seeing."

Jeremy and Maya nodded. Lucy closed her eyes and entered Silver's waiting mind. Silver immediately took off and Lucy was once again soaring over the trees. She was trying to keep track of where she was but as Silver glided over the thermals she was soon turned around. After a few minutes Silver descended into a tree overlooking a stream.

A large steel drum was oozing a sludgy liquid into the water. The stream was shimmering with a slick surface of an oil-like substance. As Lucy peered through Silver's eyes, she saw dead fish floating in the scum. Further down, a sickly-looking duck was struggling against the shore, trying to get out of the water.

Lucy relayed the scene to Jeremy and Maya.

Jeremy stamped his foot in anger. "Those bastards! We get illegal dumping around here from time to time but it's hard to catch them since we don't usually find it for weeks or even months after."

"That's awful. Lucky Silver is such a smart bird. She could have gotten really sick if she went near the contaminated water or ate any prey from there," said Maya.

Lucy pulled up some aerials on her phone. Starting with her current location she followed the general direction that Silver had flown and tried to find the stream. "Where is your property line?"

Jeremy showed her and before long they figured out where the contaminated location was. The first thing they wanted to do was see if they could help the duck and if there were any other sick wildlife that needed attending. Jeremy also wanted to get Silver checked over to be on the safe side.

Lucy asked Silver to stay put in the tree and wait for them to arrive.

Jeremy led Lucy and Maya to a large barn that was used as a storage shed. Maya looked for something they could use to transport the duck and Jeremy found some old gloves they could use to avoid contamination. Then they got in Jeremy's truck and drove as far they could until the road dead ended into the woods. They took the equipment out and walked a mile to get to the contaminated site. All three were relieved when Silver flew down from the tree and landed on Jeremy's leather glove.

"Great job girl," Jeremy told Silver, "I'm glad you told me about this."

After determining that the suspicious liquid did not seem to dissolve the thick rubber gloves that Jeremy had brought, Maya scooped up the ailing duck and put it in a box lined with a towel and covered the terrified bird with another towel to keep it calm. She looked at the fish but there was nothing to be done for them. They scanned the area for other wildlife, but they didn't find any, so they headed back to Jeremy's truck.

Once they were back at Maya's car, they loaded the duck in the back seat.

"We'll take the duck to the wildlife rehab center. You make sure Silver is okay," Maya said.

"Thanks Maya. And thank you Lucy. This could have been a worse situation if I didn't find out about the spill until later. After the authorities investigate, I can get the site cleaned up so no other animals get hurt."

"Anytime Jeremy, I'm always happy to help, and to see Silver." The merlin nodded at Lucy, who nodded back respectfully.

Maya already knew the way to the wildlife rehab center because as a grad student she used to teach at a summer science camp and took the kids on field trips there. They followed the sign to the drop off area and rang the bell.

After a while, an intake staff member came out and Maya explained what had happened and showed her the duck. The intake person assured them they would do what they could for the duck, but a lot depended on what the contaminants were and how long the poor duck was exposed.

While Maya was checking the duck in, Lucy was marveling at the amazing facility. Behind the fence she could see some outdoor cages for animals that Lucy guessed must be close to release. She saw a coyote, a turkey, some racoons, and a fawn.

Lucy picked up the brochure for the facility and saw tiny baby squirrels, wide-eyed ringtails, even a porcupine. Lucy didn't even know porcupines lived in this area.

It warmed Lucy's heart that in this world with dark magicians using animals to destroy a forest and careless people dumping chemicals into streams, that there were also a host of wildlife rehabilitators and tireless volunteers devoted to helping injured or abandoned wildlife. It inspired her to be even more committed to using her animal magic for good.

Chapter 17

LUCY WAS ALWAYS PARANOID WHEN she searched the internet, worried that she was going to get in trouble for things she looked up out of curiosity, like how to pick a lock, or if arsenic is really an undetectable poison. She just liked to know things. Today she was researching how to set up a fake profile so she could apply to the suspicious lab assistant position they had found in the Winkler Tech career services office.

It was troubling to Lucy how easily you can find step by step instructions on how to be successful doing questionable things. Lucy wondered who these people were who created these resources and if they ever got into trouble. But today she was glad these sites existed, so she couldn't be too judgmental.

She did a search for 'most popular girl names of 2002'. Before long Lucy had set up a fake social media profile that looked reasonably like a college student by the name of Hannah Stratford, a fake e-mail address, and a phone number with an online voicemail box. She created a resume for Hannah as a student in the animal science program at Winkler Tech and used the address of the college dormitory.

In her e-mail to the job posting address, she said that she always had a special relationship with animals since she was a little girl when she used to catch lizards and turtles and frogs, and her mom would be mad that she brought them into the house. The fake Hannah also volunteered as a dog walker at the county animal shelter.

Lucy attached Hannah Stratford's resume and sent the e-mail applying to the position. Now she just had to wait and see if they e-mailed back or left a message on the voicemail to set up her screening test.

*   *   *

Two days later there was a reply in Hannah Stratford's e-mail. It asked her to fill out an application and stated that if she were a good fit, they would contact her to set up an interview.

Lucy opened the attachment and was surprised to see that it didn't ask for her employment history, references, or skills. Instead, it was a questionnaire. As Lucy read through the questions, she was even more certain that this was the company employing dark magicians.

The first part was open ended prompts that seemed to be about intuition relating to animals, how to read them, and understand them, like:

Q2. I can tell when an animal is stressed by _____.

The next section was multiple choice and asked about past relationships with animals, like:

Q9. I think of pets as
a. Friends
b. Family
c. Possessions
d. Subordinates

The last section asked the respondent if they agreed or disagreed with a statement on a five-point scale, like:

Q15. Animals have the highest value when serving people.
Strongly Agree   Agree   Neutral   Disagree   Strongly Disagree

Lucy thought the third section seemed to test the ethical side of practicing dark magic on animals and might be a way to screen out candidates who would never be tempted to use animals for personal gain.

Lucy had to think carefully about how to respond to the questions so that she would pass the screening test and get an interview. She didn't want to seem like a diabolical madwoman, but she didn't want to seem like too straight an arrow.

She settled on trying to emphasize that she clearly had potential for animal magic, and was ambivalent, middle of the road, on the ethical concerns and views on the roles of animals in the social hierarchy. Lucy read it over several times, changing her answers until they were what she imagined they would be looking for in a dark magician. She sent the application back to the sender and closed her laptop.

She and Maya hadn't thought too far ahead as to what they would do if they got an interview. Since Hannah was a fake college student, neither Lucy nor Maya could pretend to be her. Not to mention that someone there might recognize them from Sienna Falls Forest and the lodge.

All this assumed that the ad was really from some diabolical company training people to control animals. Lucy figured if they could at least get a physical address then they would be able to find out more and confirm if the posting was the same company owned by Missy Zimmer, Grady McWalter's niece.

*   *   *

"Oooh—she's so cute! OMG. Squee!!!!" Bethany shrieked so loud that Lucy could hear it all the way from her cubicle on the far side of the office. She heard other staff joining in with oohing and aahing and her curiosity was getting the better of her.

Lucy left her cubicle and walked down the hallway towards the front reception area. To her surprise, there stood the corporate efficiency consultant, Hyun Shim. She was dressed in a severe black pantsuit, and looked every bit the consummate professional, but Lucy could feel a different energy about her today.

As she turned her attention to the little baby blue pet carrier resting on the front desk, she saw what everyone was cooing over. Hyun had brought her tiny little purse dog, a brown and white Papillon, with adorable, oversized wing-shaped ears and a fluffy, plumed tail.

Both Hyun and the dog seemed happy with the adoration it was receiving, and Lucy all at once realized that Hyun was just a regular person and not some corporate harbinger of termination. Hyun smiled as Bethany and Tyler complimented the dog and Hyun seemed happy to answer their questions about the unique looking breed.

Bethany beckoned her over. "Come meet Cookie, Lucy! She's, like, the cutest thing I've ever seen," she gushed.

Anyone who had such an adorable dog named Cookie must not be at all like the tough exterior that Hyun displayed during her unfinished interview a while back. Lucy felt bad again for causing the cockroach to fall in her lap, even though that did end her interrogation quickly.

Lucy went over to Hyun and Bethany and the other staff who were all petting the soft dog's head and scratching its chin. Lucy knew that some tiny dogs were nervous around strangers, but Cookie seemed to love being in the limelight and panted with happiness at all the adoring faces.

Still, Lucy felt there was something off about Cookie, but she couldn't tell what, with all the commotion surrounding the dog.

"Welcome back Ms. Shim," Anuk said warmly as he entered the reception area. "Would you like to set up in the same conference room?"

"That would be fine, thank you." Hyun collected her dog and briefcase from the desk and followed Anuk down the hallway.

With a return to her business persona, polite, but distant, Hyun Shim once again seemed like a threat to Lucy. And that threat was soon heightened when Anuk returned after escorting Hyun.

Anuk pulled Lucy away from the other staff and lowered his voice. "Ms. Shim is back to do a follow up with department managers, but since she didn't complete your interview, it needs to happen today."

Lucy paled. "Should I be worried?"

"Honestly Lucy, I would be lying if I said everything is fine. Corporate is breathing down my neck, the stolen equipment hit our office overhead, and the lost contract made our numbers even worse than they were before. I have given my recommendation that everyone in this office is critical to our success, but by hiring an efficiency consultant like Hyun, they have made it clear that it won't be up to me."

Lucy nodded and tried to make a brave face, but a large lump was welling up in her throat. She wasn't sure what else there was to discuss with Hyun, but it made her nervous about her job that Hyun felt she needed to talk with Lucy again. Lucy didn't want to leave TerraPlaya.

Did Hyun blame Lucy for the stolen equipment and lost contract? Did she think Lucy's basic mapmaking was a redundant position that could be better served by the centralized mapping division at corporate? Her thoughts started to spiral, and she felt like she was falling into quicksand.

Would she lose her job? After fourteen years?

She liked having Anuk as her manager, and she liked working with Maya. In fact, she liked all her colleagues in the office, even the ones she didn't know that well. She would miss her little cubicle that looked out into the courtyard. Maybe she would even miss the Monday morning meetings. Well, maybe not, maybe she was getting unnecessarily nostalgic.

With the distraction of the sweet dog removed, the staff wandered back to their cubicles. Lucy went back to her cubicle as well, but then straight back to the kitchen. This morning would need some tea.

As she sipped, Lucy considered that she wasn't the same person she was during her first interview with Hyun. She was more confident, she had a great friend who had her back, and she had powerful animal magic. She was still nervous, but not as much as she had been the first time she met Hyun.

Luckily, Lucy didn't have to wait too long, because Anuk called her to the conference room just after she finished her tea. Lucy took a deep breath, pulled back her shoulders, stood up straight, and marched towards her meeting with Hyun.

Hyun waved her in and beckoned for her to take a seat. Before Lucy finished sitting down, Hyun's phone rang.

"I'm sorry, but I need to take this. Will you excuse me for a moment?" Hyun exited the conference room and walked past the front desk to the main hallway that leads to the building lobby.

Lucy was alone with Cookie, who was not looking as bright now that she wasn't being showered with affection. Inside her mind, Lucy reached out to Cookie. "Hi Cookie, pleased to meet you, I'm Lucy."

The dog's enormous ears perked up in disbelief at the communication, but after the initial shock wore off, Cookie was calm enough to chat with Lucy. Lucy asked the dog if anything was wrong. As often happened when Lucy talked with animals, even when they were pets around humans all the time, Cookie didn't have the human vocabulary to describe what the problem was.

After some experimenting, Lucy was able to get Cookie to lick at the spot that was ailing her. Lucy considered that she should probably learn more about animal anatomy if she was going to be of more help, but it looked like Cookie was trying to point to her front right knee.

But how could Lucy tell Hyun Shim that something was wrong with her dog without arousing suspicion? With Mrs. Kleinbaum and her cat Frederica's ear infection Lucy was able to tell her directly what was wrong, knowing that Mrs. Kleinbaum would accept it without explanation. The same was not going to be the case with Hyun.

Lucy did a quick internet search on her phone for common ailments in Papillon dogs. Scanning the search results, one entry caught her eye— patellar luxation, a type of kneecap dislocation common in Papillons. She could work with this. Even if that wasn't the problem, getting the dog to a vet was the best chance at proper diagnosis.

When Hyun returned, Lucy was purposefully patting Cookie's head. Before Hyun could resume her questioning Lucy jumped in, "Papillons are such great dogs."

"Yes, they are. Now back to—" Hyun tried to continue the interview, but Lucy was not giving up.

"My aunt had one that looked just like this. Scooter lived for sixteen years and was in great health the whole time, except for some issues with his kneecaps that my aunt had to keep an eye on. He started getting a slight limp and wasn't eating as much and she found out that is a common problem in Papillons."

Now Hyun was distracted from the task at hand. "Really? My Cookie has been eating a little less and was walking funny. I thought she had a splinter in her paw, but I couldn't find anything. That's why I took her with me on this trip—I didn't want to leave her in doggy daycare, but I didn't have time to take her to the vet."

Lucy nodded. "Give me one minute—let me ask someone a question." Lucy texted Maya, guessing she might know a good veterinarian nearby.

In true Maya fashion, she immediately responded that her second cousin's husband had a veterinary practice just fifteen minutes from the office. In a matter of minutes, Maya had confirmed that the vet had a last-minute cancellation and could see Cookie if they could make it there by 10 a.m.

"Maya, one of the biologists who works here knows a great vet and they have an opening at 10 a.m. if you want to bring Cookie in," Lucy told Hyun.

Hyun didn't even pause to consider it or worry about the interview or whatever other tasks she had left to perform at the TerraPlaya office today. It was clear to Lucy that her only consideration was the health and happiness of her little companion. Hyun thankfully put the vet's address in her phone, picked up her beloved Cookie, and left for the vet appointment.

"Good luck—I hope you feel better, Cookie!" Lucy said as they dashed out.

"Thank you, Lucy!" both Cookie and Hyun replied.

Chapter 18

LUCY OPENED THE DOOR LEADING to the office courtyard to join Maya for lunch. Even though it was bordering on unbearably hot to eat outside, she was anxious to share a new development. "Guess what?"

Maya looked up from eating. Before she could even reply, Lucy answered her own question.

"Hannah Stratford just got an interview. 11 a.m. on Thursday."

Maya's eyes widened. "No way! Did it give an address?"

"Yep. I already checked it out. It is in Winkler, not too far from the college. But I checked the appraisal district website and the land the building is on isn't owned by either ZRC Laboratories or Sepharine Holdings."

Maya looked disappointed. "Huh, okay. That just means they don't own the land though, right?"

Lucy nodded. "Yep. The land is owned by Winkler Commercial Properties. They own several office parks in Winkler, so they probably aren't part of this. If it is ZRC at this address, they probably rent the space."

"Which is good for a company that needs to lie low sometimes and have the flexibility to move around."

Lucy considered this. It probably wasn't a coincidence that the location on ZRC's original business filings was an empty lot now or that their website didn't have any contact info. A company like ZRC wouldn't want their name on a property deed. "Good point. Still, we don't know for sure if it is ZRC who placed the ad."

"I know. That's what we need to find out. What's your schedule Thursday? I'm back from fieldwork and I could take a long lunch that day."

"Just making maps." Lucy tightened her lips and frowned slightly. "What did you have in mind?"

"A good old-fashioned stakeout."

"I was afraid you were going to say that." Lucy wanted to uncover the mysteries surrounding ZRC Laboratories and Sepharine Holdings Inc. and Sienna Falls, but she felt much more comfortable doing research behind the scenes, rather than being on the front line.

Maya leaned back in her chair. "It will be fine. We'll just check out the place and see who goes in and out. We can take your car since we had mine in Sienna Falls. We can wear baseball caps and sunglasses too—it's the middle of summer, so that will look totally normal."

"Fine, I'm in. Again."

*   *   *

Lucy and Maya sat in the car across from the building where Hannah Stratford was supposed to be interviewing. Luckily, there was a strip mall where Lucy was able to park under a tree while they surveilled. The parking lot was over half full, so they weren't too exposed. Both women were wearing sunglasses and Lucy had a baseball cap on and Maya was wearing a floppy sun hat.

Lucy tapped her hand impatiently on the dashboard. "It's nearly eleven." She felt like she was late to her own interview even though she knew Hannah didn't exist. Even knowing they were likely dealing with some bad people, Lucy still felt slightly guilty for the deception.

Just then a young woman walking down the sidewalk paused to look at a piece of paper, pulled on the door of the building, and entered. A minute later a young man went in the same building. Two more women who looked like college students followed him in a few minutes later.

"I wonder if they're all going to the same place?" Maya asked.

"Maybe they interview multiple candidates at once. Makes sense if

131

they are looking for people who have natural affinity for animal magic. They did mention a screening test."

Maya nodded. "That's true—they probably have to screen ten to find one viable candidate."

Lucy considered this. She knew that Maya had said that anyone who could be in the moment could learn animal magic, but Maya had also said Lucy had a knack for it. Lucy didn't realize that only one in ten people might be naturals. She couldn't help but feel special in spite of herself.

Lucy and Maya chatted about work and movies while they waited for something to happen. No one came in or out of the building for forty-five minutes. Just as Lucy was starting to get bored, the door swung open and the first woman who had gone in rushed out of the building. Even from across the street Lucy could see she was crying since she was dabbing her eyes with a tissue.

Maya looked over at Lucy. "What do you think happened to her?"

Lucy shook her head. "I don't know. Poor woman. I hope she's okay."

The young woman crossed the street and was heading right for them. Lucy tensed up, and even Maya grasped the door handle. The woman walked past Lucy's car and headed into the coffee shop in the strip mall behind the car.

Maya tapped Lucy on the arm and opened the car door. "Let's go!"

Lucy was confused. "Go where?"

"Just come on!" Maya closed the car door behind her. Lucy grabbed her keys and followed Maya as she walked towards the coffee shop.

Before Lucy could get a word in edgewise, they were inside the store. The young woman they followed was second in line at the counter. Her tears were starting to dry up, but she kept blotting them with her tissue.

Maya walked up and got in line behind her. "Excuse me miss, are you okay? I don't mean to intrude, but it looks like you are having a difficult day. Can we buy you a cup of coffee?"

With that, the poor woman started sniffling again. "That's so kind. I am having a terrible day," she said between blubbering.

"Aww, it's going to be okay. What would you like?" asked Maya.

"A caramel latte?"

"Okay, good." Maya smiled at the barista behind the counter. "One caramel latte, one black coffee, and one hibiscus tea, please." Maya paid and then turned back to the young woman. "Now let's sit down while we wait, and you can tell us what happened."

Lucy couldn't believe that Maya was talking to a total stranger like this. And that the young woman seemed to appreciate it. Lucy knew she bordered on the loner side, but still, if she were upset and someone started talking to her, she would probably tell them to leave her alone. Better yet, she would probably not be out in public in the first place, and she definitely wouldn't go into a coffee shop crying.

Maya handed the woman some napkins to wipe her face with.

As her tears dried up again, she looked sheepish. "It's nothing serious. I'm a college student and I just interviewed for a job. I really need the money and I was so excited about it. But they told me I'm not a good fit, whatever that means."

"I'm sorry—that stinks. I've been there for sure. I've been rejected for probably a dozen jobs at least. My name's Maya, and this is Lucy." Lucy smiled and waved at the woman.

"I'm Prue. Thanks again for the coffee."

The barista called out Maya's name, and Lucy got up to fetch the drinks so Maya could continue talking with Prue. Lucy handed Maya her coffee, Prue her caramel latte, and was grateful that Maya ordered her a nice soothing hibiscus tea.

Once Prue started sipping her drink she began to relax. "I probably didn't want to work there anyway. The whole thing was super weird."

Maya leaned forward. "How so?"

"The job was supposed to be for an animal laboratory assistant, but they asked me to do strange tests, like tell them which toy this dog would prefer to play with, without touching the toys. How would I know that? There were three other students applying and they had us all compete to get our mouses to run through a maze the fastest. Mine came in last. How is it my fault that the mouse didn't know how to get through the maze? After that they sent me home. None of it made any sense."

"That is pretty strange. What happened to the other students?"

asked Maya.

"I don't know. I guess they had more tests lined up for them. This mean lady was in charge. She walked back and forth with a clipboard watching us the whole time and she was the one who dismissed me before all the others."

Maya stroked her chin, then focused back on Prue. "Well as you said, it's probably for the best, who wants to work for a bunch of crackpots, right?"

"Yeah, I just really wanted a job that was related to my degree so I could get some experience."

"I might know someone who can help you. I have a friend who works in a large veterinary hospital nearby, and they are always looking for part time lab techs if you already have taken your lab courses and can identify samples."

"Yes, I have—that would be amazing—thank you so much!"

"My pleasure, Prue. Give me your phone and e-mail and I will talk with Greta and have her give you a call."

Lucy marveled again at how Maya seemed to be a connector, constantly helping the right people find each other. She never got tired of watching it unfold.

*   *   *

That evening Lucy considered the events of the day. Now she was reasonably sure that the company that rejected poor Prue was screening students in hopes of training them to use animal magic for nefarious purposes. ZRC Laboratories cosmetic testing business was clearly a front company that Missy Zimmer created to hide her dealings with dark animal magic. But how that related to Sepharine Holdings Inc. was still a mystery.

On a whim, Lucy tried looking at job boards at other colleges with animal sciences programs, but that wasn't always easy because they often required a student id and password. Lucy broadened out and searched the more popular job sites for "lab assistant" and "animal" and "affinity." Lucy gaped at the results on the computer screen, her mouth hanging open. Then she grabbed her phone and called Maya.

Before Maya could even say hello, Lucy blurted, "They're all over the place!"

"Whoa, slow down, Lucy. Who?"

"ZRC! I found job ads like the one we saw asking for special affinity with animals. Not just here, but all over the country. Seattle, New York, Atlanta, Chicago."

"Oof. That's big and not good. That means there must be hundreds of students being trained to do dark animal magic."

Lucy sighed. "I know. This is bigger than we thought. I don't know if we should be meddling in some national evil corporation's affairs."

"We're not messing with their affairs; we're just trying to protect Sienna Falls Forest. Did you find out anything else about Sepharine?"

"Not yet."

"I'll ask my corporate lawyer friend again how we can find out if they are connected. In the meantime, get some sleep. We learned a lot of good information today."

"That's true. And you helped a poor college student find a job."

"That too. Goodnight."

*   *   *

Since that day on the ferry, Lucy had been practicing trying to control her expressions while she was seeing through animal eyes. She still needed to have her eyes closed because it confused her brain to receive two sets of visual information at once. But she was learning to have a serene look on her face as if she were just taking a moment to rest. Maya helped her practice during lunch in the courtyard.

Lucy had bought a small resin bird bath to provide water for the critters that lived in the garden. It also was great for attracting diverse types of wildlife. Today Lucy was enjoying the view from a mockingbird.

Lucy snapped back to herself and focused on Maya. "Hey—that reminds me. That first day I saw you in the courtyard, you picked up a stunned bird and put it in a shoebox. What happened with that?"

"That already seems so long ago. I forgot you saw that. Not creepy at all that you were spying on me!" Maya chuckled.

Lucy turned bright red. "I told you—I look out the window a lot, plus you were right next to my cubicle."

"I'm just teasing you, Lucy. I brought the bird home and gave her food and water, and the next morning she had recovered. I brought her back here and released her."

"What about the other bird you were arguing with?"

"That was her mate. He was super pissed that I was taking her away. I had to convince him it was the best thing for her. He forgave me the next day."

Lucy nodded. A cardinal swooped down to the bird bath and caught her eye. "I'm going back in. Tell me if I do anything weird looking." Lucy knocked on the door of the cardinal's mind and with his agreement she was soon looking down at the water dripping from the end of the bird's orange beak. The cardinal then shook out all his feathers, making Lucy feel like her brain was rattling around in her skull.

"You're making a face, Lucy."

"Ugh. It's hard not to sometimes." Lucy focused on relaxing her face while she watched through the cardinal as he flew up to a branch on the oak tree. Lucy vacated the bird and opened her eyes.

"You're getting pretty good at this," Maya said.

"I guess I am."

"Like, what are you doing?" Bethany's voice startled the women as she and Tyler walked towards them from the courtyard gate.

Crap, thought Lucy. She was trying to imagine what they had seen from their vantage point. Her mind was blank, and she couldn't think of a response. She looked down at her feet.

Maya stepped in calmly. "Just helping Lucy with her bird identification."

Bethany arched her eyebrows. "With her eyes closed?"

"Sure, you know it helps to focus on the calls rather than visual ID."

Bethany didn't sound totally convinced. "I guess. You two seem to, like, have a lot of secrets."

"I have no idea what you're talking about, but you're welcome to practice with us out here anytime. You too, Tyler."

Tyler didn't seem overly interested in the conversation. "Thanks, but

I'll pass."

Figures, thought Lucy, why would he want to get better at his job? But it was good that he didn't take them up on the offer—if either of them did then they wouldn't be able to train in animal magic or work on the Sienna Falls mystery during their breaks.

"Maybe when it, like, cools down," said Bethany. She and Tyler turned and walked into the building, Bethany turning back to look at them one more time while whispering to Tyler.

Lucy unfolded her arms and relaxed. "That was close. We need to be more careful about how we look to others and also what we talk about out here."

Maya shrugged. "But really, what's there to see? Us talking, or concentrating, or you closing your eyes?"

"I guess. I just don't like people talking about me."

Maya leaned back and put her hands behind her head. "Who cares what Bethany and Tyler think? You don't even like them."

Lucy pursed her lips. "How do you do that?"

"Do what?"

"Not care."

Maya's laughter filled the whole courtyard. "I don't know, I just don't."

Lucy leaned forward. "No, I'm serious. Like that first day in the courtyard when I asked if you could talk to animals, and you said yes. How could you not worry that I would think you were crazy?"

Maya turned serious. "I wouldn't have admitted that to just anyone, Lucy. I knew from the beginning that I could trust you, and that we would become friends."

Lucy was taken aback. Lucy didn't make friends that easily, but maybe everyone seemed like a potential friend to someone outgoing like Maya. "Do all your family and their friends know about your animal magic too?"

"No, of course not! Lita and Jeremy know. Some of my other family who knew of my great-grandmother may believe it exists, but we don't talk about it. No one else in the family does animal magic that I am aware of."

Lucy had just assumed that Maya was an open book, but now she realized how silly it was of her to think Maya was going around telling people she could talk with animals. Now she knew how special it was that Maya had trusted her enough to share it with her, and that one decision had changed everything.

"I'm glad you told me," Lucy said earnestly.

"I'm glad I did too. Can you imagine if Bethany had almost gotten run over by a deer at Sienna Falls?"

That image made Lucy laugh so much she snorted, which in turn caused Maya to laugh hysterically.

When both women were finally all laughed out and all the tension caused by Bethany and Tyler had dissipated, Maya turned serious again.

"I think we're ready to go back to the forest," Maya blurted.

Lucy knew this was inevitable, but she had waited for Maya to bring it up so she could have as much time as possible to mentally prepare. Her animal magic was getting stronger every day, and her success controlling the mouse at Mrs. Perez's apartment gave her confidence that she could do what needed to be done. "What did you have in mind this time?"

"A little surveillance mission. Use your magic to get a better look at what is going on at the facility on the McWalter property. Even get a look inside, if possible," Maya suggested.

Lucy shivered thinking about their last trip to Sienna Falls, fleeing a stampede of terrified forest creatures. "But what if the same dark magic happens in the forest again?"

"It's a chance we have to take."

Chapter 19

IT WAS ALMOST EVENING IN Sienna Falls Forest. The women had timed it so they would be close to the McWalter property by nightfall. They wanted as much cover as possible just in case they needed to hide.

"Are you ready, Lucy?" asked Maya as they neared their target location, close enough for Lucy to quickly fly a bird to the location, but far enough that they couldn't be seen or heard.

"I'm ready." Lucy had connected with a few different birds this time, searching for the right one, and settled on a barred owl that was amenable to her proposal. Lucy nudged the bird with her mind towards the suspicious building they wanted to investigate. Lucy wasn't sure she was going in the right direction, but then she saw the clearing and had the owl swoop down into a tree near the access road.

Lucy gasped. "There are people here. At least two. The men we saw at the lodge. Loading crates from a van into the building."

"I bet those bastards stole our stuff! Can you see what they are carrying?"

Lucy asked the owl to quietly fly across to another tree so she could get a different angle. "Yes. Cages. With live animals."

"That's not good! What could they be doing in that building?"

"Let's try to find out. First, I'm going to explore outside some more." Lucy prompted the owl to circle around the side of the building. "Whoa— what is that? There is a big, fenced enclosure next to the building, and it's not empty."

"What's in them?"

Lucy had the owl swoop as close as she dared to the fence. "Wolves! There are angry looking wolves in cages. What the bat told us was right."

Maya let out a deep sigh. "Lita was right too—if they are controlling wolves, that is some serious dark magic."

Lucy was trying to stay focused, but her mind was jumping to all sorts of dark scenarios. She just had to get in the building and find out what they were dealing with. She knew that it would be much easier for her to connect with another animal if she could see it from the owl. Something that could help her get a look inside.

She had the bird move to a tree so she could scan the area for options. Lucy saw a moth, but she didn't think she could control its fluttery flight pattern. She saw a frog but figured the leaping would be too noticeable. Finally, she saw a beetle close to the front door of the building. The door started to open as one of the workers exited the building. This was her chance. "I'm going in!"

Lucy took a leap of faith as she left the owl with her thanks, and jumped abruptly into the beetle, hoping with all her might that the beetle would not reject her. Lucy made her quickest plea to the insect, and luckily it relented, and she scurried inside just before the door slammed shut.

As her mind cleared from the jump, she tried to adjust to the beetle's vision, but struggled. "Ugh!"

"What's wrong?" asked Maya.

"I'm inside, but I can't see well. It's kind of blurry up close but I can see things moving. It's like my brain can't make sense of what I'm seeing."

"Who are you looking through?"

"Some kind of beetle."

"Oh—I bet it has compound eyes. Can you see things further away? You might be able to see some directions and distances more clearly."

Lucy experimented with moving the beetle's head different ways and focusing on different parts of its vision. After a while, her brain started to adapt and understand the basic outlines in the room. Tables, chairs, a person moving towards them. Aaah! Lucy maneuvered the beetle out of the way before the footsteps approached them.

From a dark corner she took in what she could see from the floor. The door had opened and closed again, so she knew two workers were outside. Inside she could see one pair of feet under a table on the other side of the small main room. The room was lined along the outside with a ring of laboratory rooms with thick plate glass windows. She needed a better look.

She crawled up the wall and on top of a tall filing cabinet, peeking her head out from beneath a manila folder. From here she could see the back of a woman's head. Luckily beetles have decent hearing, Lucy thought as she listened in.

The slightly blurry woman spoke into a microphone on the desk in front of her. "Proceed with test procedure 9c."

From her position Lucy could see stacks of animals in cages in one of the rooms with the glass. A man sat upright on a tall metal stool in the middle of the room, looking into the adjacent room, which was also reinforced with thick glass.

Lucy strained to see what was in the next room. It looked like a small zoo habitat with a fake tree and branches. One of the fake limbs held a bird's nest with a mother bird and several pale-yellow eggs.

A latch slid on one of the cages, releasing a raven into the room. "Oh my god—no!" Lucy cried as the raven tore into the small bird's nest, clawing open eggs and viciously mauling the mother bird.

Lucy felt sick to her stomach as the raven relentlessly tore the family to pieces, eating both bird and eggs, leaving a gory mess of entrails and broken shells. The man in the other room seemed to be concentrating, but also to Lucy's utter disgust, he seemed to be enjoying the gory scene.

Lucy forced herself to concentrate even though she wanted to vomit. She needed to know more so they could stop this. She managed to tell Maya what she saw.

Maya clutched Lucy's arm. "Stay with it, Lucy—this is important. Was the man controlling the raven?"

"Yes, it looked like it. I think this is some kind of training, and this woman is leading it."

"What's happening now?"

Lucy focused again on the scene inside. The raven was back in the cage, and both the man and woman seemed pleased with the experiment.

"Well done, Alfonse. You are growing stronger each day," said the woman seated at the table.

From Lucy's vantage point she couldn't see the woman's face, but the severe, blonde bun twisted on top of her head gave the impression of an ambitious, powerful force of nature. Underneath the table, Lucy could also see she was wearing black high heeled shoes with dark gray slacks. Who wears high heeled shoes to some makeshift building in the middle of nowhere, Lucy wondered.

"I know, I can feel my power growing with each experiment," the man replied with an undertone of arrogance.

"Will everything be ready in time?"

The man smiled through the glass. "Trust me, Bridgit, this should be the last push we need to clear Sienna Falls Forest for a long while. The forest repairs itself quickly, but this third wave will make certain that it is known far and wide that no creature should return."

No, no, no! Lucy panicked. These dark magicians were going to destroy the forest ecosystem and the Silver-winged Warblers would never return. She got Maya quickly up to speed.

"When Lucy? We need to find out when so we can stop them!"

"I don't know. I'll stay as long as I can and try to find out." Lucy returned her focus to the room with the dark magicians.

"How is Mercy doing with the wolves?" asked the woman called Bridgit.

"She has more training sessions with them scheduled over the next few weeks. Losing Franco was an unfortunate setback, but Mercy is learning faster than he ever did, so good riddance."

"Indeed. Not everyone is cut out for this. I'll never understand how a little power scares some people. The stronger I become, the more it feeds my hunger."

Lucy shuddered as the woman practically cackled like the wicked witch of the west. It seemed that the big event wasn't going to happen for at least two weeks, so they had a little time, but they still didn't know the exact date of the attack on Sienna Falls Forest.

Lucy was starting to feel exhausted and felt her hold on the beetle slipping. She wanted to make sure it got out safely though, so she headed back down the wall and for the exit. She wasn't sure how long she could wait, but thankfully the door opened again, and she scurried out, leaving the beetle hidden safely in the brush.

*　　*　　*

Lucy was quietly sipping her Irish breakfast tea in the lodge café the next morning. She had barely slept after what she had witnessed the day before. She feared she would have nightmares about birds being torn apart, and she worried the image would haunt her forever. She had to be careful how she used her animal vision in the future as she'd already seen several things she wished she hadn't.

"Did you eat already?" Maya asked as she sat down across from Lucy.

"No, just getting my first tea of the day in."

"We could eat here, or we could head towards Northbrook and stop on the way."

"Yeah, I guess let's—"

A sudden scream from the kitchen filled the café.

"What the holy hell??? Get it!" a voice shouted.

Maya jumped up and almost collided with Sylvia, who had rushed from the reception area to see what the fuss was all about. Sylvia pushed past the cashier behind the café counter and swung open the kitchen door.

"What is going on in here?" Lucy could hear Sylvia saying from behind the door.

Maya waited impatiently in front of the counter.

"Oh! Let me call someone right away," Sylvia was saying as she swung the door back into the café.

Maya blocked her path. "What is it, Sylvia?"

Sylvia was clearly alarmed but answered with a forced calmness. She spoke loudly so the entire room could hear. "Nothing to worry about folks. Please go back to enjoying your breakfast."

143

Maya raised her eyebrows and gave Sylvia a look. She lowered her voice to a whisper. "That scream wasn't nothing. We're not just any guests—maybe we can help."

"You are a wildlife biologist, aren't you?" asked Sylvia.

"That's right," said Maya.

"Come with me." Sylvia pulled Maya back to the reception area. Maya beckoned to Lucy to follow her.

Sylvia spoke in a hushed tone so the other patrons in the café wouldn't hear. "There's a very large snake in the kitchen. I'm going to call animal control. The staff is trying to kill it, but it is hiding behind a cabinet."

"No!" Maya shook her head vehemently. "That's a terrible idea. People often get bitten while they are trying to kill snakes. Most snakes aren't aggressive if you leave them alone. There's no reason to kill it. Let me at least see what kind it is—if it is venomous or not."

Sylvia furrowed her brows. "You're a guest—I can't let you do that. Think of the liability if something happened to you."

"I'll sign a waiver—whatever. Or tell everyone you tried to stop me, and I wouldn't listen," Maya pleaded.

Sylvia looked imploringly at Lucy, who shrugged. "There's pretty much no stopping Maya when she gets it in her head to do something, especially when it concerns wildlife."

"Okay, fine, but just try to identify it. If it is venomous, I will have to call animal control immediately and clear the café," said Sylvia.

Maya nodded and the three women walked back towards the kitchen. As they approached, Maya turned to Sylvia and said, "I'll need the kitchen staff to step out for a minute to give me some room to work."

Sylvia gingerly opened the kitchen door and looked around inside. "They're gone already—it's all yours now. Please be extra careful."

Maya pulled Lucy by the arm into the kitchen. "Alright Lucy, ready to do your thing?"

Lucy's eyes practically bulged out of her head. "Me? What am I going to do about a snake? You're the one that volunteered."

Maya stared at her. "Um, are you forgetting that you can control animals?"

"Right, that's true. I can try…" Lucy looked unsure. She took a deep breath in and out. "At any rate, let me sense where it is hiding first. Then maybe you can get a look to see if it is venomous."

Lucy closed her eyes and brought her awareness to the space around her, to the smells of greasy bacon and buttery eggs and the sound of the dishwasher running. "It's over here." Lucy pointed to a tall stack of aluminum shelving. The bottom shelf was at ground level and contained canned goods and sacks of rice.

Maya cautiously approached the shelves. Keeping her distance, she quietly peeked behind the shelves. The three-foot snake had brown blotches on a gray background, no rattle at its tail end. "It's just a rat snake. A big one too!"

"So not venomous?" asked Lucy.

"Nope. Can you ask it to leave?"

"Let me see." Lucy focused again, then reached out to the snake. She sent it feelings of assurance, but she could sense that the snake was terrified after being chased and almost killed. "I don't think I can communicate with it right now. Can we just shoo it out with a broom? You said it isn't poisonous."

"I did, but we still don't want to get bitten. The bite of a large non-venomous snake could still get infected or even cause tetanus. And sometimes a bit of tooth even gets left in the bite."

Lucy frowned. "You could have led with that."

"And let you miss out on a great opportunity to practice your animal magic for a real, in the moment, emergency? Think of it like live training," Maya said with a twinkle in her eye.

"Point taken. Let me see if I can control it. Prop open that back exit for me and stand back."

Maya went to the back of the kitchen and opened the door. She put a rock beside it to keep it open so the snake could find its way out. Then she moved to the side of the kitchen so she wouldn't accidentally be in its path.

Lucy recentered. This time she found the door to the snake's mind, but instead of knocking on it she forcefully pushed her way in, imagining she was throwing her entire body against it. As she fell through the door, the snake instantly revolted.

Hissssss!

Lucy jumped back, smashing into the stainless-steel sink behind her. She rubbed her back. She knew the snake was just showing its displeasure at her intrusion the only way it knew how and realized she should have expected its reaction. She needed to focus more intently to stay in control no matter what the snake did this time.

She pushed her way into the snake's mind again.

Hissssss!

This time the snake's protest did nothing to deter her. She focused on willing it to move out from behind the shelves. Looking through the snake's eyes she could see its pink, forked tongue flick out in front of her, another sign that it was resisting. Lucy hated controlling an animal against its will, but the alternative was unthinkable.

The snake was different from the other animals she had controlled. She had gotten used to birds and four-legged animals and she knew how they moved. But with the snake it wasn't as easy as trying to lift one leg, then the other. Of course she had seen plenty of snakes on television slither in an s-pattern, but it was another thing to understand which muscles it required in a body that isn't your own.

Lucy tried to throw the snake's head forward, then grip underneath to pull the rest of its body along. The snake was still resisting, and it would take too long to get to the exit this way. She needed to use a combination of communication, reassurance, and control to make this work.

She sent out calming energy to the snake and told it she was trying to help. She pleaded that if it stayed here the other people would be back and may harm it and he needed to let her guide it to the exit. Then she tried again to force the snake forward by controlling its muscles, at the same time asking it to cooperate.

Finally, after the third forcible toss of the head, the snake started to move of its own will, allowing Lucy to guide it gently through the open door and out into the yard. She didn't stop there though. She wanted to get some distance between the snake and the kitchen.

When they were far enough away, Lucy cautioned the snake not to return to the building or he would meet his demise. The snake seemed to understand, and Lucy left him in peace at the edge of Sienna Falls Forest.

When Lucy opened her eyes, Maya was grinning. "I knew you could do it!"

"I almost couldn't—its resistance was strong, but I broke through."

"You probably saved its life. Let's give Sylvia the good news."

Lucy nodded, and the women walked through the café and back towards the reception desk, where Sylvia was anxiously waiting.

"What happened? Was it venomous?"

Maya shook her head. "Nope, it was just a large rat snake. We chased it outside into the forest."

"Rat snake? I haven't heard of that."

Maya took out her phone and brought up a photo.

Sylvia leaned over the desk and glanced at the picture. "Oh, we always called those chicken snakes because they would raid our hen houses and swallow whole eggs."

Lucy squished up her face in disgust. "They do? An egg is bigger than its whole head!"

"Sylvia's right—they do eat eggs. They can open their mouths wider than their bodies. It's pretty amazing," said Maya.

Sylvia laughed. "Amazing? If you say so, wildlife lady. I'm okay with snakes as long as they stay out of my house and place of business."

"Fair enough."

"Thank you so much for helping us out today. I'll put a credit for a complimentary meal for you both in the restaurant."

"Aww—thank you!" Maya said.

"Yeah, thanks Sylvia!" Lucy smiled.

She helped save a snake from getting killed by panicked kitchen staff *and* got a free meal. It didn't erase the bad experiences from the day before, but it gave her another chance to focus on something positive she could do with her animal magic. It wasn't easy to find good justifications for using her animal control, and she didn't want to stress unwilling animals just to practice the skill. Still, she noticed that each time she used it successfully, she grew more confident and more powerful.

Hopefully it would be enough to help the animals of Sienna Falls Forest.

Chapter 20

LUCY SEARCHED THE INTERNET FOR a student named Franco in the Winkler Tech Animal Sciences Program. It didn't take long for her to find his social media page, and it wasn't even private. She thought about how hard it would have been to track someone down like this when she was in college.

An online presence has its pluses and minuses, but right now it was a plus for Lucy. Might be a minus for Franco, depending on how things go. Now she had a name, Franco De Luca, and a photo of a young man, early twenties, shaggy light brown hair, and brown eyes.

Sure, Lucy felt like a creepy cyberstalker trying to find this young man, but she knew he could be the key to uncovering ZRC Laboratories' plan. She intensified her internet sleuthing and deduced that he should be on campus on Tuesday afternoons based on some recent posts complaining about school. Lucy looked at the campus schedule and found a couple of animal science courses around that time, with two starting at 11:45 a.m. and ending at 1:15 p.m.

By 1 p.m. Tuesday afternoon, Lucy and Maya sat nonchalantly outside the animal sciences building at Winkler Tech. They wore blue jeans and baseball caps and carried some books to try and blend in. Lucy had Franco's photo up on her phone and both women were scanning each student who left the building as covertly as they could.

"That's him!" Lucy said as a student with a red shirt walked down the steps.

Lucy and Maya strode over to him. "Are you Franco De Luca?" asked Maya.

Franco's raised an eyebrow. "Who's asking?"

"We wanted to talk with you about a job you had recently. Um, training animals," Lucy said, trying to use a less accusatory word for what they knew was happening at ZRC.

The color drained out of his face. "I don't know what you're talking about. If you're cops, you need to show me your badges. If you aren't, you need to back off."

Lucy looked at Maya. Franco was definitely hiding something, but he was right—they weren't cops and they couldn't make him talk. Lucy tried to appeal to his sense of decency. "Look Franco, we just want to get some information. We already know about Sienna Falls. We just want to stop them from destroying the forest."

"If you know about Sienna Falls, then you know what these people are capable of. I'm lucky I got out early. I promised I wouldn't talk about it to anyone, and they let me go. You two are going to get me into trouble."

"We don't want to get you into trouble. We just want to know when the final attack on Sienna Falls is going to be and how we can stop it," Maya pressed.

"I don't know, okay? I don't. I was just a low-level trainee. Once I found out the type of stuff they were doing I quit."

Lucy couldn't help wanting to know more. Did Franco have animal magic before he worked at ZRC, or did they teach him? "Can you talk with animals, Franco? Can you control them?"

Franco looked as white as a sheet by now. He shook his head. "I just want to finish school and live my life. Put this behind me."

Maya gently touched his shoulder and looked into his eyes. "It's okay. We can talk with animals, and she can control them. We aren't like ZRC. We use our skills for good and so can you. Now please, tell us something we can use to stop them."

Franco's jaw clenched. "You can't stop them. Missy Zimmer is ruthless and ambitious. The people who work for ZRC are soulless. They are power hungry, straight out of a comic book, evil villain types."

Lucy decided to appeal to his sense of morals. "We know you're scared, but you must have gotten into animal science for a reason. And if you have learned to communicate with animals, as I suspect you have, can you really leave the innocent creatures in Sienna Falls Forest to be slaughtered?"

Franco's head drooped and the conflict was apparent on his face. "What can I do? My powers are nothing compared to theirs."

Maya replied, "You can start by telling us everything you know and everything you saw. Any little thing might be a lead for us to figure out how to stop them."

Franco clenched his teeth in defiance but looking at the women's earnest faces he reconsidered and finally relented. "Fine, I'll talk, but after today you have to promise to leave me alone and never contact me again."

"We promise," agreed Lucy and Maya. The three of them moved out of the sun and looked around for a good place to sit and talk. Franco pointed around the corner towards some stone benches.

Franco confirmed everything they knew about ZRC. They were training people to control animals. Franco had indeed been tested at the same site that Hannah was supposed to have her interview. He knew of at least four other technicians that were in training before he quit, and he knew of at least two trainers.

Franco had never met Missy Zimmer, but he had heard her name in passing. She was way too high up in the corporation to be part of a lowly training class, but he had the impression that she controlled everything from afar, and her name was spoken with fear and respect.

He warned them about Bridgit Whelan. Bridgit was Missy's eyes and ears for the ZRC branches in this region. She was in charge of the Sienna Falls operation and the recruiting and training at multiple ZRC branches, including Winkler. Franco dreaded when she sat in on his training sessions because she was strict and swift with harsh criticism when trainees performed with anything short of perfection.

Lucy thought Franco seemed like a decent person and wondered how he passed their screening test. She learned that Franco had grown up on a cattle ranch with a healthy respect for animals but was also comfortable with the idea that they were there to feed humans. He had a pet pig that was raised to become holiday dinner, so he had to distance himself from his barnyard friends to protect himself. ZRC must have recognized that perspective and thought it could be manipulated into a view of human dominion over the animal kingdom.

The initial training at ZRC taught him how to control animals in seemingly innocent ways, like directing mice through a maze, or making a bird pick up a metal button in its beak. Franco started to question what the ultimate purpose of the training was.

He had, of course, found the same company website as Lucy had, and didn't see how any of this could be related to cosmetics testing. But he was a student and they paid good money to train him, significantly more than any other job a college student was qualified for, so he went along. Plus, like Lucy, he thrived on practicing his skills and getting better at animal magic. Franco told them that the trainees were referred to as "animal handlers," which made the position sound more like zookeepers or animal control responders.

A few weeks ago, his trainer felt he was ready for his first assignment, and they sent him to Sienna Falls to work with the wolves. Up until then, the animals he controlled were always small and harmless. The wolves were the first animals he worked with that could be dangerous to humans and that scared him. Franco could feel their power and feel his power growing after working with them. That scared him even more.

He went to school to learn more about livestock production so he could take over his father's ranch someday. He wasn't interested in controlling wolves for some evil corporation, so he quit.

Alfonse threatened him with his life if he ever told anyone what he had learned. He also had signed a non-disclosure agreement that threatened legal action if he told anyone about their business practices. He turned in his training manual and swore that he hadn't copied it.

Like Lucy and Maya, Franco knew the whole thing was too unbelievable to go to the police, and they technically hadn't asked him to do anything illegal, so he agreed to keep quiet in exchange for going back to his normal college student life.

Lucy and Maya had listened intently to his story. There was a lot to digest. They knew what a risk Franco had taken in confiding in them. Lucy had just a few more questions she needed to ask before they let him go.

"Have you ever heard the name Sepharine Holdings?" Lucy asked.

Franco thought for a few seconds. "I don't think so—doesn't sound familiar."

Lucy's face fell in disappointment. She was still trying to link the two companies. Now that they knew for sure ZRC was involved in the Sienna Falls attack, it didn't make sense that the men staying at Sienna Falls Lodge used a different name. Unless it was to purposely distance themselves from ZRC. As she considered it more, it would make sense that Missy Zimmer wouldn't want there to be any records tying ZRC to the Sienna Falls area where she grew up.

Lucy refocused on Franco. This was their one and only chance to get information from him and she didn't want to waste it. "How about Mercy? Do you know her?"

Franco scrunched up his face. "Ugh! Mercy is working for them now? Yes, she's a student here too. I guess I'm not surprised. She's not a very nice person—I bet she'll fit right in."

"That's helpful to know. One more question. You mentioned a training manual?"

Franco nodded. "Yeah, but I had to give it back. It had the exercises we were supposed to work on at home in between sessions to get better at communicating with the animals."

Lucy looked over at Maya and she could tell they were thinking the same thing. They needed to get their hands on this manual.

Maya took a business card out of her purse. "Thank you so much for sharing all of this with us—it was brave. We really don't want to cause trouble for you, so we won't bother you again. But if you think of anything else that could help us, please call me." Maya handed Franco her business card and soon he was lost in the crowd of students heading to their next class.

*   *   *

As soon as she was settled into her cozy little house for the night, she sat on her purple loveseat and opened her laptop. She had been waiting all day to find out more about Bridgit Whelan. Who would be friends with a person like that? Does her family know what she does for a living? What was Bridgit doing right now? Was she watching a movie on a purple loveseat of her own?

Bridget Whelan turned out to be a much more common name than Lucy had expected, but she had become quite adept at internet sleuthing over the past few months. And she knew that Bridgit probably didn't live too far from Winkler if she frequently supervised the training classes there.

Finally, she found something. It appeared that dark magician Bridgit Whelan had two children in Winkler Elementary, and not only that, but she had at one point been president of the PTA.

Lucy stared at a newsletter photo of Bridgit at a fundraiser. It was definitely the same woman she had seen in the building on the McWalter property. Her blonde hair was pulled back with a headband instead of a bun, but it still somehow looked highly controlled. In the photo she was wearing a white cable knit sweater with tan pants.

Now that Lucy saw her standing, she could see Bridgit was a very tall woman, yet she still wore high heels that made her tower over the other women, and even some of the men. Lucy thought that was certainly by design.

Lucy zoomed in to take a closer look. Bridgit was holding a tray of cupcakes, decorated in pink and white frosting.

She was smiling.

There was no reason for Lucy to think that a dark magician never smiled or baked cupcakes, but she was still surprised to see it.

Lucy kept digging and found that Bridgit also ran benefit races for cancer research and other causes. Lucy found a photo of her with a medal for coming in first in her age group in the Winkler 5k. She was starting to see a pattern here—no other office than president would be good enough for her, no other medal but gold. Lucy wondered what the pinnacle of animal magic was. She wasn't sure, but she bet Bridgit was trying to get there.

She didn't know what she was expecting to find about her online, but this was not it. No evidence of the cackling woman who ordered the killing of innocent birds and spoke of her quest for power.

Instead, Bridgit seemed like a very ordinary woman. Lucy guessed that her husband and children probably did think she worked for a cosmetics testing company.

Brigit probably set up play dates for her kids and went grocery shopping just like everyone else. When she could find the time between destroying a forest, massacring endangered birds, and training the next generations of dark magicians.

It dawned on Lucy that this also meant that regular people could be powerful and dangerous.

As weird as it was to discover that Bridgit wasn't a full-time villain, it was also encouraging. Bridgit wasn't some mythical sorceress. She was just a regular person like Lucy. And that meant that Lucy could beat her.

Chapter 21

"I CAN'T THANK YOU BOTH enough for helping Mrs. Perez. Not only was she losing her mind wondering what that strange noise was but having bees in the wall could have led to a dangerous situation," Mrs. Kleinbaum said.

"I'm glad we were able to help," Lucy replied, "and it made me realize there are so many ways I can use my animal magic for good."

Maya nodded in agreement and added, "And we even helped the bees, thanks to Lars. They are happily relocated in a safer place."

"Thanks to you, Maya. How lucky that you knew a beekeeper, and that Lucy knew you. Lucy has changed so much since she met you, and for the better, I'd say."

Maya looked slightly embarrassed. "Aww, thank you. Lucy is a great friend and I'm glad we met."

Mrs. Kleinbaum nodded, but then took a serious tone. "Now just don't get her into too much trouble with this Sienna Falls matter. It sounds dangerous and I don't want you young ladies to get hurt."

"We'll be careful," Maya and Lucy promised. Lucy hadn't filled Mrs. Kleinbaum in on the latest events because she didn't want her to worry too much.

A knock at the door made all three women put the mysteries and dangers out of their minds. Mrs. Kleinbaum opened the door and beckoned

Mrs. Perez to enter.

Lucy reached out her hand. "Mrs. Perez, I'm so pleased to meet you. I'm Lucy, and this is my friend Maya."

"The pleasure is mine, ladies. Mrs. Kleinbaum has been so welcoming and it's wonderful to meet her friends."

Mrs. Kleinbaum invited the women to sit down and have tea and pastries. She looked the happiest that Lucy had seen her, with delicious food and a living room full of good company.

"Mrs. Perez was telling me a few days ago that she used to be an opera singer," said Mrs. Kleinbaum.

Lucy's eyes widened with respect. "Really? I'd love to hear more about it. I've always wanted to sing, but I never studied it until now. I'm taking voice lessons and trying out for the Northbrook Community Choir in the fall."

"That's wonderful! You are never too old to learn music. At my age, my voice isn't what it once was, but I still love to sing. When I was young, I played the ingenues, but in truth, my favorite parts were the ones I performed after my voice was mature. I travelled all over the country and met all sorts of people. It was truly an adventure."

"I'd love to see some photos and hear some recordings if you have them," Lucy said.

"I would also!" Mrs. Kleinbaum declared.

"Me three!" said Maya.

Mrs. Perez beamed with joy at the idea of sharing her treasured memories with her new friends. Within minutes she had returned from her apartment with a box full of photos and programs. Lucy, Maya, and Mrs. Kleinbaum fawned over the collection showing Mrs. Perez in fabulous costumes on grand stages, newspaper clippings of rave reviews, and even a spread in an opera magazine.

Mrs. Kleinbaum took down her record player and the three women listened in admiration to a young Mrs. Perez singing a heartfelt aria that transported them to another time and place and nearly brought tears to their eyes from the emotions pouring out of her voice. At the end, Lucy, Maya, and Mrs. Kleinbaum all stood up clapping, giving Mrs. Perez a standing ovation. Mrs. Perez took a deep bow, her cheeks flushed with pride.

Lucy felt the warmth in the room and smiled to herself as she imagined herself at eighty. Just a few months ago she didn't think she would have any stories to tell about her life. But now, she felt like her story was just beginning and where it would take her was a wide and wonderful unknown.

*   *   *

Stealing ZRC's animal magic training manual from Mercy wasn't going to be easy. Lucy felt uncomfortable. Since she had learned animal magic she had spied and eavesdropped on people, pretended to be someone she wasn't, and cyberstalked a college student. Now she was going to steal. It didn't make her feel like she was one of the good guys.

Lucy knew Mercy was working for the dark magicians and was training with the wolves for the Sienna Falls operation. She didn't deserve Lucy's consideration, but Lucy still hated to break the law.

Where would Mercy keep the manual, Lucy wondered. If it was meant for everyday practice, then she might keep it with her, in a backpack. Especially if she went from class straight to training at ZRC. Lucy thought that was a better chance than trying to sneak into Mercy's dorm room only to find out the manual wasn't even there.

The question was where to intercept Mercy when she would have her backpack and how to get the manual without anyone seeing. Lucy considered using an animal to help her take it, but she didn't know how far along Mercy was in her training. Mercy might be able to sense all the animals near to her just like Lucy could.

Lucy had no trouble finding Mercy on social media. What was with people checking in places? It's like young people volunteered to walk around with tracking devices. It was fortunate for Lucy because she discovered that Mercy went to the same coffee shop near campus every Tuesday and Thursday at noon.

Lucy and Maya were lucky that Anuk didn't mind staff having a flexible schedule as long as they completed their assignments on time and worked at least forty hours per week. Still, with corporate breathing down their necks and losing the contract, it probably wasn't the best time to be absent at odd hours during the workday.

Lucy filled Maya in on her plan and they agreed to travel to Winkler on Thursday.

As far as they knew, Mercy didn't know what they looked like, so they could just be two friends sitting in a coffee shop. They arrived early and ordered a black coffee for Maya and a tea for Lucy.

Lucy pointed under the table. "There she is." Just like in her profile picture, Mercy was what Lucy would have referred to as goth when she was in high school. Black boots, black hair, black tights, thick eyeliner, and mascara. Some things never change. Lucy had gone through a goth phase herself, but frankly she was too lazy and cared too little about fashion to keep it up.

Mercy ordered from the counter and sat at a table next to the window.

Lucy gave Maya the signal, and Maya took her coffee to the milk and sugar station. She slowly poured sugar in her coffee, then some milk, then stirred it, taking her time, stalling for the right moment. Finally, the cashier called Mercy's name. As Mercy grabbed her coffee off the counter, Maya shouted "Mouse!" and turned around abruptly, knocking into Mercy, and spilling both of their drinks.

Mercy scowled as she shook hot coffee off her shirt. "What the hell? You stupid bitch—watch where you're going!"

Maya's temper flared as Mercy snarled at her, but she feigned sweetness. "I'm so sorry. The mouse startled me." Maya grabbed some napkins and handed them to Mercy.

As everyone turned to the two women, Lucy took control of the mouse Maya had released on the floor and sent it running across the room.

"See—there it goes!" Maya shouted. Patrons started freaking out and one woman put her feet up on her chair.

While everyone was either trying to avoid or catch the mouse, Lucy grabbed Mercy's backpack off the back of her chair. Blocking the view with her body, she quickly rummaged through it. There were a few textbooks, some notepads, and then she found it—the training manual. She shoved it in her jacket, returned the backpack to the chair, and left the café.

"Look—it's leaving!" Maya pointed as the mouse ran under the door and escaped outside.

Lucy had the mouse turn the corner towards her and then scooped him up into her pocket. She strode to her car, where she deposited the mouse in the cage, and put the stolen manual on the back seat. Maya soon joined her, and they sped away back to Northbrook.

As Lucy drove, she thought now I'm an impersonator, a spy, a cyberstalker, and a thief. Who would have foreseen that? She laughed to herself, and Maya just looked at her and shook her head.

*   *   *

The manual was different from what Lucy expected. She was hoping it would explain how animal magic worked. But as Franco said, it was only training exercises. It wouldn't be useful to someone who found it if they didn't already know about animal magic.

She supposed that was by design, and perhaps it was for the best— did the world really need a manual teaching any random person how to use animal magic for evil?

Still, the manual gave her an understanding of the types of things that the dark magicians at Sienna Falls would be capable of doing. The beginning exercises were simple, communicating with animals in a friendly way. The intermediate exercises practiced controlling willing animals. The advanced exercises covered controlling animals against their will.

Lucy noticed there were no exercises about seeing through an animal's eyes. She wondered if that was a rarer skill, or if it just wasn't something ZRC often needed to employ. It didn't seem likely that the ZRC trainers didn't know that was possible.

At any rate, Lucy came to two main conclusions after reading the manual. The first was that even though it went against every moral fiber of her being, she needed to know how to control an animal against its will in order to fight against the dark magicians.

The second was that she needed Maya to upgrade her skills if they had any chance of winning. Lucy felt weird that the tables were turned and now she would be the one instructing Maya. She shared this concern with her friend as they sat in the office courtyard.

"Don't be ridiculous, Lucy. I'm not too proud to accept that you have surpassed me in animal magic. I just want to protect Sienna Falls Forest. So be tough with me—nothing else will do if we want to win."

Lucy appreciated that her friend had such a great attitude. This was not a competition; it was a battle of good versus evil. "All right, I will be tough. I know you purposely avoid animal magic in natural settings so that you don't upset the balance. I thought we could focus on domestic animals or those in urban settings."

"That sounds good," said Maya.

"From now on, we're training during lunch in the courtyard every day we're both in the office. Starting today."

"Yes ma'am." Maya gave Lucy a cheeky salute.

Lucy rolled her eyes. "I know you can do the beginner exercises, so let's start with an intermediate one. Have you ever been successful with controlling a willing animal?"

Maya quickly turned serious, then sighed. "I've tried a few times since we met but I can't do it."

"That's okay. Let's try again. First let me find an animal that is agreeable." Lucy focused on sensing all the nearby animals. She saw the squirrel that she had given nuts to that first day, the first time she had ever communicated with an animal.

She reached out to the squirrel and asked him for permission. He remembered her kindness and agreed to her request. Then Lucy asked the squirrel if he would allow Maya to enter his mind. Lucy wasn't sure that he understood what she was asking, but it was worth a try.

"Okay Maya. See the squirrel on the limb over there? Try with him. Go into you place of mindfulness like you taught me. Then connect with the squirrel and ask him for permission. To me it feels like pushing a door."

"I'll try." Maya closed her eyes and started to concentrate on the sounds around her. Lucy could tell she was starting to relax and focus. After a few minutes, Maya opened her eyes and stared straight at the squirrel. The squirrel blinked, then darted up the trunk of the tree.

Maya turned back to Lucy, defeated. "It didn't work. I can't find this door you keep talking about."

Lucy bit her lip. "I'm not sure how else to explain it. Maybe it will be different for you. The door is just a construct I use so it makes sense to me, and I can visualize it. Did you visualize the door?"

"I don't know. Maybe not." Maya shrugged.

"Try again," Lucy said firmly.

Maya went back to her focused state. Lucy looked back and forth between Maya and the squirrel, looking for any sign that she was successful. She could tell Maya was getting impatient.

"It's not working." Maya threw her hands in the air in frustration.

"Don't give up, Maya, it might take a while to get it. Let's try something else. Do you still have peanuts in your desk?"

"Yep. Let me go get them—I need a break anyway." Maya walked back into the office building.

While she was gone, Lucy reached out to the squirrel and told him what she had planned. She promised him he could have his fill of peanuts in return for his cooperation. Lucy did notice that urban animals seemed more amenable to her requests than animals who had less frequent contact with humans. Perhaps it was because the squirrel benefitted from having humans around.

Maya returned with the peanuts. Lucy took some out and put them in two piles. Then she reached out to the squirrel. He climbed down the tree and stood centered behind the two piles of peanuts.

"Get to your place of mindfulness. Then at the count of three send the squirrel to the pile on your side. I will be trying to do the same," Lucy directed.

Maya tilted her head in thought. "I don't know, that might be upsetting for the squirrel."

"He's already agreed and is happy with his reward. We need to do this if we want to help Sienna Falls Forest."

"Fine. You're right." Maya closed her eyes and relaxed. Lucy did the same. After about thirty seconds, Lucy opened her eyes and glance at Maya. Maya was focused on the squirrel. "One, two, three," Lucy whispered.

Lucy was pushing the squirrel to the pile on the left. She didn't feel any resistance and the squirrel immediately moved left and started eating the peanuts. "Focus Maya. Send him to the right."

"I'm trying," Maya grunted, her face contorted in concentration.

Lucy knew she was trying her hardest, but maybe Maya just couldn't perform this type of animal magic. But she knew she needed Maya's help to defeat the dark magicians. "No problem. Instead of trying to control him, focus on breaking my influence over him. I'm going to make him move over to the pile on the right."

The squirrel started to move to the pile of peanuts on the right. Maya scrunched up her face and imagined blocking Lucy's powers by creating a big domed shield over the squirrel. Suddenly the squirrel stopped and blinked his eyes. Lucy tried again to move the squirrel, but it looked dazed. She turned to Maya with pride. "I think you did it—you blocked my magical hold over him. That's big!"

Maya let out a giant exhale and then grinned. "Progress."

Lucy nodded. Then she thanked the squirrel profusely for his help and put all the peanuts beneath the tree where he could access them away from the path of people entering and exiting the building. She figured that was enough human interaction for one day.

As promised, Lucy was relentless in Maya's training. Some days Maya had field work, but on the other days they were out there practicing. Maya still wasn't able to control an animal, but she was getting great at breaking Lucy's control.

Lucy figured since the animals they would be battling at Sienna Falls Forest were only doing the bidding of the evil magicians, it was equally useful to target the handlers as it was to try and control the animals. This way it would be a two-pronged attack. She hoped.

Chapter 22

EVER SINCE LUCY HAD DROPPED off the injured duck at the rehabilitation center, she had thought about ways she could make a difference with her animal magic. The Northbrook Animal Shelter was always looking for volunteers. She looked at all the opportunities on the website and she discovered that the shelter had expanded the adoption program hours to include five-thirty to nine on Friday evenings. They were having a volunteer training session this Friday and she decided to attend.

Lucy arrived at the white brick building. The front wall had a large mural showing different breeds and colors of cats curled up sleeping, and dogs catching frisbees, and children playing, with little birds and ladybugs scattered among the figures.

Lucy's heart warmed when she saw the image and was excited as she entered through the glass double doors. She knew she was going into a place where there were good people trying to do good things. And that is exactly what she needed while her life was burdened with dark magicians.

A super-smiley, enthusiastic man said, "Are you here for the volunteer session? Great! Head down this hallway to the left."

Lucy thanked him and walked down the hall. She turned left into a room full of chairs. There were already five other people there to volunteer. She smiled shyly at the people already sitting and took a seat in the back.

The smiley man entered and stood at the front of the room. "Thank you all for volunteering! My name is Owen, and I am the volunteer coordinator for the adoption program. Our ultimate goal is not only to rescue and adopt out cats and dogs, but also to make sure each adoption is a perfect match that will result in a forever home."

This sounded like a worthy cause to Lucy, and she was excited to figure out how she could apply her animal magic to the situation.

"There are two main components to this program. One is having volunteers to get to know the animals and write accurate descriptions for the website. The second is interviewing potential adopters to find out what they are looking for, what their households are like, and if they would be able to provide a forever home. Then we try and match the personality of the animals with those of the potential adopters."

Lucy loved this idea. She wanted to help every animal find the perfect home. She couldn't wait to get started. Her heart felt full of love for all these needy animals.

"Kittens and puppies are much easier to adopt out—everyone wants them. But we in the biz know that adopting an older animal can be extremely rewarding, and since their personalities have already developed, it can be easier to find a match. Nevertheless, you will see that it is challenging to find adopters for adult animals. If any of you would like to focus on them, let me know."

Lucy knew immediately she wanted to try working with the older animals. Maybe she could talk with each one and find out more about their personalities and what type of people they would enjoy living with.

After the introduction was over, Owen went through the safety procedures. There were a lot of rules in place to keep the volunteers and animals safe, as well as to minimize the risk of spreading any illnesses.

Finally, at the end of two hours, Owen said "Okay, who wants to meet a few of our current occupants?" The volunteers all responded enthusiastically and followed Owen down the hall to the other side of the building where the animals lived.

The room was lined with a glass wall towards the front of the building so that potential adopters could see the animals. The volunteers had to go around the back to access the kennels. There were several adoption rooms and Owen explained the procedures for taking an animal from the kennel to the adoption room. He then invited each of the volunteers to spend some time with one of the animals.

Lucy chose a handsome gray cat named Cloud. She read the description on Cloud's kennel.

Sweet 4 yr old male. Loves playing with wand toys. Unknown if good with children or other pets.

Poor boy, Lucy thought. How can they find him a good fit if they don't know enough about him? Surely families have passed him by looking for cats that would tolerate existing pets or small children. Lucy took Cloud to one of the adoption rooms and opened the carrier. Cloud popped right out, glad to stretch his legs. Lucy sat down on the floor and held out her hand. Cloud walked over and sniffed her fingers. Lucy scratched his head and he started to purr. What a sweetie, Lucy thought.

Cloud flopped over on the floor, enjoying getting pet and kneading his paws in the air. Lucy realized it was going to be hard for her to not adopt every animal she came in contact with here. But her job was to find many pets their perfect home and that is what she would do.

Cloud, I'm Lucy. How are you today?

Cloud's ears perked up and he rolled over to sit up like a sphinx statue. Lucy felt his confusion and she didn't want to stress him out, but she knew this was an opportunity to find him the perfect match.

Cloud, I'm here to help you. I want you to find a great home with toys and cat trees and all the attention you deserve.

Cloud rubbed against Lucy's leg. *I'd like that.*

Yes! Now she was getting somewhere. *Do you want to live in a home with other cats?*

Cloud looked thoughtful for a moment. *Maybe, if could be in charge.*

Okay, so maybe no other male cats. How do you feel about dogs?

Cloud arched his back and hissed.

Lucy jumped back. *Okay, okay, no dogs! Do you like children?*

No, they put their grubby hands on my clean fur.

165

So, no children. I can work with that. Do you want to play for a bit, Cloud? Lucy picked up the wand teaser toy she had taken from his kennel shelf and bounced it up and down.

Cloud started leaping in the air, attacking the little mouse on a string. He swatted it with his paws and pulled on it with is teeth. He looked like he was having tons of fun and Lucy was sad when Owen came by to say they were closing up for the evening and Lucy needed to put Cloud back in his cage.

Don't worry Cloud—I'm going to find you a great home.

Thanks Lucy.

Before Lucy left, she updated Cloud's kennel card.

Sweet, dashing, super soft 4 yr old male is ready to be king of the castle. Affectionate and loves playing with wand toys. Prefers a home without young children. No dogs. Okay with female cats. Cloud is smart and friendly and can't wait for his forever home.

*   *   *

Lucy and Maya had brainstormed ways to find out when the attack on Sienna Falls would take place. They didn't want to risk getting too close to the facility on the McWalter's property again for fear of bringing unwanted attention to themselves. Plus, the chances that someone would happen to mention it while Lucy was spying again with an animal seemed small.

Instead, Maya suggested that since the two men that stole their equipment were booked as Sepharine Holdings Inc. at the lodge, maybe that would give them a clue. But Lucy pointed out that Sylvia had been reluctant to give out any information concerning guests in the past and had only done so because of the fabrication Maya came up with about Lucy's romantic interest.

This time they would have to find a way to look in the computer for reservations. That involved more subterfuge than Lucy was comfortable with. Lucy pointed out that they weren't spies, after all. But in the end, Lucy couldn't come up with an alternative idea, so she agreed to give it a try.

While they were in Sienna Falls, they could also stop by the Southwest Regional Conservation Coalition and see if Skye knew anything about Grady McWalter III setting up a conservation easement.

Since Maya was a better liar than Lucy, whose face would get bright red and couldn't stop from sweating, Lucy had to be the one to look in the computer while Maya distracted Sylvia.

Lucy and Maya were greeted by Sylvia and then checked into their rooms as usual. After a few minutes, Maya left her room and returned to the front desk. "Sylvia, I need to speak to you for a minute."

"Of course. How can I help you—is everything okay?"

"Well, I'm not so sure. You know I'm a biologist, but my area of expertise is birds and not insects. There is an insect in my room, and I want to make sure it isn't…," Maya lowered her voice to a whisper, "bed bugs."

Sylvia's face contorted with concern. "Oh dear. I hope not. We take that issue very seriously and have many protocols in place to prevent them." Sylvia grabbed her keys and hurriedly followed Maya down the hall to her room.

When Lucy heard the door to Maya's room click shut, she opened the door and ran down the hall. Luckily, the reception area was empty, and she quickly snuck behind the counter. Sylvia had been in such a rush to determine if the lodge had a major pest problem that she forgot to log out of her computer.

Lucy had to make a few attempts before getting to a screen that let her search for reservations by name. She entered "Sepharine," and their account pulled up with all the dates the company had employees stay there, plus all the future reservations, and the number of rooms.

Lucy scanned the entries, most of which were two rooms at a time. Then she saw it—Sepharine had 5 rooms reserved two weeks from now. That must be the weekend they planned to have extra staff at the facility to do their final attack on Sienna Falls Forest.

She backed out to the main screen, darted out from behind the counter, and went around the corner to the café just before Maya and Sylvia returned to the front desk.

"I'm sorry again for wasting your time, Sylvia," Maya was saying.

167

"Oh no, don't think twice about it—we'd always rather be safe than sorry. An infestation could shut down our whole place for several days or more."

"Okay, well thanks again."

"No problem, have a pleasant stay."

Maya joined Lucy in the café and Lucy filled her in on what she had found in the reservation database.

"Nice, great work! Two weeks from now. That's not much time to prepare," Maya mused.

Lucy purposely hadn't let herself think about what they would actually do to stop the attack because it scared her too much. She was taking one step at a time. First, they found out Sepharine Holdings Inc.'s plan, then they located Franco, then they found out the date.

All of those pieces were low in risk, so Lucy could keep her focus narrow, like a horse with blinders on. But now that they were near the end, it started to dawn on her what Maya was proposing.

How could Lucy and Maya stop a group of dark magicians and an evil corporation from destroying their beloved Sienna Falls Forest? The whole idea was preposterous, she thought. But she could hardly tell Maya now, could she? Lucy's hands started to feel clammy, and her head began to ache.

"Why don't we go talk with Skye, and then come back and have dinner?" Maya suggested.

Lucy was grateful to have another tangible, safe step to focus on. She pushed all her thoughts and anxieties down and smiled back at Maya. "Sounds like a plan."

The Southwest Regional Conservation Coalition office was open, and Skye greeted them. "Hi there. I'm surprised to see you again. I am still really sorry there is nothing I can do to help you and TerraPlaya."

Maya waved her hands. "It's okay, really. We are here for a different reason today. A friend of mine at the wildlife department thought that Grady McWalter III had started setting up a conservation easement about ten years ago for his property. We don't know which land trust organization it was with, but I know that is something that your group does, and since the Coalition was founded over twenty years ago, maybe it was with you."

Skye's mouth fell open. "Oh goodness. That would be huge if that were true. Since his land is adjacent to Sienna Falls Forest, that would essentially triple the acres of habitat that are protected from development. Unfortunately, I don't know anything about that."

"Maybe there is someone else who worked here back then we could ask?" Lucy suggested.

"I'm afraid not. I took over this office about a year ago, and the previous executive director retired to Costa Rica. If you can't tell, she left quite a mess, and I'm still going through all of these papers and working on a project to digitize our records." Skye gestured to the metal filing cabinets and boxes full of unfiled folders.

Lucy and Maya looked at the many boxes and files and their hearts sank. It would be easy enough to lose track of papers in this office, and they weren't even sure the conservation easement was with this group, or even that it existed. They knew that non-profit staff were always overwhelmed with a variety of duties, and they couldn't very well ask Skye to look for a needle that might not even exist in this messy haystack.

"Maybe we could help you organize and digitize your files?" Lucy offered.

"That's a very generous offer considering our history, but I don't even have time to supervise volunteers right now with our current priorities," Skye responded remorsefully.

Lucy looked disappointed. "I understand. Let us know if you change your mind."

Lucy and Maya drove back to Sienna Falls Lodge to eat dinner. Then they were going to strategize about how to defeat the dark magicians.

Lucy was quiet throughout dinner. Since they knew some of the dark magicians could be in the dining room, they were careful not to discuss their plans out in the open. The food at the lodge was simple but always delicious and usually Lucy enjoyed every bite.

But this time a nagging in the pit of her stomach made her lose her appetite, and she just pushed the food around on her plate. She was too anxious to eat and couldn't think of any small talk to make because all she could think about was how crazy it was to believe they could make a difference.

Maya eyed Lucy's untouched plate and lifted her brows in concern. "Are you okay, Lucy—you've barely touched your food."

"I don't feel very well. I think I need to go lie down. Can we talk in the morning instead?"

Maya looked concerned. "Of course. Do you need me to get anything from the drugstore?"

"No, I'll be okay. Goodnight."

"Goodnight, Lucy. Text me if you need anything."

*   *   *

The next morning Lucy went out to her car to get her phone charger. As she stepped onto the gravel in the parking lot and neared her car she jumped back. Her front tire had been slashed.

Not an innocent nail in the tire, but three deep gashes across the side, clearly cut on purpose. In fact, the gashes looked like claw marks more than anything else.

She stood frozen for a moment until she saw a folded piece of paper on her dashboard that wasn't there the day before. Oddly, her car was still locked when she pulled on the handle. She pressed the unlock button on her key, opened the door and unfolded the piece of paper. A black feather fell out. There was a message scrawled in black ink.

You're in over your head. Fly away while you still can.

Lucy dropped the note as if it burned her hands. She looked around frantically but no one else was in the parking lot. She slammed the car door and ran back into the lodge, down the hall to Maya's room.

Lucy knocked desperately. "Maya, open up!"

The door swung open. "Are you sick—what's wrong?" asked Maya.

Lucy explained about her tire and the note. Maya's face paled. "That's messed up. I'm sorry about your tire. I'll ask Sylvia if they have someone who can help put on the spare and if there is a tire place nearby."

"I don't care about the tire!" Lucy yelled. "They're threatening us now. Why aren't you more upset?"

Maya's eyes narrowed. "I *am* upset, I'm angry. These people need to be stopped."

Lucy threw her hands up in the air. "And we are the ones who are going to stop them? We couldn't even keep my car safe for one night. We couldn't keep our GPS and laptops safe."

"I understand you're distraught, Lucy. Let's take care of your tire now and we'll figure everything else out after."

That calmed Lucy down a bit because she could go back to focusing on one simple and safe task at hand. Sylvia asked one of the maintenance staff to help the women put on the spare tire because Lucy's hands were shaking too much to do it herself, and Maya was so angry that she couldn't focus.

Sylvia couldn't believe what bad luck the women had at the lodge but assured them they probably ran over some barbed wire or something. After the spare was on, they headed to the nearest tire store to get the ruined tire replaced.

Before long, the women were driving back to Northbrook. Lucy made it clear she didn't feel like talking, so Maya stared out the window the entire drive home. Lucy dropped Maya off at her house and headed home.

Back in her little house she finally felt safe again. She made tea and popcorn and curled up on her little purple velvet couch. Tonight she just wanted to escape from all the dark things in the real world to a fantasy of romance and music, so she watched the 1940s musical *Meet Me in St. Louis*, starring Judy Garland, set around the wonder of the 1904 World's Fair. Lucy let the enchanting singing and dance numbers distract her mind from anxious thoughts and she was soon lost in the movie.

Chapter 23

MAYA WAS WAITING FOR HER in the courtyard on Monday morning. It was early and Lucy was tired. She hadn't slept the night before. She was still rattled by the incident at the lodge and feeling like she was in way over her head. For the first time she wasn't happy to see her friend. She wished she could slip past her and get to her cubicle and be safe in her world of maps.

"Good morning, Lucy!"

"Good morning."

Maya didn't seem to notice Lucy's lethargy and started talking enthusiastically. "I was thinking last night, and I came up with a plan, we should—"

Lucy involuntarily winced, then tried to cover it with a neutral expression, but it was too late.

Maya put her hands on her hips. "Spill it Lucy, I can tell you have something to say."

Lucy took a deep breath, looked up at Maya and said firmly, "I can't do this. I just can't."

"Can't do what exactly?" pressed Maya.

"I can't deal with this Sienna Falls nightmare." Lucy's voice was raised and starting to tremble. She hated going against Maya, but in this moment her fears and anxieties outweighed the risk of disappointing her friend.

"I know you're scared. I'm scared too. But we're invested in this, and we're the only ones who can stop it."

"We don't know that we can stop it. And yes, I'm scared. They slashed my tire and threatened us. Franco warned us that they are ruthless, and I don't know how far they are willing to go. They will kill innocent animals, and destroy nature to meet their needs, is that all? Would they kill a person? I don't know and I don't want to find out!"

"So that's it, you're just out? You have all this power and you're just going to *waste* it?" Maya shook her head in disbelief.

"Why should it be up to us to try and fight some giant evil corporation?"

"You know the saying 'With great power comes great responsibility'? You have that great power now, or at least you have more than the rest of us."

"I didn't *ask* for this power. Six months ago my life was fine, it was calm. I didn't ask for it to be turned upside down."

Maya's eyes sparked with anger and hurt. "You weren't complaining about it when you were swimming with the dolphins. Now you're sorry we met?"

Lucy's eyes started welling up with tears. She didn't mean to hurt her friend, but she just couldn't be the person Maya wanted her to be. "I didn't say that. Of course, I'm not sorry we met. But I'm not a spy or a superhero. I'm just Lucy."

"I know who you are, you—"

Lucy shook her head violently. "No, you don't. That's the problem. You don't know me at all."

"So, what—you're just going to go back to your little quiet life hiding in your little cubicle, drinking your tea?"

Maya's remark felt like a knife to the gut. "Maybe I am—I don't know, but it's none of your business if I do. I can't do this right now." Lucy stormed out of the courtyard towards her car, tears streaming down her cheeks as she fled.

*   *   *

Lucy called in sick to work for the third day in a row. Or e-mailed, really, as she didn't want to talk with anyone. She was seldom out so she knew Anuk wouldn't begrudge her some time off, even if she only gave a vague explanation of "not feeling well."

It wasn't a lie because she wasn't feeling well at all. Lucy was deeply depressed. She had messed up her friendship with Maya by blaming her for the current challenges in her life when she knew in her heart that she would always be beyond grateful for learning about animal magic.

She was depressed because she knew that her anxiety was controlling her once again, after making so much progress over the years. Lucy was aware that her anxieties weren't unfounded—there was a real risk that they could get physically hurt if they pursued the Sienna Falls situation. But she also knew that her anxiety made her withdraw into herself and hide, instead of talking it through with Maya like she should have.

She was depressed because she was letting all the creatures in Sienna Falls Forest down. Every deer, cardinal, and squirrel was going to suffer because she wasn't brave enough to step in. She wasn't a warrior, or a superhero prepared to battle an evil corporation employing a bunch of dark magicians.

This wasn't some comic or movie where the shy woman transforms into a powerful force. This was Lucy being Lucy, just trying to muddle through life. She waffled back and forth between feeling like she was a coward and a failure and feeling like it was never fair of the world and Maya to ask her to be so brave in the first place.

For three days Lucy wallowed under a blanket in the middle of summer, eating stale chips and frozen cookie dough, watching television, and purposely ignoring her phone and e-mails. Even her favorite movies barely held her attention. She didn't feel like taking a shower and her hair was getting stringy and her clothes were starting to smell.

The more she stewed about the argument, the more hurt she was and angrier she became. There is a special way that only people who know you really well can hurt you. Lucy was always aware that is part of the risk of letting people in. Maya's snarky comment about Lucy going back to sit in her cubicle and drinking tea was hurtful on that special level, because Maya went for the core of what Lucy felt unsure of about herself.

Lucy knew from her years of therapy that she shouldn't overanalyze and attribute any underlying meaning to what Maya said, but it was hard not to think Maya must have thought she was just a pathetic person who needed saving. It's not like Maya needed more friends, right?

Well, Lucy was still good at her job making maps, she still had Mrs. Kleinbaum, she still had her voice lessons, and she still had her old movies. She was fine before she met Maya and she would be fine after her.

On the fourth day she was making herself some tea in the kitchen. Out of habit, Lucy said good morning to the cardinal at the bird feeder. She didn't get a response. That wasn't abnormal because not all animals talked back to her. She tried again with another bird. No response.

She stepped out onto her back patio and stood still, listening for the soundtrack of nature that she had gotten so accustomed to that she often didn't notice it anymore. But today she realized that it wasn't there. Yes, she could hear a bird chirping, but she couldn't feel the creatures around her like she could before. She couldn't sense the insects in the ground, and she couldn't inventory each creature in her yard like she could before.

She tried to knock on the mind of a squirrel on the fence, but nothing happened. She couldn't even get to the place where the door would have been. She had never felt so lonely in her entire life. Not only was Lucy broken and depressed, but she had lost her animal magic.

*   *   *

"Glad to have you back Lucy," Anuk said brightly at the staff meeting. It was Monday yet again, and Lucy had been out all of the previous week. She wasn't feeling better, but she couldn't stay home forever. She needed the income, after all.

When she looked in the mirror that morning, she thought her eyes still looked red from a week of crying, and her skin looked more sallow than usual. She figured at least no one would question that she'd been sick. She purposely came in late and avoided seeing Maya. Luckily, there was an empty seat far away from her, so Lucy could do her best to avoid any contact.

"Thanks," replied Lucy sheepishly. Anuk went on about the assignments that week and Lucy knew she had a lot of maps to catch up on. She was relieved because that would keep her mind busy and give her a sense of purpose. She had looked at her phone that morning before work, and she was disappointed that Maya had not called to check on her.

She knew Maya was headstrong, but she secretly hoped that Maya would understand why Lucy had to bow out. Apparently, Maya was still angry. That made Lucy a little angry too because Maya had no right to push her into a dangerous situation.

Both women successfully avoided each other for the next two days. Lucy ate lunch at her desk instead of the courtyard, and Maya did the same. She knew that Maya would be out doing field work starting Wednesday, so if they didn't talk before the end of Tuesday, then the next time she would see Maya again would be at the next Monday morning meeting. And that meant it would be after the day of the attack on Sienna Falls Forest.

Lucy was a lot of things, but she was definitely stubborn. And Maya was the same way. Neither one gave in and tried to talk to the other.

Late Tuesday afternoon, as Lucy was packing up her things, Bethany stood and whispered over the cubicle wall. "Hey Lucy, is everything, like, okay with you and Maya?"

Lucy froze. She hated to think other people in the office were gossiping about her, or that they looked like teenagers in a petty fight. Keeping her voice smooth she replied, "Yeah, why do you ask?"

Bethany walked around and leaned against the wall knowingly. "You two are, like, two peas in a pod. Now all of the sudden you're sitting on opposite sides of the table?"

Ugh, thought Lucy. It was probably obvious to everyone—how embarrassing. "Thanks for asking, Bethany, but it's nothing, really."

"'Kay, if you say so." Bethany turned the corner out of sight.

Lucy sighed deeply. Since Lucy had lost her animal magic, she reasoned that perhaps it was a sign. Maybe she was supposed to go back to her old life, the one she had before she met Maya. It wasn't so bad, she thought.

Then she remembered the ferry ride and the dolphins, and the ice cream shop, and finding the Silver-winged Warblers, and watching the *Picture of Dorian Gray*, and Jeremy and Silver, and dinner with Carmela, and she could feel the tears starting to stream down her cheeks again.

She didn't want to lose all that. She didn't want to stop having adventures. But she had lost her animal magic and she didn't know what she could do about it.

*   *   *

Lucy was sobbing, her face red and eyes puffy. Mrs. Kleinbaum patted her arm and Frederica sidled her leg.

"Poor Lucy. I know how much Maya means to you. To lose a good friend is a terrible thing. But I can't believe this is the end. You two have a special friendship that can weather a greater storm than this," said Mrs. Kleinbaum.

Lucy sniffled and nodded. "I thought our friendship was strong too, but now I'm not so sure. I can't be who she wants me to be. And if she can't accept that I'm not as brave as she is, then maybe I don't want her friendship anyway."

"True friends will like you for who you are. But from what I saw when I met Maya, and from all the stories I have heard from you, she does."

"I guess so."

"Forget for a moment what you think Maya wants, or who you imagine she wants you to be. What does Lucy want? Who do you want to be?"

Lucy shrugged her shoulders and let out a pained sigh. "I don't even know."

"I don't believe that. Here, let's try something. Answer me as quickly as you can without thinking through it first, okay?"

"Okay."

"Do you want to be friends with Maya?"

"Yes."

"Do you want your animal magic back?"

"Yes."

"Do you want to help stop the dark magicians in Sienna Falls Forest?"

"Yes, but—"

"No buts, Lucy. Sounds to me like you want the same things Maya wants. So, what are you going to do about it?" Mrs. Kleinbaum had never spoken so firmly to Lucy, and it took her by surprise.

"I can't go back to Sienna Falls. I'm not brave enough."

"I'm sure you know the saying, Lucy, that bravery doesn't mean you aren't scared to do something, it means you do it even though you're scared. I don't like the idea of you going back there, but I also don't want you to have regrets."

"I don't know if I can."

"What can't you do? Can you drive there? Can you walk into the forest?" Mrs. Kleinbaum demanded.

"Yes, of course, but—"

"You can do whatever you set your mind to. I don't know what the outcome will be, but you are only in control of your own actions."

Lucy considered this. Much of her therapy over the years focused on setting values and then behaving according to those values, regardless of how she was feeling in the moment. Therapy also taught her to focus on what was in her power and to let go of trying to control other people. She was starting to feel a little better, and her tears were beginning to dry. But then she remembered.

"But Mrs. Kleinbaum, I lost my animal magic. I can't help at Sienna Falls even if I wanted to." Lucy's eye welled up with tears once again.

"Now Lucy, didn't you tell me that animal magic wasn't a gift, but a skill that requires concentration and practice? How can you lose something like that? I don't think you lost it. I think you rejected it."

Lucy stopped crying as her face lit up. "You're right! I can't lose my magic because it's not a gift! I must have blocked it since I was so upset."

"Well, try it now. Talk with Frederica!"

Lucy scrunched up her face in concentration. Go back to basics, she told herself. She focused on what sounds she could hear. Mrs. Kleinbaum's fan making a rattling noise, the hum of the refrigerator, a car leaving the parking lot, a bird outside in the tree.

She then focused on what she could feel, her thigh against the chair, Frederica headbutting her leg. She noticed the smell of herbal tea, fragrant with chamomile and mint. She was back in her familiar state of mindfulness. Then she opened her eyes and looked directly at Frederica.

"Sweet friend," Lucy spoke in her mind to the fluffy white cat, "can you hear me?"

Yes. Can I have treats now? Frederica swished her tail.

Lucy laughed for the first time in almost two weeks.

Mrs. Kleinbaum shook her finger at Frederica. "She asked for treats again, didn't she?"

"She sure did! Can I give her some?" Lucy said with a grin. She had never been so happy to hear a cat beg for food.

"Of course! What a spoiled cat." Mrs. Kleinbaum plucked the treat pouch from the cabinet and handed it to Lucy. Lucy gave Frederica some treats and pet her soft head, making Frederica purr.

"Thank you so much Mrs. Kleinbaum. You helped me see everything clearly."

"My pleasure. You are always trying to help others, so it's great to be able to help you for a change. Now that you have your animal magic back in order, what are you going to do?"

"I'm going to fight for Sienna Falls and fix things with Maya." Lucy spoke with more certainty than she ever had. She was still scared but couldn't help thinking that Maya coming to work at TerraPlaya, Tyler coincidentally spraining his ankle, and her knack for learning animal magic so quickly, meant her destiny was to defeat the dark magicians at Sienna Falls. Now she just had to make things right before it was too late.

*   *   *

It was time to put on the war paint. She had been controlled by her fears for long enough and now it was time to fight. She looked through her closet for anything that might make her feel like a warrior. The best she could find was pretty close to her field clothes—khaki pants and hiking boots.

She found a studded bracelet from an old Halloween costume, and she threw that in her luggage for the heck of it. She packed a pocketknife, her water bottle, some snacks, and a first aid kit. She didn't have much of a plan so she just threw in anything that might be remotely helpful.

But that was it, wasn't it? She needed a plan and currently she didn't have one. Being spontaneous was for people like Maya. That was fine, but wars were won with plans, and that is what Lucy excelled at. She took out her notepad and started writing down everything she knew about the dark magicians, what she learned from the training manual, from Franco, and from her experiences at Sienna Falls Forest.

Then she started writing ideas. True brainstorming, where no idea was too stupid. The entire situation was so surreal anyway that it would almost be silly to rule anything out. Before long, Lucy had the makings of a plan. There were a lot of unknowns, since she didn't even know if Maya would be there, but it was more than she had a few hours ago.

Lucy knew she wouldn't be able to sleep so she watched a classic movie, but not a 1940s classic like usual. No, this called for something a little different. This was a 1980s classic, *The Legend of Billie Jean*, where Helen Slater plays a Texas teenager who becomes a martyr after she is inspired by Joan of Arc to stand up for her and her brother.

By the time the movie had ended Lucy felt like she could conquer the world. As long as she kept from thinking about what she planned to do tomorrow, she felt fine.

Chapter 24

LUCY TURNED ON HER ROAD trip playlist. She had to do something to distract herself from questioning if she was acting crazy. No, she had made a decision, and she was sticking with it. She needed to focus on strategizing and less on fear and doubt.

Lucy had called Maya last night and again this morning, but she didn't answer. Her gut told her to head to Sienna Falls anyway, so that is what she was doing. She knew she couldn't fight the dark magicians alone, but she had to trust her instincts and let the chips fall where they may.

When Lucy arrived in the lodge she checked in at the front desk with a familiar face.

"Hi Sylvia!"

"Hi Lucy! Welcome back. Your friend already checked in. I think she is in the café."

Lucy's face lit up. Maya was here already! "Great! Thanks." Lucy took her room key and went to put her luggage away.

She had practiced in her mind what she would say to Maya, but now that she was here, she was nervous. What if Maya didn't forgive her? Lucy looked at herself in the bathroom mirror and pointed at her reflection. You can only control your actions, she told herself. You can't control how Maya responds.

She took a deep breath and headed to the café. She scanned the room quickly and spotted Maya drinking coffee and looking out the window. Suddenly Maya turned around, in that strange way you do when you feel you're being watched. Maya caught Lucy's eyes and her face broke out into the widest smile Lucy had ever seen. Maya stood up and ran over to Lucy and hugged her.

Lucy felt such a sense of relief since she knew immediately that her friendship with Maya was secure.

"I'm so glad to see you, Lucy!"

"I'm glad to see you too!"

Lucy had a whole speech prepared, but none of that seemed to matter anymore. She was back with her friend at Sienna Falls, where she was meant to be.

For once Maya looked more unsure than Lucy. "Are we doing this, then?"

"Let's kick some butt!" Lucy said. She might not feel brave, but she was determined and knew they would fight as hard as they could to protect the forest.

Maya laughed at Lucy's uncharacteristic response. "Awesome! Let's go make some plans."

The women headed back to Maya's room so they could talk without anyone eavesdropping on them.

Maya began. "I have some great news! Guess who called me a few days ago?"

"Who?"

"Franco! What we said to him really sunk in and he said he wanted to help."

"But isn't he worried about what ZRC might do to him when they find out he isn't keeping their operations a secret?"

"Yes, he's scared, but he said he couldn't live with himself if he stood by and did nothing."

"That's courageous."

"He and Jeremy will be here by seven to go over the plan. In the meantime, you and I have work to do."

"We do?"

"Yep. We need to raise an army."

*   *   *

As Lucy stepped into Sienna Falls Forest, the familiar calm washed over her again. Even with the trial they faced tomorrow, the serenity of the forest penetrated her soul and soothed her nerves. She wondered how she had ever considered not fighting for the forest as an option. With her newfound animal magic, the natural world was more a part of her than ever, and all the forest creatures felt like extended family.

Once they passed the curve in the bend of the stream, Lucy knew they were about halfway to the McWalter property, close to where they had first experienced the dark magic and where Lucy and Maya had hidden in the cave. Maya stopped.

Lucy turned to her friend. "Now what?"

"This is our chance to warn the creatures of the forest about what is coming tomorrow. We need help protecting the most vulnerable animals and we need others to commit to joining the fight." Maya dropped her backpack on the ground.

Lucy did the same. She knew what needed to happen next. Both women dropped to the forest floor seated cross legged with their knees touching, like they had the first time they had sent out peace to the forest, the day they had found their first Silver-winged Warbler. It seemed like another lifetime ago to Lucy, the joy of finding the endangered bird, before it was tainted by the discovery of an evil plot.

Lucy and Maya joined hands and closed their eyes. Lucy knew connection was extra important today, so she took her time centering, focusing on all the sounds and energies of the forest as she slipped into her state of mindfulness. Lucy could feel Maya's energy and connection enhancing her own, like a radio antenna boosting a signal.

When Lucy felt the connection to the forest was powerful and the signal was at maximum strength, she started broadcasting a message to all the creatures. She warned them that after the sun set tonight, after the night faded away and the sun rose again in the morning, that the dark magicians would return with their wolves and their ravens.

She asked the creatures to join her and Maya and their friends in fighting the dark magicians. She asked the stronger creatures to protect the weaker ones. To put aside the differences of the natural order of animal hierarchy and food chain to protect each other for one single day. For large birds to protect the nests and eggs of smaller birds that would usually be prey. She asked that animals that had claws or other weapons band together to fight against the dark magicians.

Lucy knew that a single raccoon or possum was no match for a full-grown wolf, but the combined attack of a dozen animals could drive one away. She warned that there would be bloodshed and injury, but that Lucy, Maya, and her friends would do their best to help any injured animals.

Lucy could feel the response of the forest. First there was fear and hesitation. Then she felt some of the braver animals heed her call and vow to join the fight. As the forest began to chatter with discussion amongst themselves, she could feel the energy of a determined army of creatures amassing. Lucy knew that some creatures were planning to abandon their homes and escape with their families while they had the chance. That was okay, and Lucy didn't blame them for their choices.

She also heard commitments to protect each other and even to fight to the death. The creatures knew the forest was theirs and they weren't going to let the dark magicians harm it again.

When Lucy opened her eyes and looked around, she blinked in disbelief. The sun shone down through the forest canopy like a picture from a fairytale, and there stood a wide array of forest animals surrounding them. A majestic buck nodded his head towards the women, the sun glinting off his antlers. A raccoon stood straight up like a soldier. A red-tailed hawk let out a shriek of solidarity as it swooped overhead. There were mice and squirrels, cardinals, snakes, beetles, and skunks, all gathered together.

Lucy bowed deeply to the animals and sent out her thanks. *Til we meet tomorrow*, she told them, *prepare, and wait for my call.*

Lucy and Maya repeated this process several times throughout Sienna Falls Forest. Each time they had a small portion of creatures who decided to flee and a larger portion who committed to stay and fight. Lucy started to

184

feel like the general of an army of forest creatures, and she supposed that was exactly what she was.

The women were at the last site they needed to cover before heading back. Just when Lucy thought she had seen every type of creature in the forest, she opened her eyes this time to see a mountain lion among those who had heeded her call. Lucy jumped up from the ground in terror and quickly glanced at Maya. All the smaller creatures were frozen, waiting to see what the intimidating animal was going to do.

Maya stayed seated and signaled with her hand to stay calm. "This is big, Lucy," Maya whispered, "if we have a mountain lion on our side, that will be a huge help in defeating the wolves."

Lucy nodded. She was trembling in fear as just twenty feet away from her stood an animal that could tear her to shreds. Lucy had never seen a cougar in real life, but she had seen plenty on nature shows, and this one was huge.

He stood three feet high with a muscular back and stocky legs. His paws were enormous, and Lucy could only imagine the claws that were hidden beneath the tan fur. Lucy marveled at his dark heart-shaped nose and long white whiskers. This mountain lion would be a formidable opponent and she was thankful he was on her side. At least, she hoped that's what the situation was.

Lucy reached out to the giant cat with her mind. *We are honored that you will join our fight tomorrow*, Lucy told him.

She was surprised when the mountain lion responded clearly. *Anyone who fights against the evil ones to protect my home is a friend, even a human. I will fight with you to the end.*

Lucy bowed to the mountain lion. *My name is Lucy and I thank you for your friendship. Is there a name I may call you?*

My name is not easily repeated in human tongue, but you may call me Rex.

She nodded in deference towards the majestic creature. *Rex, we do not think the dark magicians will be defeated easily tomorrow, but with your help we may be able to banish them from the forest for good.*

I have no doubt, Lucy. Til tomorrow. Rex turned and bounded back into the woods out of sight. The other forest animals relaxed and returned to their chattering.

Lucy couldn't believe what just happened. She just made friends with a cougar. In her wildest dreams, she never imagined this scenario. Maya was still sitting there in amazement. Lucy pulled her up and both women just stared slack jawed for a minute.

"I think you are officially queen of the forest now," Maya said with a glint in her eye.

Lucy beamed. "Were you able to hear what he said?"

Maya nodded. "Yes, I think because your energy was amplifying my animal magic, I heard him too. Rex, the mountain lion. You really are something else, Lucy!"

*   *   *

Lucy and Maya were sitting at the small table in Maya's room at the lodge. Even Maya's anxiety levels were high enough that she looked through the peephole after there was a polite knock at the door, even though they were expecting someone any minute. Lucy looked on in anticipation.

"It's Jeremy." Maya opened the door, and he entered holding a large traveling carrier. "Hi Jeremy, hi Silver."

Jeremy put the carrier holding Silver the merlin on top of the dresser. "Hi Maya." The corners of his mouth turned up when he saw Lucy. "It's great to see you, Lucy—glad you made it."

Lucy blushed. She should have known that Maya would have told Jeremy about their argument and that she didn't expect Lucy to be at Sienna Falls for the big battle. "Thanks, it's nice to see you too. And you too, Silver." She nodded to the merlin in the carrier. "I wasn't sure about coming here, but I realized at the last minute this is where I belong."

Jeremy nodded. "What's important is that you're here now. So, what's the plan?"

Maya beckoned Jeremy to sit down. "Franco should be here soon— let's wait for him before getting down to business."

Jeremy looked incredulous. "The Franco that used to work for the dark magicians? Is that a good idea? Can we trust him?"

Maya looked at Lucy and Lucy nodded firmly. "Absolutely," Maya replied. "Franco is our secret weapon. Without him we wouldn't know how they work. And he trained with the wolves."

"We need him to have any chance of winning," Lucy added.

Jeremy sat back in his chair. "Okay, I trust your intuition. If you say Franco is with us, then I'm good."

That settled, Maya and Jeremy caught up on family gossip while Lucy listened in, wondering what it would be like to have such a large family. On one hand, Maya always had people to support her, but on the other hand, she had a lot of people offering her unsolicited advice on every move she made in life. Maya had told her about how many times high school suitors were scared away by her intimidating male cousins. It seemed funny now, but as a teenager it drove Maya crazy.

Maya's phone lit up. "Franco's in the lobby. I'll tell him to check in then join us here." Maya texted back and the three of them waited for the knock on the door. Maya looked through the peephole again before she opened the door. "So glad you joined us. Come in, come in."

Franco looked around. He smiled and waved to Lucy. Jeremy stood up and walked over to Franco. "I'm Jeremy, Maya's cousin."

"Nice to meet you." Franco stuck out his hand and Jeremy shook it firmly while staring Franco straight in the eyes. It did not escape Lucy's notice that Jeremy still seemed mistrustful of Franco.

"Now that we are done with introductions, let's get started." Maya filled Jeremy and Franco in on the work she and Lucy had done earlier in the forest.

Franco looked shocked. "A mountain lion? I didn't know they lived around here. That's unbelievable."

Maya smiled. "Well, believe it because Lucy made a new friend, and his name is Rex."

Jeremy laughed. "I believe it knowing Lucy. She has a real knack for animal magic."

Lucy shrugged. She was starting to believe that her skills in animal magic surpassed those of many others, including Maya, but she didn't know how she compared to the dark magicians, who had been doing magic way longer than her.

She turned to Franco. "Tell us about ZRC. Who do you think will be there? When I spied in the facility there was a guy named Alfonse, but Bridgit appeared to be in charge."

Franco nodded. "Alfonse will definitely be there. He's one of the more advanced animal handlers they have. Bridgit too—she's in charge of the Sienna Falls operation and the Winkler training branch. I'm sure Mercy will be also there since you overheard they have been training her to work with wolves."

Lucy had taken out her notepad and was adding to the plan she had devised the previous night. "They reserved five rooms, so I expect at least that many people. How many wolves are there?"

Franco paced back and forth. "There were four in the cages when I trained here. And there were about a dozen ravens. There were a couple of other students in my training class, but I don't know that they all made it through the course. I didn't see any other students training in Sienna Falls."

Jeremy turned from the window and focused on Franco. "You have all the insider knowledge—so how do we beat them?"

Franco looked flustered. "I don't have all the answers, but I have some ideas. One of the wolves that I called Shadow was reluctant to be controlled. He didn't feel naturally evil to me like some of the other animals."

Lucy looked up from writing. "Maybe we can convince him not to fight?"

"Maybe. There is another wolf I called Spike. I've felt that he hates Alfonse, so maybe we can use that against them."

Lucy nodded. "I like that idea. I want as few animals hurt as possible. Even the ones trained by the dark magicians. Maya, do you know anyone who could rehabilitate wolves?"

"I think so. I may know of a place they could be released safely, but I'd have to check. And it depends if they were captured from the wild. Do you know, Franco?"

"I believe the wolves are wild, but they have a breeding program for the ravens."

"Okay. The ravens would have to go to a bird sanctuary. I can ask the people at the wildlife rehab center for recommendations."

Franco turned to Jeremy. "Can you talk with animals too?"

Jeremy stood next to Silver's carrier. "No, I can't talk to animals like you three can. But Silver can talk with other birds, and I can send commands through her. We can focus on the ravens while you deal with the wolves."

Lucy finished writing and put the pen down with satisfaction. "Looks like we have a plan, folks."

Maya looked sober as she made eye contact with each one of them. "I'm not going to lie. The odds are against us. At least five dark magicians, four wolves, twelve ravens. Against four of us."

Jeremy patted the carrier. "Five counting Silver."

Lucy's eyes sparkled with determination. Maya needed her to be the brave one right now. "Five dark magicians against us *and* an entire army of forest creatures, including a mountain lion. I think they're the ones in trouble."

*　　*　　*

Lucy was wide awake in her bed. She knew that she needed to get some rest before the battle tomorrow, but there is nothing like trying to will yourself to sleep that somehow makes sleep impossible. Lucy couldn't help thinking how somewhere in this same lodge dark magicians were sleeping peacefully.

She always thought of villains like they are depicted in the movies, sitting on a throne-like chair, in an impenetrable fortress overlooking the sea, petting a black cat, and cackling about how they are going to take over the world. She never imagined villains were just people like her who made different choices. Franco was the perfect case in point, just a regular college student who almost ended up on the wrong side. And who knows what led Bridgit to this life? Was she recruited as an innocent student too?

How could she possibly sleep with so many unknowns facing her tomorrow? Six months ago, she would have been so anxious that she would have gotten in her car and driven home. But oddly enough, tonight she had no thoughts about running away. Even though she could get torn apart by wolves tomorrow, or her friends could get seriously hurt or worse, she would stand her ground. Even knowing they could do their best and the forest creatures could still be massacred, she had made her choice to fight for what she believed in.

Her resolve came from knowing she had trained hard to learn animal magic. She had three humans, a falcon, a mountain lion, and other countless creatures who would stand with her. She had a plan, she was prepared, and she would see it through to the end. Now she was just waiting for tomorrow to come.

Chapter 25

SILVER SWOOPED DOWN FROM THE forest canopy in front of them and returned to the leather glove on Jeremy's arm. "They're coming!" Jeremy called out.

"It's go time!" Maya clasped hands with Lucy and they sent out the battle call to the army of forest creatures. Within seconds animals started to appear. Scorpions crept out from under rocks. Wasps formed in clouds. Skunks, deer, and raccoons gathered near them.

Lucy could feel the energy of the forest shifting. Behind her and to the sides there was a sense of unity and determination. Coming towards her from the front she felt the dark energy of the evil magicians and their animal counterparts.

Within minutes, the dark magicians were upon them, accompanied by four wolves and a dozen ravens. A willowy man narrowed his eyes when he saw Franco. "You! How dare you! You will regret this choice."

Franco stood tall, his face showing no fear or hesitation. "Alfonse. I was hoping I'd never see you again, but here we are. I will never regret taking you down." He put one fist in the other hand and cracked his knuckles.

A tall, blonde woman that Lucy recognized as Bridgit cackled. "Enough talk. This will all be over soon. Alfonse, teach our old friend a lesson. Mercy, you take the dark-haired woman. I'll take the blonde. Kayla, Raul—you know what to do."

A woman stepped out from behind the four evil magicians and spread her arms wide. She opened her mouth and started singing. Her voice echoed throughout the forest, the tones reverberating through their bodies.

Lucy was shocked as she saw several of her animal friends turn and retreat into the forest.

Bridgit cackled again. "Nice work, Kayla." The woman bowed her head slightly and moved back behind the trees.

Mercy stepped forward, focused on Maya.

Franco whispered to Maya, "Mercy controls Shadow."

Maya nodded. She knew what that meant. Maya looked across the forest clearing and saw Mercy, eyes glaring. At Mercy's direction, Shadow began loping towards her.

Maya reached out with her mind to Shadow. *I know you don't want to be here. You don't have to do what she says. Run away while you still can.*

Shadow paused. Maya couldn't hear what Mercy was saying to the wolf, but she imagined Mercy was imploring him to continue. He took a few steps towards Maya.

Don't listen. She doesn't own you. You are in control. Run away, my friend.

Maya focused her energy on breaking Mercy's control over Shadow. She could tell Mercy wasn't as strong compared with Lucy.

Shadow stopped again. The wolf looked back at Mercy. Mercy waved her hands violently at Shadow, urging him to obey.

Maya stood frozen as Shadow hurtled towards her. *Please. Trust me.*

Shadow was barreling right at her. At the last moment he turned, leapt above the wall of small forest creatures, and fled into the forest.

Mercy screamed and punched a tree. Maya took a deep breath and turned her focus to what was happening around her. The scene was gruesome. Bloody feathers fluttered through the air. Raul was controlling a dozen ravens, sending them to attack any forest animals within reach.

Jeremy was sending orders through Silver. A great horned owl screeched as a raven's beak tore at its wing. A hawk swooped down and went for the raven's eye. It shrieked in pain. Five smaller birds pulled at its tail feathers. The raven spied the hawk incoming again through its good eye and swooped low to the ground. A raccoon swiped up and shredded the raven's belly as it flew overhead. The raven fell to the forest floor, its entrails staining the soil. One down, eleven to go.

On the other side of the clearing Alfonse sent Spike to get his revenge on Franco. As Spike approached, Franco could tell that the wolf recognized him. Franco reached out with his mind. *It's me boy—do you remember?*

Spike snarled and bared his teeth at Franco.

Alfonse laughed and ordered Spike to attack. "Did you think he would listen to you, stupid boy?"

Franco tried again. *Remember how Alfonse hit you? How he yelled at you and threatened you?*

"Get him, you worthless piece of shit!" Alfonse yelled at Spike. Spike pawed at the ground like a bull ready to charge.

Franco ignored Alfonse and focused on Spike. *Remember how I gave you extra meat? I used to be with them, but now I'm not. Alfonse is a bad man. He will never stop hurting you.*

Alfonse screamed, "Attack him now or no food for a week!"

See, he's evil. He's the one you need to take down. We will help you. I promise.

Spike howled like he was in pain. Franco could see the poor wolf was torn between his old master and a chance at freedom. He didn't know who to trust. "Maya—help me out here. Vouch for me," Franco said.

Maya focused in on Spike. *Franco is one of the good guys now. We will find you a new home if you help us.* Maya concentrated on trying to break Alfonse's control over Spike, imagining she was projecting a dome over Spike that blocked Alfonse's commands.

Alfonse screamed in desperation. "What are you waiting for, you idiot animal? Get him now or I'll give you the thrashing of your life!"

That was the final straw. Franco and Maya watched as Spike turned around to face Alfonse. The wolf pawed the ground and snarled again. Alfonse's expression turned from anger to terror as Spike bolted towards him. Alfonse turned to run, but it was too late.

The wolf jumped on his back, knocking him to the ground. Spike took a chunk out of Alfonse's shoulder, blood gushing down his arm. Before the wolf took a fatal bite of Alfonse's exposed neck, Franco reached out to stop him. *That's enough Spike. Just keep him down, but don't kill him.* Spike stood tall, put one paw on Alfonse's bloody back, and howled so loud it seemed to fill the entire forest. Lucy shuddered at the sound.

Jeremy and Silver were still making steady progress with the ravens. Maya stepped in to try and help break Raul's control over the ravens. It was easier because he was trying to control so many animals at once. Maya was able to get two ravens to abandon the fight. A duo of hawks took down another raven, tearing a hole in its neck with their claws, and dragging it to the ground where the smaller mammals ripped it to shreds.

Maya directed the forest creatures to aid in the battle. They didn't want to kill the dark magicians, but that didn't mean they couldn't harm the human handlers at all. Maya watched as a sleek little skunk snuck up to Raul. At her direction, the little creature lifted his tail and sprayed. Raul screamed in disgust as the spray drenched his pants, and the foul odor flooded his nostrils, and the vapors burned his eyes. The distraction allowed Maya to break his control over another raven who flew off in retreat.

Lucy was aware of all her friends fighting around her, but she was focused on Bridgit.

"Bridgit's wolves are pure evil. They will kill you if they get the chance," Franco warned.

"Understood," Lucy responded, without taking her eyes off of Bridgit and her wolves. "Maya—try to break their connection if you can. Franco—help Jeremy and Silver take down the rest of the ravens."

Bridgit looked like evil incarnate standing behind her two wolves. Her eyes were narrowed and focused as she concentrated on controlling her evil companions.

Lucy knew as soon as Bridgit gave the order to attack she was in serious trouble. She would need help from her friends both animal and human to win.

Bridgit sneered at Lucy. "You're out of your depth here. Last chance to run away with your life."

Lucy stood her ground. She could feel the energy of all the forest creatures standing with her. She had one chance to stop Bridgit from giving the orders. Lucy called for her army to attack. A scorpion stung Bridgit on her shin. A swarm of wasps went for her face. A mockingbird divebombed her head.

Bridgit screamed in terror as she waved her hands to ward off the animals, but the attack enraged and motivated her. "Now!" she screamed. The two wolves started moving towards Lucy.

Lucy asked the forest creatures to help her fight the wolves. Lucy watched in despair as one of the wolves slashed a raccoon with its razor-sharp claws and the raccoon fell to the ground. The larger birds tried pecking at its eye, but it swatted them away with a fearsome snarl. Lucy was in trouble.

"Maya—how's it going breaking the connection?" Lucy cried.

"I'm almost there with the one on the right. Bridgit's not focusing as much. But this wolf is still full of hate—he might not respond to you."

"I have to try." Lucy concentrated on controlling the wolf on the right. She could feel Bridgit's dark influence in the wolf's mind. She could also feel Maya trying to build a protective shield against Bridgit. Finally, Lucy felt Bridgit's control expelled. But the wolf was still angry and baring down on her.

I don't want to hurt you, she told the animal. The wolf snarled. Lucy reached into its mind and tried to soothe its dark thoughts, but it resisted fiercely. She felt like she was pounding on the door to the wolf's mind, trying to break in. At first it seemed locked tight, but then she broke through and the resistance fell away. Getting in its mind was one thing, but controlling a furious wolf was another. She concentrated on willing his legs to halt. She thought he was slowing his sprint towards her when she was snapped out of focus.

"Lucy—look out!!!" Franco pointed towards the second wolf that had started barreling towards Lucy in a frenzy.

Lucy froze.

This was the end. She had no way to stop this wolf from mauling her. She stood still, desperately trying to think of a plan while bracing for impact. Just when her life was finally getting interesting, she was going to die. Then out of the corner of her eye, she saw a flash of brown.

A mountain lion leapt through the air and smashed into the wolf, knocking it to the side just before it reached Lucy. The lion and the wolf tore at each other, a furious pile of claws and teeth. The mountain lion growled as it sliced through the wolf's back. The wolf snarled and tore at the lion with its jaw wide. The ground was littered with chunks of fur and splattering of blood.

Lucy turned her attention back to Bridgit and the other wolf. Both were taken aback by the unexpected appearance of the mountain lion. Lucy refocused on taming the wolf and directing the forest creatures to keep Bridgit occupied so she couldn't regain control. Bridgit was surprised again when a deer came out of nowhere and kicked her in the back, toppling her forward.

Three squirrels jumped on her as soon as she hit the ground. Bridgit flailed her arms around, but she couldn't fend them off.

You're outnumbered, Lucy told the wolf. *Let me in and we can end this.* Lucy looked around and took in the sight. Jeremy, Silver, and Franco had subdued Raul and the ravens. The mountain lion and second wolf were still battling.

With one fearsome roar, the mountain lion grabbed the wolf by the throat and smacked him against a rock, breaking his neck. The wolf fell silent.

Lucy felt her heart break at the sight, but there was nothing to be done. *It's over,* she told Bridgit's remaining wolf. This time the wolf backed away from Lucy. It looked briefly at Bridgit, then snarled one last time and loped off into the forest.

Lucy called off the animals who were still attacking Bridgit and Raul. She noticed Mercy and the singing women were nowhere to be seen. As soon as Bridgit could stand again, she limped off with Raul's help, then they struggled to collect Alfonse, blood still pouring from his wound, and dragged him back towards the McWalter property.

Lucy breathed a sigh of relief and turned towards the mountain lion. *Thank you, Rex.*

The mountain lion nodded, then grabbed the wolf's carcass and ran off into the forest.

Lucy looked around at her army of forest creatures. *Thank you, friends of the forest. You were all very brave. We will help those who are injured and*

196

mourn those who were lost. The forest creatures began to dissipate, returning to their nests and burrows, caves, and hives.

Lucy turned to address her friends, but there were no words to describe what had just happened. They had all experienced the same fear, triumph, and loss. Maya simply walked over and hugged Lucy.

Chapter 26

LUCY WAS HAPPY TO BE sitting on the couch again while Carmela sat in her big green armchair. Maya had just finished filling her grandmother in on what happened at Sienna Falls.

"I'm so happy you are both safe." Carmela stood up and hugged her granddaughter. "And Lucy, I can't believe how far you've come with your animal magic. I'm proud of you both!" Carmela gave Lucy a big hug too.

Lucy wasn't much of a hugger, and usually shrank back when people hugged her, but Carmela was starting to feel like her grandmother too and she welcomed the embrace. Without Carmela's guidance, Lucy would never have learned more than simple animal communication. She wouldn't have known she could learn to look through their eyes or control their movements, or the protocols of permission that helped make sure she wasn't using animals like the dark magicians.

Maya knitted her brows. "The one thing I don't understand is what was with that woman singing in the forest."

Lucy nodded. "I wonder about that too. I got a weird feeling from it, but I can't explain it."

"I might be able to shed some light on that." Carmela took a long sip of her tea, then took a deep breath as if collecting her thoughts. "You see, girls, there are other types of magic besides animal magic." She paused to let that sink in.

Lucy's mouth hung open. "There are? I guess I shouldn't be surprised, since just a few months ago I didn't know animal magic existed, but..."

"First tell us more, then we can discuss why you never told me this before." Maya looked both shocked and hurt.

"Fair enough, cariño, I will tell you what I know. Many practitioners divide magic into five types. In truth they often overlap, but they each have a core foundation. You already know animal magic is one. There is also chant, or song magic, which I suspect is what you encountered in the forest. It's safe to assume that someone who is aware of one type of magic may also know other kinds as well."

Realization dawned in Lucy's face. "Yes, when I heard that singing in the forest, it did feel like magic, but at the time I didn't recognize it. It was like the singing sent out a certain energy."

"That's exactly right. Singing is made up of sound waves, and sounds waves are energy." Carmela explained.

"People can learn to control the sounds waves to create certain energies to make things happen?" Maya questioned.

"I'm afraid I don't know much about chant magic, but yes, that is my understanding. Not just singing or chanting but playing instruments as well."

Lucy nodded. "Okay, so animal magic and chant magic. What are the other three?"

"The others are ones you've heard of so often in books and movies. There is herbal magic, which has long been part of eastern medicinal practices, and is now what we call alternative medicine here. Not just for healing though, but for all sorts of outcomes. Then there is elemental magic, that's the traditional magic of working with air, fire, earth, and water. And lastly is psychic or spirit magic."

"Like ghosts?" Lucy asked.

"Not just ghosts. Astral projection, telekinesis, telepathy, divination. The types of things we think of as supernatural."

Maya sunk back into the couch. "I think we need a moment to digest all of this." Lucy nodded in agreement.

"Of course, I understand. Let me make you some more tea." Carmela took the women's cups and went into the kitchen.

Lucy had so many thoughts swimming in her head that she didn't even know where to begin processing them. Her world had been widened so much just by finding out about animal magic, and she was only just starting to accept that it was magic, and that there were dark magicians using these skills for nefarious purposes. But still, animal magic seemed rooted in the natural world and like a skill that could be learned by anyone with discipline. But these other types, they sounded like fiction, like stories she read about witches and wizards.

If what Carmela said were true, the world was even wider than Lucy could imagine. She loved animal magic and using her skills to help both animals and people. But she loved learning and studying and even in this moment she knew she would be compelled to find out more about the other four types of magic.

Carmela returned with the tea and handed each woman a cup. "There you go ladies, drink up. This will help soothe your nerves, a little herbal magic. I'm sure that was a lot of new information to take in."

Maya swirled the tea around in the cup, avoiding Carmela's eyes as she asked, "All these years you never told me any of this? Why? And why all of the sudden share it now that Lucy is in our lives?" Maya's voice trembled with hurt and betrayal.

"Dear Maya, I didn't mean to hurt you. I didn't tell you because you chose your path as a little girl. You were always going to protect animals. When you were a little girl, your mom bought you a goldfish. Do you remember?"

Maya looked up. "Sure, I remember. Pinky the goldfish."

"Yes, Pinky. I never saw a goldfish so well cared for, how often you cleaned the water, never forgot to feed him, and I never knew a little goldfish to live so long as Pinky. From then on it was animals all the time—lizards, hamsters, toads—you would take great care of all of them. When a little bird fell out of its nest you called the local wildlife rescue center and got directions on how to nurse it back to health. And you did and it flew away, stronger than ever."

"So... you never told me because I didn't need to know?" Maya asked slowly.

Carmela nodded firmly. "Exactly. You already had your calling. Perhaps I should have told you, but you always seemed content with animal magic."

"You're right, I am content. So why tell Lucy? She has already far surpassed my skills in animal magic. Isn't it her calling too?"

"That is not for me or you to say. We haven't known Lucy for long. I don't know her heart like I knew my granddaughter's."

Carmela turned to Lucy. "You only just learned about animal magic. Your path is yet to be determined." Carmela looked back at Maya. "Lucy can choose among many paths and therefore she should know about the other types of magic so she can choose one or many of them to be part of her life."

Lucy felt a tiny fire growing in her belly, a thirst for knowledge. Now that she knew about the other types of magic, she would have to learn more, even if it was just enough to find out they weren't for her. She would never abandon her animal magic. It had already become a part of her.

*   *   *

Lucy looked crestfallen staring at the empty kennel at Northbrook Animal Shelter. She ran down the hall towards the main office.

"Where's Cloud?" she asked Owen. Lucy had been looking forward to seeing the gorgeous gray cat again at her next volunteer session.

"Great news—someone scheduled an adoption appointment with him. It's happening right now."

Lucy felt a pit in her stomach and her throat felt tight. She had made a huge mistake.

Even though she knew the point of volunteering at the shelter was to help as many animals as possible, and she couldn't adopt every single one, she had fallen in love with sweet Cloud after just one visit.

It was okay, though, because she just wanted him to be happy and if someone else gives him a good home that is all that matters.

Lucy walked down to the adoption rooms and saw Cloud with a young couple. She pretended to be writing something on a clipboard while she eavesdropped.

"I don't know—he's pretty cute and all, but maybe I want a kitten," said the woman.

"Whatever you want, babe—it's your cat," the man replied, looking down at his cell phone.

The woman poked him. "It'll be our cat. You have to like him too."

"Yeah, yeah, of course, I know," the man responded without looking up.

"I don't know. This one's kind of gloomy, don't you think? And if I wear white, he's gonna get gray fur on me."

Lucy's insides started to boil. These people did not deserve her little Cloud angel. The guy didn't even sound like he wanted a cat, and the woman wanted a fashion accessory, not a cat. She couldn't let this happen. She reached out to Cloud.

Cloud, it's Lucy.

Cloud's ears perked up. The couple didn't even notice since they had started bickering. *Lucy! I missed you.*

I'm sorry buddy, I realized you should live with me. I want to be your forever home. What do you think?

Cloud's eyes lit up. *I'd like that.*

Me too. But first we have to get rid of these people.

I think I can take care of that. Cloud went over to the woman's leather purse, stretched out his long sharp claws and scratched down the side.

The woman swatted at Cloud. "Oh, hell no. Get away from that! That purse is expensive. I can't have a cat who scratches things."

Cloud arched his back and hissed. The couple jumped up and pressed back against the wall.

The woman knocked on the window and saw Lucy. "We're done in here—can you take the cat away?"

Lucy smiled. "Of course." She opened the door and the couple jetted down the hallway towards the shelter exit. Lucy hoped they both grew up a little and did some soul searching before they thought about adopting another pet.

She went into the adoption room and pet Cloud's chin. Nice job. We're going to get along great.

Cloud purred.

*   *   *

Maya had alerted Buck Henshaw with the wildlife department that there were three wolves in Sienna Falls Forest. Since they were not native to the area, they captured and relocated them. Jeremy and Silver helped Maya recapture the ravens and they were sent to a sanctuary for birds who were born in captivity and can't be released into the wild.

For good measure, Lucy and Maya decided they should make one more visit to Sienna Falls Forest to be sure it was safe and that the dark magicians were truly defeated.

A familiar smile behind the desk welcomed them. "Ladies, welcome back. I just read something you might be interested in." Sylvia handed the women a copy of the Sienna Falls Herald.

The front-page headline read "McWalter Estate Settled."

The longstanding legal dispute over the estate of Grady McWalter III came to an end as the court gave sole possession to Peter McWalter after additional documents were uncovered. Prior to his passing, Grady McWalter III established a conservation easement with the Southwest Regional Conservation Coalition limiting development rights on the property. The terms of the trust allow for continued residence in the main dwelling on the property, as well as standard ranching operations. "I'm pleased with the outcome," Peter McWalter said about the verdict, "My uncle loved this land, and he loved Sienna Falls. He always made it clear that he wanted the property to remain in a natural state." Peter McWalter, a history teacher at Sienna Falls High, said he plans to move his family to the house on the ranch, and to work with the Southwest Regional Conservation Coalition on best practices for preserving the natural integrity of the land.

Lucy and Maya beamed with joy. "That's fantastic!" Lucy exclaimed. "Woo hoo!" said Maya.

Sylvia chuckled. "You two really have become attached to our little town, haven't you?"

"We just love Sienna Falls Forest, and we know how important the adjacent McWalter land is to keeping it healthy, especially with the development on the west side," Maya explained as she handed the paper back.

Sylvia tucked the paper back under the reception desk. "I heard that what happened was after the other kin found out they couldn't sell the property to a developer because of the conservation easement that they dropped their claim. The land wasn't worth anything to them otherwise. Peter is a good soul and I'm glad it went to him. I think he'll do right by it."

"I'm so glad to hear it. I'm going to miss this place," said Lucy.

"Oh? No more surveys? You two were becoming my favorite regulars."

Maya and Lucy smiled. "We're done with work for now, but we'll still come back to hike just for fun sometime," Maya promised.

*   *   *

To be on the safe side, Lucy suggested that they check in on the McWalter property remotely using Lucy's animal vision again. They hiked one last time close to the property line, and Lucy found a willing bird to spy through. She navigated the bird to the facility where Bridgit and Alfonse had been training animals to ruin Sienna Falls Forest. Through the bird's eyes she saw that the outside cages had been dismantled and removed. The area outside the building was completely empty.

She asked the bird to perch in the tiny window located at the top of the side wall and she peered in. The inside was dark and deserted. The tables, chairs, and filing cabinets had all been removed. The cages that had held the ravens and other birds were gone. It looked to Lucy like they had abandoned their operations and had no intent on returning.

She wondered what Peter McWalter would think when he came upon the building, since there was no evidence of what it had been used for. Lucy hoped he would tear it down so the last of the dark magic could be erased from the property.

"No trace of them except the building itself," Lucy reported back to Maya.

"That's good. Between us kicking their butts in Sienna Falls Forest and Peter McWalter now owning and living on the property I don't think they'll be back here."

"Does that mean we won?" Lucy asked cautiously.

Maya laughed. "Yep. And it doesn't surprise *me*, because we are winners!"

"I don't know about that. Maybe you are but I never was before I met you."

"That's rubbish." Maya suddenly looked serious. "Lucy, I never did apologize for the things I said to you in the courtyard."

Lucy shrugged. "You don't have to. It was true that I was hiding in my cubicle. And I was scared."

"Nah, you should have been scared. I was too. I'm sorry I wasn't more understanding."

"As long as we are apologizing, I'm sorry that I implied I was sorry we met or that you introduced me to animal magic. Just a few months ago I was too anxious to leave the office but now I can talk with mountain lions. And that is because of you."

"No way. From the first day we met, I thought you were awesome. Even Anuk said you were the person to know in the office. You're an expert mapmaker, everyone in the office likes and respects you. And from our very first trip you were one of the best field assistants I've ever worked with. Plus, you like very cool movies."

"Aww, thanks Maya!"

On the way out, they stopped in to see Skye at the Southwest Regional Conservation Coalition. They were dying to know who had found the conservation easement.

When Lucy and Maya entered the office Skye's face lit up and she ran over to them and gave each of the women a hug. "My heroes!"

Lucy blushed and Maya beamed with pride.

"Tell us everything. Was it you who found the conservation easement?" Maya asked.

Skye beckoned for the women to sit at the table. "After you visited last time, I e-mailed the former executive director in Costa Rica to see if she remembered anything about it. It took a few days for her to respond, but she knew all about it."

"So where was it? Was it here in the office?" said Lucy.

"No, actually. As much of a mess as it is here, I found out there is another whole storage facility with documents from ten to twenty years ago. She told me where the key was, and I went to the storage unit. Luckily, the boxes were labeled by year and type."

"What a lucky find!" Maya responded.

Lucy wrinkled her forehead. "Why wasn't the easement part of the land record when the executors of Grady's estate first went through everything?"

Skye shook her head. "I don't know the answer to that. The document was completely executed, signed, notarized and everything. I submitted it to the court working on the case and they determined it was valid."

"That's great. I am sure he will rest easier now, knowing his wishes are being followed," said Maya.

Skye nodded in agreement. "I hope so, we owe him a debt of gratitude. And as if that weren't enough, I also found a management plan that Grady had started. His property is special because it's not only vast with thousands of acres, but part of it is forested and part of it is grassland. He was a true conservationist and he wanted to manage his land for both ranching and preservation. He had paid to have biological surveys done for endangered species. The reports are from over ten years ago, but at the time there were two types of rare birds in the forested area adjacent to Sienna Falls Forest as well as karst invertebrates in caves on his property."

Maya's eyes lit up. "That's fantastic! This makes it even more special that the land is protected from development now."

"I know. It's really a dream come true for us from a regional conservation standpoint."

After celebrating the victory with coffee and tea and snacks that Skye kept on hand for volunteers, the women bade Skye farewell and wished her the best of luck.

On the drive back, Lucy couldn't stop thinking about what it all meant. She still had so many unanswered questions. What did Grady's will have to do with Sienna Falls Forest? Why did men from Sepharine Holdings steal their equipment and sabotage their Silver-winged Warbler survey? What did they stand to gain from hurting the forest?

As Maya drove, she glanced over at Lucy and saw she was lost in thought. "What's on your mind, you look serious."

Lucy stroked her chin and turned from the window. "I'm still trying to understand why all of this happened. What was their endgame?"

"Well, I think it is safe to assume that Missy Zimmer thought she would win the court case and inherit the land, and once she did, she planned to profit off of it in some way, logging the forested part, or selling the property for development, or some combination."

Lucy nodded. "I agree with that assumption. But what did that have to do with our bird survey and why did they need to try and damage forest that wasn't even part of their property?"

"I can only guess at that. Missy clearly knew there were endangered species on the McWalter property and probably suspected they were also in Sienna Falls Forest. When she found out we were doing the survey, she was probably afraid that if we found Silver-winged Warblers that would mess up her plans."

"So she tried to destroy them before the area could be designated as habitat for an endangered species?"

"I think so. Documenting an endangered species in Sienna Falls Forest would make local news and environmental groups would rally to protect the forest and the adjacent land. And it is likely that even on the adjacent private property there could be some restrictions on activities that could disturb the habitat. At the very least, getting the right permits would delay development."

Lucy crinkled her nose up as she looked out the window. "Missy would not like that at all."

"Nope. She doesn't sound like a woman who lets anything stand in her way."

"Except us."

Maya laughed. "Except us."

Chapter 27

IT WAS HARD TO BELIEVE that after their big adventure at Sienna Falls and finding out the world is full of more magic than Lucy ever dreamed possible, that she would be back in the Monday morning staff meeting yet again. She felt like her world had changed in a deep and meaningful way, yet here she was. She could barely concentrate on what Anuk was saying because her mind kept drifting away.

Anuk finished going over the assignments for the week. As he wrapped up the meeting, he said "Lucy and Maya, can you please stay a moment?"

Lucy immediately panicked like she was in middle school and the teacher told her to stay after class. She even heard the whispers of Tyler and Bethany filing into the hallway, gossiping that the two women must be in trouble. Maya shifted uncomfortably in her chair.

Anuk waited for the rest of the staff to exit then closed the conference room door. "Hyun Shim completed her review of the office."

Lucy cringed. "Did she say anything about my interview?" Lucy had worried that Hyun would show up again unexpectedly, but she hadn't heard anything from her since the day she brought Cookie into the office and left Lucy's interview unfinished for a second time.

Anuk nodded. "Yes, she said you are an asset to the office and had only positive things to report. She said anyone would be lucky to have you on their team."

Lucy was amazed. Maya's cousin's husband, the veterinarian that they had recommended to Hyun, said that Cookie the Papillon dog did have kneecap problems, but they would be able to treat it and Cookie could live a long, happy life. Lucy was pleased to have helped Hyun and her little dog, but she didn't imagine it would change Hyun's assessment of her.

Maya chimed in, "I second that motion. I'm glad to be on your team too!"

Lucy blushed, embarrassed by the unexpected praise.

"That's not all. The Southwest Regional Conservation Coalition restarted our contract and also extended it to include bird surveys for two more years. And they wrote about TerraPlaya and your survey documenting the Silver-winged Warblers in their newsletter. I got a call from another non-profit who wants to talk to us about working with them."

Maya's entire face lit up. "Yes! That's amazing! I can't wait to get back out there to do more surveys."

Lucy grinned. "I wouldn't mind helping with at least a few of those surveys."

"Of course, Lucy, we'll work all that out. You still are our best map maker, but we can work with Tyler to make sure you both get field time."

"That would be great, thanks!"

Anuk looked serious for a moment. "I also owe you both an apology. I still don't know what happened with the Southwest Regional Conservation Coalition and why they cancelled the contract, but clearly neither of you did anything wrong, or they would not have restarted it. I promise in the future I will support you."

"I appreciate that. We know you were stressed by the pressure from corporate," Maya said.

"That's true, I was, but that doesn't excuse my behavior. And this news about our two-year contract and the potential for similar work with new clients is one of the main reasons that our office strategic plan has been approved, and Hyun is recommending that our office be left untouched. No layoffs or restructuring, at least for now. Our future is bright."

Lucy was practically bursting with excitement as she went back to her cubicle. Even though she was making maps the rest of the day, she also knew she would get to go back to Sienna Falls Forest someday and maybe even find some more Silver-winged Warblers. And who knows what other adventures awaited her and Maya doing surveys for other non-profits.

Hopefully, future projects would have more birds, and fewer evil magicians. She never wanted to stop making maps, but it was nice to have some balance and variety.

*   *   *

Maya stopped by Lucy's cubicle before the end of the workday. "I heard back from my corporate lawyer friend. Jason did some digging on Sepharine Holdings Inc."

Lucy tapped her desk with her finger. "Yeah? What did he find?"

"ZRC is a subsidiary company of Sepharine Holdings."

Lucy frowned. "That's scary. If ZRC really has branches all over the country and they are owned by an even bigger company..."

"It's even worse than that. Sepharine has four other subsidiaries too."

Lucy paled. "I bet all four are fronts companies too."

"Probably."

"What if each one of them has a Missy Zimmer and a Bridgit Whelan?" A shiver ran down Lucy's spine.

"It's possible. I have the company names written down." Maya handed Lucy a piece of paper.

Lucy shook her head and refused the paper. "I don't want to know. The Sienna Falls mystery is over. I'm out of the spy business now."

Maya smiled and put the paper back in her pocket. "You're right. We did awesome and we both deserve to relax and enjoy ourselves for a while."

Relief spread across Lucy's face. She had no plans to spend her life thwarting plots by evil magicians. But she did accept that now that she had this power, she was compelled to use it to help people.

If evil magicians crossed their path again, she'd worry about that if and when it happened. For now, she was going to enjoy helping with fieldwork and spending time with her friends, and her sweet new companion, Cloud.

Chapter 28

LUCY SHOOK OUT HER ARMS to release some tension. She felt sick to her stomach and her hands were trembling. She was up next.

As the applause died out for the singer before her, her voice teacher stood next to her backstage. Carlos high fived his student as he came off the stage and then turned to Lucy. "You got this, Lucy! You have practiced diligently, and you couldn't be more prepared. Now go out there and enjoy sharing your beautiful voice!"

Lucy took a deep breath in and exhaled slowly, as Carlos had taught her. She shook out her limbs one more time and then stepped out onto the stage. She stood tall and straight, with her shoulders back and her head high, as she had imagined so many times in her visualizations of this moment. Even with all her preparation, there was a voice in the back of her mind that said "Run!" but she knew this was a typical fight or flight response. If she could battle wolves and dark magicians, she could sing in a recital.

Lucy allowed herself to look out at the audience. There she saw the smiling faces of Maya and her grandmother Carmela, Mrs. Kleinbaum, Mrs. Perez, and Jeremy. She knew they were all there to support her and it meant the world to her.

She nodded to the pianist that she was ready. The introduction music began, a melancholy progression of rich harmonies. Lucy worried that people could see her hands shaking. Her throat suddenly felt parched and tight. Remember your practice, Lucy.

She took a breath in and started to sing. Hearing her own voice in a recital hall with natural reverb was surreal. Was that really her? Concentrate Lucy, stay in the moment.

Lucy centered herself and focused on telling the story of a love so deep that it surrendered all logic. She sang with passion about the willingness to endure pain for even just a chance at love. She fought to let go of tiny mistakes that the audience would never notice and instead enjoy sharing the result of her hard work with her friends.

Before she knew it, she was at the last phrase of the song. She held out her final note as the pianist hit the final chords. Then she was done. She had performed in her very first recital.

Lucy took a bow as her friends cheered for her. She then waved to acknowledge the fine playing of the accompanist and bowed one more time. She exited backstage, still standing tall, pleased with her accomplishment.

After the recital, the singers and audience were encouraged to mingle by the punch bowl and have their fill of cookies and brownies.

Maya ran over and hugged Lucy. "Great job! That was awesome."

"Thanks Maya. It means a lot to me that you came."

"Of course! Wouldn't miss it for the world."

Carmela, Mrs. Kleinbaum, Mrs. Perez, and Jeremy all told Lucy how beautiful she sounded and how proud they were of her. Lucy briefly considered that they were obligated to say that, but then she decided to accept the compliments at face value and enjoy herself.

She felt fairly good about her performance overall. She had practiced hard and although she knew her voice wasn't polished sounding yet, she did her best to express the emotion of the song. She was looking forward to more recitals, and even to her audition with the Northbrook Community Choir. But most importantly, she was thankful that she had so many people come to support her.

She was also proud that she had conquered her anxieties enough to not only take voice lessons, but to sing in a recital. She couldn't believe that this year she had made several new friends, learned animal magic, defeated dark magicians, and helped win a new contract at work. Singing in this recital was the cherry on top.

Lucy stood munching on a cookie as Maya and her other friends mingled with the other students and audience members. She hadn't eaten all day due to her nerves and she was famished. She took a nibble as she saw Carmela waving her over to the corner. Lucy walked over, curious as to what she wanted.

"I believe one of your fellow students knows song magic," Carmela whispered.

Lucy scanned the room. "Really, who?"

Carmela pointed subtly to a tall woman wearing a yellow flowery dress. Carmela opened her recital program and pointed to a name, Noor Khanna.

"Oh! I didn't hear her sing because I was backstage at that time."

Carmela nodded. "As I said before, I don't know much about song magic, just enough to recognize it when I hear it. It's not just that she had excellent technique, or such rich emotion, but her singing was transcendent. It's as if her voice fell over the audience like snow, blanketing us with peace and tranquility."

"I'm sorry I missed it. I wish I had some reason to talk to her." Lucy was eager to learn about song magic, but she hadn't gotten far in figuring out how she would pursue it.

As fate would have it, at that moment, her voice teacher Carlos walked over with Noor. "Lucy, I want you to meet one of my other adult students. Noor, this is one of my newest students, Lucy."

"Pleasure to meet you, Noor," Lucy said.

"You as well. You sang beautifully. I would never have guessed this was your first performance."

"Thank you. I didn't get to hear you sing, but I heard from my friends that you were wonderful."

Noor smiled with a twinkle in her eye.

Carlos chimed in. "Noor has a way with an audience, that's for certain. I wanted you two to meet since you are both auditioning for the Northbrook Community Choir this fall. I have no doubt you both will be accepted, and now you'll both know someone there."

Lucy grinned. She felt like twirling and dancing around at her luck. She knew Carmela wouldn't be wrong about Noor, since Carmela was the wisest person she knew.

Lucy didn't know what was in store for her next, but she had an odd feeling that fate had just intervened, and that song magic was in her future. And she couldn't wait for her next adventure.

CASTLE BRIDGE MEDIA RECOMMENDS...

If you liked *ANIMAL CHARMER*, you might also enjoy reading the following titles from Castle Bridge Media available on Amazon or by order at your favorite book store:

Animal Charmer
By Rain Nox

Austinites
By In Churl Yo

Bloodsucker City
By Jim Towns

THE CASTLE OF HORROR
ANTHOLOGY SERIES
Volume 1
Volume 2: *Holiday Horrors*
Volume 3: *Scary Summer Stories*
Volume 4: *Women Running From Houses*
Volume 5: *Thinly Veiled: The 70s*
Volume 6: *Femme Fatales**
Volume 7: *Love Gone Wrong*
Volume 8: *Thinly Veiled: The 80s*
Volume 9: *Young Adult*
Edited By Jason Henderson
and In Churl Yo
*Edited By P.J. Hoover

Castle of Horror Podcast
Book of Great Horror:
Our Favorites, Top Tens
and Bizarre Pleasures
Edited By Jason Henderson

Dream State
By Martin Ott

FuturePast Sci-Fi Anthology
Edited by In Churl Yo

GLAZIER'S GAP
Ghosts of the Forbidden
By Leanna Renee Hieber

The Hermes Protocol
By Chris M. Arnone

Isonation
By In Churl Yo

MID-LIFE CRISIS THRILLERS
18 Miles From Town
By Jason Henderson
Lost Angel
By Sam Knight

Nightwalkers: Gothic Horror Movies
By Bruce Lanier Wright

THE PATH
The Blue-Spangled Blue
By David Bowles
The Deepest Green
By David Bowles

SURF MYSTIC
Night of the Book Man
By Peyton Douglas
Dark of the Curl
By Peyton Douglas

Yesterday's Tomorrows:
The Golden Age of
Science Fiction Movies
By Bruce Lanier Wright

Please remember to leave us your reviews on Amazon and Goodreads!

THANK YOU FOR SUPPORTING INDEPENDENT PUBLISHERS AND AUTHORS!
castlebridgemedia.com

www.ingramcontent.com/pod-product-compliance
Lightning Source LLC
Chambersburg PA
CBHW020949180626
46814CB00003B/1001